A KIND OF COMPASS
STORIES ON DISTANCE

A KIND OF COMPASS
STORIES ON DISTANCE

edited by Belinda McKeon

TRAMPPRESS

First published 2015 by
Tramp Press
Dublin
www.tramppress.com

1 3 5 7 9 10 8 6 4 2
ISBN 978-0-9928170-5-3

Tramp Press gratefully acknowledges the financial assistance of the Arts Council.

Set in 11pt on 15pt Hoefler by Marsha Swan
Printed by GraphyCems in Spain

Contents

CONTENTS

INTRODUCTION

Belinda McKeon

D istance is inherent to the short story.
   Or, the short story is made out of distance, out of the problem
of it. A story must be 'the depth of a novel, the breadth of a poem,'
Amy Bloom writes, and it must be these things within the space allowed
by a clutch of pages, or maybe even a single page; space which eats itself
up greedily, like a life. And yet the short story is a form which contains
within itself acres, 'a faraway deep inside,' to borrow a second phrase from
Rebecca Solnit's *A Field Guide to Getting Lost*, the book from which this
anthology takes its title. The distance from here to there is never what it
seems. The difference between those two places – those two illusions? – is
always more than a country mile.

   I asked these seventeen writers to think about distance because I am
obsessed with it, and because I wanted to outsource that obsession for
a while, or maybe to exorcise it. This did not work. I read the stories as
they arrived from down the road and across the oceans, from Ireland and
England and Italy and France and Iceland and Australia and Japan, and
from America, where I live now, and from writers who live now in America
but were born in Nigeria and the Philippines and Iran; I read these stories
as they showed up in my inbox, and I became even more obsessed. With
the faraway deep inside; with the faraway glancing off every surface. With
the spaces – the acres – between people, between places, between the
parts and versions of the self. With the stuff of feeling at home, and how
that never produces interesting fiction, and with the stuff of feeling at sea,
and how that so often produces fiction that will not leave you alone.

Short stories, Richard Ford writes, are 'daring little instruments'. I always read 'daring', there, as 'darling' at first − and if that's not an attempt to take the pinch of fear, of anxiety, of seasickness or jetlag or compass-needle-spinning out of the business of writing a story, I don't know what is. Because they're not *darling*, short stories − or at least, they should not be; they're *daring*. They go places. They leave for places, and their creators had damn well better go along. And those places, if a story is doing what it needs to do, are hardly ever comfortable − for the writer *or* the reader. This idea of a story allowing its readers to go to places they'd otherwise never have had the chance to experience; this idea gets trundled out a lot, on the jacket copy of books for instance, and actually, didn't I trundle that idea out myself, writing the jacket copy for this book? Yes, I did. Because it is such a jacket copy way of talking about what stories do; it is the kind of description you pull, unthinkingly, out of your jacket pocket.

Well, forget I said that, will you please? Or consider me a liar, a lazy jacket-copy-writer, whatever works for you, because I don't really believe in that idea. It casts the story in too much of a do-gooder, humanitarian sort of role; a sort of Make-a-Wish Foundation for readers. But readers looking for good stories don't want to make a wish. Readers like this want to take a plunge, make a wrong turn, find themselves lost and feel their hearts thumping as they scrabble around for a field guide. As they look at the cracked glass of an unlikely compass. 'Art,' Deborah Eisenberg has said, 'is destabilizing. It undermines, rather than reinforces, what you already know and what you already think. It ventures into distant ambiguities, it dismantles the received in your brain and expands and refines what you can experience.'

A good story takes its readers to places to which they didn't particularly want to go. It takes its readers to those places and it says, *look; see*. I've never particularly wanted to go into space, for instance; given that it is usually quite an undertaking for me to get out of the house and go to yoga, Mars or even (I may be googling the phrase 'map of outer space' right now, by the way) the earth's outer atmosphere are a bit of a stretch for me. But I went there; I was taken to those places, or to the possibility of those places by two stories in this anthology − two stories the shared resonances of which struck me at first as uncanny and then as quite devastating. Elske Rahill and Maria Takolander both thought about distance and came up with women drawn to the idea of splitting off from everything, to the opportunity to leave everything behind, everything known, everything thought worthy of treasuring or losing; there is something, I think, so very telling in that.

And there is maybe, too, something very telling in the fact that I think of space as a place to which a person might go, the way they might go to a country or a continent; the way Sara Baume's troubled protagonist, for instance, might fly to London to do a favour for a relative, or the way that the eager tourist in Yoko Ogawa's story might treat herself to a holiday in Vienna. That's the thing about distance, or rather about the way we conceive of it; we always place ourselves at the origin-point of the far-away-ness, think of ourselves as the 'here' to the 'there'. But we are both at once, really, and more than both; we are not looking at space, from our solid rock, but caught in it, part of it, changing it. 'Ever the more so as I walk I take on the colours and the feelings of the places through which I walk and I am no longer a surprise to these places,' says the self-vanished man of Kevin Barry's story. It works both ways.

People travel in some of these stories, but they are in exile in all of them. Any story that digs into the human is a story about exile, in a sense; we are all at a remove from one another, sometimes trying to reach one another, sometimes trying to do the opposite. Porochista Khakpour's Henry comes to a 'famous city' with the apparent intent of avoiding other people, but the glass that keeps us separate is a mirror as much as is a window; Francesca Marciano's Stella flies to a small island in the Indian Ocean, half-hoping to step onto the sands of something she lost long ago, but the roads are made of packed dirt and a harsh tower looms over everything. The homecoming of Sam Lipsyte's Caperton may be mostly a shambles, and may be hilarious, but it is also surprisingly painful; it is also surprisingly sad. And for E.C. Osondu's Tochi, meanwhile, a distance crossed becomes a door that refuses to open, and a night which looks different to other, darker nights but is actually the same.

Part of what makes these stories so moving is the tenacity with which their characters insist on holding onto hope, or onto some battered version of it, even as they tell themselves they have let hope go. Is it bound up with the experience of distance, that human tendency? Kristín Ómarsdóttir's young characters seem at first foolish with hope, almost drugged with it, but the strange dance of her story shows how madly they have had to battle to sustain it. Éilís Ní Dhuibhne gives us a character who knows what has happened, who knows what has changed, what has been lost – she knows that a distance deep as a ravine has opened up in her life – and yet her character makes out of that knowledge, and out of her continuing desire to look away from it, something extraordinary. On the Northumberland island from which Ross Raisin's story takes its name, a girl does her work and keeps her watch – over the sea, over the dunes, over the young man who has appeared just at the time an older man has vanished; even a ripple of change feels to her like a swell of boiling sea. David Hayden's character, adrift in New York, tries hard to find a compass, looking for it in reminiscence, in art, even in guilt – don't we so often use guilt as a compass? – but the needle will not move. It is only, after all, a kind of needle.

Formally, the short story allows for the enactment of distance as well as for its interrogation; here, the stories of Gina Apostol and Suzanne Scanlon find their shape, their manifestation, in the shape and manifestations of their character's estrangements from each other, and from their pasts. Communication is fractured, at the level of the sentence – how an utterance looks on the page, how it is placed, which mouth it seems to fall from – and at the level of evidence handed down on other pages, other gathered artefacts. And because the shrinking, the snatching-away of distance can be even starker than its expanse, Mark Doten and Niven Govinden have given themselves only the space of a page, only the space of a realisation and of a shock and of a reality, newly dawned, within which to create their imagined worlds. Are these worlds to which we want to pay a visit? The force and the vividness of these stories leaves us with little choice.

So find your compass. Or your kind-of-compass; that vagueness, that sense of the improvised are both so fundamental to the nature of the thing. Because the needle always points in the same direction, and yet it hardly ever looks like the same direction; almost always, sitting there in your hand, this magnet to the pull of the world, it looks like a direction you've never taken before. And you don't have to go there. You don't have to take the path at which the needle nudges. Knowing that path is there, you can veer off course. Knowing it's there, you can go anywhere. The needle will still know what it knows.

Kind of.

A KIND OF COMPASS
STORIES ON DISTANCE

TERRAFORMING

Elske Rahill

A group of men applauds the landing, their claps and whistles drowning the grumble of the earth as it passes beneath. Caitriona lifts her face out of the cup of her palm. Wet. There is drool down her neck, drying to a tight crust along her jaw. Beyond the window, only a syrupy yellow mist. She wipes her hand on her leggings and uses the end of her sleeve to rub at her neck and face. She knows there must be marks on her; chalky tide lines mapping the shapes where the saliva has dried.

The plane sighs to a halt, but over the speaker comes an announcement that the doors can't be opened yet and phones are to be kept off. Some of the passengers come out into the aisles, removing bags from the overhead lockers, pulling coats out from under haunches and feet.

It's been years since she was in London. What she remembers are the dark veins of the underground, deceptive landmarks made by café chains, brisk men who did not offer to help with bags. She stayed a night – no, two – with her sister, before either of them were married. They shopped for clothes and Boots cosmetics, saw a musical, ate chocolate cereal in their hotel room and talked a lot in a way they hadn't done since.

The man next to her leans into the aisle, trying to tug something out of the overhead locker. In the twist and stretch of the effort, his t-shirt rises over the khaki canvas belt. Billow of flesh; oblong navel; neat thatch of hair that cleaves the belly in two as it runs from umbilicus down to the neon blue band of his trunks.

Caitriona looks away. She does not want to glimpse the knot where this man was once tied to his beginnings. While she dozed on the flight, she was thinking about her son: the delicious creases at the back of his neck, his incongruence with the adult world of airport lounges and foreign currency.

'Sir, please remain in your seat until the seatbelt light goes off!' It is the air hostess who tore their boarding passes at the gate. She has turquoise eyelids and big, crunchy hair. When they boarded she was calm and smiling, but now a dangerous shade of red is rising from beneath her powdered complexion.

The man produces a long rucksack with many straps and flaps. He turns to the air hostess.

'There now,' he says.

She snatches the bag from him with two hands and pushes it back into the overhead locker. 'Wait for the seatbelt light to go off!'

The man sits down, muttering. He shakes his head, turning towards Caitriona, his palm flat on the empty seat between them, but Caitriona keeps her face towards the window. Her hand luggage is at her feet, and she has the directions written out clearly on a piece of paper. A bus, one tube stop and a three-minute walk. She will find a bathroom and remove the signs of dried drool from her face. Then she will go straight to the hotel and check in. She has packed a sandwich. There will be no need to leave the room until morning.

It was after her father's death that the dreams began. They arched up like a nest of waking cats, all purr and acid hiss. They licked at her ears, tongues at once gentle and scouring, and with their claws they tore deep stars into her night.

She has followed them here to this compact hotel room, clean and cool with a bed hemmed by a wall at the head and foot. There is a flat television screwed onto the wall, a row of green and red lights glowering up its side. The screen shows a picture of stones on a beach and a bubble with the words, 'Welcome Ms C. Dawson. We hope you enjoy your stay,' moving about the parameters of the screen like a wandering buoy. She should have used a different name. There is a small desk with a block of Post-its, a pen, a phone and a card with the numbers for Reception and Emergency and Room Service. Caitriona has never been in a room like this before.

She sits on the side of the bed, takes her mobile from her handbag, and squeezes the power button until it blinks to life. She has to wait through a series of texts as the phone acclimatises to the new location. Then it settles down and she can call. As the ringing begins she can feel her eyelids twitch; a kick of panic when she hears his voice.

'You made it?'

She smiles and nods as she speaks, because she read once that people can hear the expression on your face. 'Yes,' she says. 'Eleanor picked me up. Flight was fine, you know, as you'd expect. Get what you pay for ... But anyway there you go. Is my little man all right? We're going for a bite to eat now ... God, yeah – so good to see her ... A girly night, yeah. But listen babe, I'm on my mobile ... they don't have a landline, no. No don't upset him ... I'll be back before he notices. Don't forget the eczema cream when you're getting him into his jammies. Yeah. K. I'll phone you tomorrow ...'

Afterwards she takes a shower. Then she sits at the desk and unwraps her ham sandwich. Not hungry.

She wakes in a gaspful of sand to the low whirr of churning air. Red and green prickle the dark. She couldn't turn off the air conditioning. It has dried her skin taut to the bone, and her lips taste of blood. There is an en suite, but on the mirror a sticker says not to drink the tap water. She knows there is Coke and mineral water in the little lobby at the end of the hall. She saw the vending machine on her way to the room, but she was too keen to get in and shut the door. She will nip out quickly. A cardigan over her pyjama top. Remember the key card.

Round white sensor lights click on one by one overhead. The hallway is painted a clean shade of grey. There is a charcoal carpet underfoot, and along the walls, tall sprigs of straw in slate-black, pyramid-shaped vases.

Her feet are bare. No slippers, and no clean socks for tomorrow either.

There they are. Too late to turn around. Two of them right there, sitting on a black wicker couch beside the machine. Deep in conversation, they dip their heads together like a pair of swans. Caitriona recognises the girl from the cover of the bright magazine that comes in the Sunday paper – an oval face set in a perfect bob. In the picture she wore a red jumpsuit, metallic powder shimmering on her cheekbones, a space helmet under her arm. Her hair looked set in plastic, peroxide white and mortis stiff. In real life she is smaller, her colouring mute. A haze of frizz and a stubborn cow's lick kink her hair to life. Her feet are folded up beneath her, and one of the couch's silver cushions is nestled on her lap. Caitriona doesn't recognise the girl's companion – a narrow-chested man with a vague beard – but he is one too. She knows from the t-shirt, red with black letters: *MISSION MARS – Let's Get This Future Started.*

The two lift their eyes as she passes. Fat sag of pyjama bottoms. Naked feet. She crosses her arms over her nipples and makes for the vending machine. It's a big old beast with lots of empty metal swirls where packets of sweets and chocolate bars once were. It lows softly, illuminating its stock. There is a lot of water and only a few bottles of Coke.

She reaches into her cardigan pocket. No money. Key card and no money. She presses a selection all the same. The two candidates resume their conversation. 'The training will be hard,' says the girl, her speech quiet and moist, the confident, winding vowels of fluent second-language English. 'We can remember it is ten years away. There is much that can be learned in ten years. We will not be sent unless we are capable. We will not be chosen unless we are right.'

'The radiation,' says the man. He is English. 'I want to be sure there's medicine with us up there – painkillers. I don't mind dying up there, but it's being without access to the right medicine. Euthanasia, even. If it comes to it. I mean, it'll be new laws there, won't it? Or space law?'

'Space code,' says the girl, 'strict space code.'

Caitriona pushes her hand into the vending machine flap, then into her cardigan pocket, hoping to conceal the absence of any bottle. She shuffles away quickly and this time they do not pause as she passes.

'Somehow I'm not scared,' says the girl, leaning in close. 'It's like it's my destiny, you know? It feels right. I have told them already I want to be the first mother on Mars. Mother of the first Martian. It will happen. I know it.'

'They'll send you in one of the later groups, then. Not the first group anyway ... There's bound to be teething problems. And who knows what the radiation will do to our fertility?'

The corridor is still lit. It takes three swipes before the key card opens the door. In the dark, she puts her mouth under the bathroom tap.

Settled into oblivion in some cave of her mind, bypassed for years by the circuits and synapses that keep things going, is a pool of facts that her father left there for her:

Mars is a wandering planet.

Jupiter is a ball of gas dense as water.

Pluto – Pluto, which was once her favourite planet, a pretty little orb out there at the end of the sequence, Pluto is all ice and rock, a cool marble mottled blue and yellow like a bruise, and it orbits the sun, spinning faster and slower as the aeons pass in a cycle that takes millions of years.

'Imagine all the lives that pass in one cycle,' her father said. 'Imagine all the work that goes into each of those lives. All the harvesting and skimping and counting to make ends meet and keep food in mouths, and coats on backs, and bring babies to adulthood. You can't imagine it, can you? Me neither. You would have to be God.'

There are infinite possibilities, life on Earth is all a coincidence of gasses and heat and time that could as easily never have been.

They were rare moments that her father could sit with her and point out all the planets in a large coloured hardback. He had bought it with the help of tokens saved from Blue Moon biscuit packets. It stayed in the small good room with the *Reader's Digests* and the grandly dressed china doll that her mother had been given as a child. Her father drove a bread van and when he wasn't doing that he cleaned the gutters or windows of wealthier houses. He resoled his children's hand-me-down shoes with strips of leather he had soaked overnight, teeth clenched while he worked, lips drawing back to pull tight the stitches. Then with his tongue between his lips he positioned the glue and firmed down strips of old tires for grip.

Ashamed of living in a council estate, he wanted to own a house. When Caitriona was fourteen he had managed it.

'You can do anything, Trinny,' he told Caitriona. 'My Trinny can do anything. Don't let anyone do you down. Not for being a girl or a bit heavy – don't mind that. Hold your head high.'

It was her sister who was with him when he died. She phoned from the hospital, voice like a paper bag tossed hollow in the wind. Caitriona said 'OK' as though consenting, and got off the phone as quickly as she could. She was surprised at how little she minded. While she waited for her husband to get in, she finished the washing up and checked on the baby and made a cup of tea to sip on the couch and wait. As soon as she sat it reached up from her gut, a small, sore cry. She thought of the empty house and all the carefully shelved *Reader's Digests* with the slippery pages and wondered if there was a way to make them mean something.

She could not finish the tea, but that night sleep came easy. She slid into the gas planet as thick liquid with nothing hard to kick at. She recognised the feeling – a place where contact is impossible because nothing is divided. All yield and push, self dispersed into all matter and all of it in her. She woke in a sweat, ears and toes rippling with a queer nostalgia. She knew she must have dreamt it before.

Jupiter is the God of everything.

Sometimes she is on the red planet itself. Blood-tinted sky and the heat pressing like flesh against her face. Wind and sand ahead, wind and sand behind, and no way of knowing what way to go. Stretch of dark. Blind hand looking for touch. Spear puncturing the surface and she feels the hurt of it in her breast somehow. A little flag but with what name on it?

She made the audition tape alone on her laptop, a sort of prayer. It felt strange to declare her name. 'I am Caitriona Dawson. I dream of exploring space.' She must have expected to be chosen, some blessing from the dead, perhaps, because when she received the email she wasn't too surprised. She knew she would pass the Skype interview. 'There'll be plenty of interest in you,' said her liaison officer. 'Out of one hundred chosen candidates across the globe, you are the only mother. You'll get a lot of coverage.'

'After the next round,' she told him. 'If I get to the next round, then OK. Then I'll tell my family and I'll do all the interviews and stuff then ...'

There were qualities they saw in her, the liaison said, qualities that a new world will need; the honesty and the compassion and the fire that they were looking for.

She knew then that yes, this was what she was for. She could do anything, and no one was to do her down.

———————————————

When morning comes she discovers that there is a way to unplug the television, by reaching in behind. It is a relief to see the little lights blink away. The sliding door by the desk, which she thought was a wardrobe, in fact conceals a second sink, with a sticker saying *Potable Water*. Beside it there is a small kettle, and two black teacups, a black wicker basket with teabags, sachets of instant coffee, individually packaged biscuits and thimble-sized portions of UHT milk.

She makes a cup of tea, the wrong colour, and pours a second dose of milk in after the first slides to the bottom. She eats two counterfeit Jammy Dodgers, sitting at the desk, dipping them in the tea while it cools. As it turns out, the tea is not too bad. The cups are rather shallow and the conference is not for another two hours, so she makes a second cup.

She had an outfit picked for today. She bought it specially – a smart blouse and a waistcoat – but she knows now that she cannot wear it. It is a costume for a circus master. She will blush all through the day, squirming the clothes to comic crookedness. She brought a grey jumper dress for the flight home. The dress she wore on the way over is better – a quiet green colour and a way of cinching the waist – but she won't be able to remove the smell of plane and her own frowsy sleep from it. The grey jumper dress then. She sponges the stains from her leggings. There is nothing to be done about the socks.

———————————————

According to the website the first talk is called 'Why It's Time To Go'. The event page showed a picture of Earth with patches of blue and red and black, the surface blistered and peeling like scorched skin – something about the ozone layer. She tried to read about it at work, but she was so afraid of being caught that the blood started to pump too quickly behind her eyes and she couldn't string the shapes into letters, the words into coherence. She knew how they would all laugh at her: the open-mouthed guffaws of her manager, the stiff snorts of the front-of-house girls.

The e-vite said to come early for a chance to chat with experts and meet the other candidates.

The front entrance opens into a round room with many doors in its curved walls. Slim women with ponytails are meandering slowly through the crowd, offering something hot from large silver pots. There are more people than Caitriona expected. Some are talking in tentative pairs, but most are standing apart, flicking through pages in red pocket folders, trying to avoid the terrible quietness of the place. There is a pillar in the centre and all around it a ledge where miniature bagels, and miniature Danish pastries, and bites of marmalade-glazed toast the size of postage stamps are presented on silver platters. The walls are lined with information stands displaying bits of rock and large glossy photographs of the galaxy.

'Excuse me,' a man no older than twenty with very yellow hair touches her elbow, 'you need to register before you can enter.'

'Oh ...' Caitriona says.

'Are you here for the conference?'

He points to a banner reading *Mission Mars Orientation and Registration*. Below it, a second young man with an identical hairstyle is sitting at a long table. He is a little broader than his colleague, but he has the same look: disconcertingly symmetrical features set stiffly in an unlined face. They are both dressed impeccably: black suit, black tie, wound-red shirt and, on the lapel, a red enamel disc ringed with gold.

'Welcome to the first European Mission Mars Candidate Conference,' says the broader man. 'Can I see your ID?'

A machine no bigger than her phone prints her name onto a rectangular sticker. He peels it off and hands it to her on one fingertip. The other man hands her a red pocket folder fat with stapled papers, a *Mars One* pen, and, wrapped in a clear envelope, a pin like theirs, the sharp gold point poking hopefully at the packaging. The object has a pleasing, tight weight to it, like the smooth, old bullet her father kept in a tobacco box over the bookshelf. Caitriona hooks it into the fine-knit dress, worrying immediately that she has placed it exactly where her nipple is and that people will notice it jiggling stupidly. Too late.

The two men open their palms in tandem towards the room. 'The conference will begin in two minutes,' says the slimmer one. 'Good luck, Caitriona.'

The first half of the day is made up of a series of lectures that Caitriona struggles to follow. There is quite a lot of science, but the lecturers repeat that candidates mustn't worry; they don't have to understand it all yet. A big projection shows the houses they will live in – a row of silver domes on a crimson terrain. There is one lecture called *Our Galaxy; Our Neighbourhood*, where they are given brief summaries of the other planets in the solar system.

Someone puts their hand up. Caitriona can't hear the question but the lecturer repeats it through his microphone. 'This lady is asking about Pluto, about why it is no longer a planet ...' He explains that it never really was, but it is a good question because soon they – the men who do these things – will send a probe to take measurements and photos and find out more about Pluto. So there might be some hope for Pluto after all, thinks Caitriona, to have a place in the galaxy; to be remembered again. A colour picture of Pluto is projected onto the wall. The lady murmurs again, and the speaker repeats her question for the audience:

'Would it be possible for them to find something that would make Pluto a planet again?' He laughs. 'No, sorry, that's not how it works, I'm afraid. Right: any more questions before we wrap up for lunch? ... No? OK, chosen candidates go with Pearse. Make sure you have your ID. All other stakeholders please come with me.'

Pearse is a tall man with a whey complexion and long, milky fingers. He stands at the front of the hall while the candidates form a flock. He counts the heads: twenty-five. Then he leads them out into the main auditorium and off down a corridor to a smaller, cooler room with a whiteboard and collapsible chairs pushed back against the walls.

There are three cardboard boxes on a desk, and a water dispenser sitting awkwardly in the middle of the room. Pearse stands by the boxes and congratulates them all on being chosen. He warns that this is only the beginning of a long, hard quest for a new world.

The boxes contain their lunch – a selection of protein bars. These are samples of what they will be living on for the seven-month voyage. Pearse says there are three flavours – strawberry, chocolate and vanilla. All three are the same muddy colour and wrapped in the same red greaseproof paper. They smell like rotting wood, but the taste is inoffensive. 'Some people find they taste like pineapple,' says Pearse. While the candidates eat, a nutritionist called Camilla explains that the bars are made from tiny green sea vegetables and contain a full spectrum of vitamins, proteins and trace minerals. They will need to take fat supplements on board too, and lots of water.

After lunch the water cooler is wheeled into the adjoining room, and they are asked to help fold the chairs properly and stack them in a corner. Then they are told to form a circle. One by one they must announce their names and tell the group something about themselves.

'I am Caitriona Dawson,' says Caitriona, 'and I work in hospitality.' She can feel the heat in her face and she can't figure out what to do with her hands, so she fiddles with the Mars pin, taking the back off and pinching the little wings to open the hole and put it back on. She has an urge to push the point into her palm. Her response isn't the worst though. One woman tugs fiercely at her cuticles with her teeth and when it comes her turn she says, 'I am Delia, and I have three cats and six goldfish.'

Somebody sniggers and Pearse says, 'No laughing at other candidates please. Anything at all about yourself. Thank you Delia.'

Next they are organised into groups of four. Caitriona is asked to choose a group name and she says 'Pluto,' before she has time to think. They are each given a big round blue sticker and they write their names on it, and the name of their team: *Caitriona Dawson – Pluto*. There is one man in the group, a skinny fellow from London who says he works in a hospital but doesn't disclose his role there. She noticed him earlier because he has been wearing the black version of the *Mission Mars* cap all through the day. The more merchandise you buy, the more Mars points you get. You get points, too, for blogging, more if you interview with journalists, and there will be a documentary with the chosen candidates. They explained all this in the interview. They need publicity for funding, they said; the mission depends on it.

Also in her group are the oval-faced girl from last night, and an older lady from Scotland with big jewellery, very small hands and an enormous bosom. The lady touches Caitriona's elbow and winks warmly. 'Good name,' she says, 'I always had a soft spot for Pluto.'

Pearse sits on a high swivel chair at the top of the room; one foot tucked in his crotch and one dangling. He rotates slowly from side to side, making the hinge yelp. Their first task is to explain to each other why they are volunteering. 'Be completely honest,' Pearse says. 'This is only amongst ourselves.'

Caitriona huddles into her group. The hospital worker says his name is Eric and that he will speak first. He removes his cap to reveal a slick of thinning hair. Then he flips open a sleek black wallet to show a photo of his son, a round-eyed child with a frightened mouth.

'This is Blaze,' he says, 'my son.'

He slides the picture out and passes it around his three teammates. There is a pause while they each take a moment to look at Eric's son. 'How sweet,' says the Scottish lady, and Eric nods sadly. He takes a deep breath and returns the cap to his head. Then he begins to speak very fast, eyes pecking at the faces of his audience. His ex is a psycho, he says. She is always cutting access, always trying to make him do all the running. The courts have ordered him to give her thirty-five quid a week, which she blows on nail polish and cappuccinos. 'Thirty-five quid a week. For the privilege of seeing my own son,' he says, staring hard at Caitriona now. 'I'm going to show them all I am a dad to be proud of. He'll be able to say "my dad is a spaceman," and then she'll be sorry. Boys love rockets.'

When he is finished speaking Eric looks exhausted. There is a silence into which the Scottish lady sighs, 'Well I might as well go next ...' Then she gives a deep, sad chuckle. While she speaks Eric lowers his head, but his eyes still dart about as though he wasn't quite finished. The woman rocks on her heels, hands clasped at her belly. She punctuates each utterance with a little laugh, like relief after pain. 'I just want to be remembered. That's all. That's all really. To make a mark.'

The white-haired girl quickly takes over. She makes Caitriona nervous. She says she is an astrophysics student and she lives in Stockholm. She began her studies in marine biology, she says, but she soon decided that the answers were not on this earth. She is either mad or extremely clever, with lots of words that Caitriona has never heard before, spoken with strange authority in that alien accent. 'The next war will be the end of life on earth,' she says. 'Someone has to find a new planet or human life is finished.'

When it comes her turn Caitriona doesn't know what she will say but the words come very quickly. 'My dad died last year. He wanted me to do something extraordinary but I never knew what it should be. So ... yep. That's why I'm here.'

The groups are assigned tasks; a number of computer-simulated crises which they will have to manage together. At first Eric has a lot of opinions – 'Look girls, what we need here is to think outside the box. Who's to say plants can't pull the water from the atmosphere?' – but he soon lets the astrophysics student lead.

On the e-vite it said the conference would finish at six, but when six comes, Pearse asks them to follow him. They arrive in a dimly lit room where there is a scattering of fine black dust under a long glass case. The case is in the centre of the room and they are allowed to walk around the exhibit and peer in through the viewing panels on the side. This, he says, gesturing with both hands to the stretch of glass, is a new metal that copies itself over and over, and when it copies itself it creates a gas. One of the purposes of the mission is to take this substance up to Mars. Once it begins, the stuff will keep copying itself until, after millions of years, it has created an ozone layer around the planet. Then they will start filling the atmosphere with air. This is called 'terraforming.'

'Imagine all the lives that pass in those millions of years,' her father once told her – but did he? Or are these the things she is inventing now, to make him real, to remember a person about whom there is very little to say?

After they have looked for a while at the metal Caitriona expects that they will finish up, but instead Pearse says that each group has half an hour to come up with a presentation on the best way to multiply the metal on Mars.

She waits until seven before slipping out of her workshop group. 'Sorry Pearse,' she says, 'I'll have to excuse myself ...'

For a moment Pearse's face loses all expression. He keeps his eyes on her while his voice goes up like a siren, 'Excuse me everyone. I need your attention for a moment!'

The room falls silent. They are all looking at her now, with pity or disdain, perhaps. She doesn't know. She keeps her gaze focused on Pearse. She will not lower her head.

'A candidate ...' he peers at her badge, '... *Catreeownna* ... has just told me that she needs to leave to catch a flight. That leaves her team down one member. For this mission you need to be dedicated. You need to be able to deal with the unexpected ... Well. Let's all say goodbye and get on with our work.'

Dark, despite pipes of light running cool as drains overhead. The air is thickened by the earth that must be muffling against the concrete, dulling the faraway chirrup of the trams. Cram of bodies teeming down and up the stairs and keeping to one side for the sake of order. Which side is it she should be on? She keeps veering to the wrong side. She needs to find a bin to stuff the conference pack in. Her badge, too. Remember to take off the badge.

If she misses the flight it means using the credit card. It means inventing some excuse. Already she will have to explain the conference fee. As a chosen candidate, she was given a special rate, but it was enough to make a dent. Barry will notice it and ask and she still doesn't know what she'll say. When she squeezes between the sliding doors she is still holding the red folder.

'Mind the gap.'

So many people. Blank faces but she can tell their type by the way they dress and the things they have; a tall woman in an awkward blouse knitting with purple yarn amongst the crush of passengers; a bearded young man with a checked scarf, hugging a rolled canvas.

Wobbling at his mother's knees, hand squelched tight in hers, is a little boy in a camouflage jacket with a crest that says *Army Man*. He looks like the child in the hospital worker's photo. Huge eyes and mouth shut small until it opens wide and lets a shriek. 'Look Mummy!'

He is pointing at the floor. Some of the conference pack contents have slid out, Caitriona sees; they are sprawled down amongst the feet.

'Look! SPACE, Mummy! SPACE!'

The mother's face is flattened with a thick layer of dust-dull make-up. She rubs her son's head, pulls it to her hip. 'Shhhh ...'

There is no use trying to squat and pick them up. She will only drop other things if she tries. Panic starts in her lungs. What is it that they are breathing in and out down here? What is keeping them all standing, making the blood whoosh through, and how long will it sustain them? She clutches at a loop overhead to steady herself, jiggles to the pulse of the carriage. Only one tube stop and a bus. Then the plane and then her little boy's face slotting into her neck, ears like the singing tunnels of seashells, fragrant scalp, the rippling cable of his spine.

She tries to tidy the papers a little with her feet: the pictures of the galaxy and of the machine that will make the oxygen, and the blot of words she could not understand. She should have thrown them out right there in the conference centre. She has probably failed anyway. Of course she has.

The child is on the floor now, trying to pick up one of the pictures he has seen − the solar system, which is not a sequence of eight as she once believed, but a blur of stars and planets too vast for her mind to map. Fat sticky hands like her boy; her boy who exploded from a tiny nook; a surge of blood thrusting her body into a new space and then his birth that threw open her sky. But she will close it up neat again, as she suspects all mothers do. She will grow away from him over the ten years it will take to train for Mars, and that is right of course. A curling beat inside her and then a cord. Then a breast and then a head in her neck. Then a hand in hers and then no hand because that's how it is with time and space. Wider and wider the distance; the journey that began in her, and who will he be out there with no touch left between them?

The door slides open.

'Mind the gap.'

She pours with the shoal of passengers out onto the platform and the crowd is gone, moving blind as maggots on the steps. At the top there is only a dull light for it is evening now. She has almost reached the open.

'Hello lady.' The child has grabbed the end of Caitriona's grey jumper dress. A little shut mouth again, a little chin. Big bug eyes.

'Shhh,' the mother says, 'sorry about that.'

'Oh no,' says Caitriona, 'No, I have a little one myself ...'

'So you know how it is?'

And the woman's smile is like the swell of a dying star, the disappointed climax and the heavy joy of it, and the relief because Caitriona knows it too – the terrible detail of accidental being.

The child is thrusting a bundle of papers towards her: three sheets stapled together and on the front the picture of the home on Mars – a row of huts like silver polyps on the rust sand.

'You keep that,' she says, but the child shakes his head. The pin then. She pinches the back and pulls it from her chest.

'Look,' she says, 'do you know what that is?'

'Space,' the boy says.

'You keep that, OK?'

———————————

On the plane she allows herself a sigh of relief. The smells she carries are of packed bodies and recycled air, a sweet, fruity broth of panic brewing from the cleaves of her flesh – but she has made it, and the evidence has been disposed of. The only thing she has kept is the big blue sticker: an innocuous thing, the kind of thing they might give out in playgroups for children's names. But that too should go. She folds it into a half moon, sticky sides together, and then into smaller and smaller wedges, before tucking it into the pocket in front of her with the in-flight shopping magazine. No one will ever open it to see what is written there: *Caitriona Dawson – Pluto*.

'Oh yes, Pluto. That used to be a planet didn't it?' Barry touched the hand-painted mobile, making it wobble clumsily above their sleeping child. The mobile was a gift from her sister. It has a sun and an Earth and seven other planets, but no Pluto. She didn't notice until the day she returned from maternity hospital.

Pluto was the precious livid piece in her solar system jigsaw, and she always slotted it in last. Today she saw the planet projected huge against the white parchment. It was exactly like the jigsaw; an unfathomable full stop spinning out in space, its surface blotched brightly like the skin of an unburied corpse.

THE NATURALS

Sam Lipsyte

C aperton's stepmother, Stell, called.

'Your father,' Stell said.

'Larry?' Caperton said.

'He's dying. You can say Dad.'

'He's done deathbed before.'

'It's different,' Stell said. 'The doctors agree now. And your father, well, no grand speeches about not going gentle, for one thing. For another, he looks out of it, pushed down. He shops online. He watches TV. I think you should be here.'

'Command performance?'

'Don't be a crumbum.'

Caperton took the short flight from O'Hare to Newark on one of the new boutique lines. Shortbread, cappuccinos, and sea-salted nuts in great jars sated travellers, gratis, at the gate. The in-flight magazine resembled an avant-garde culture journal Caperton once read with fervour. The cover depicted the airline's female pilots as cockpit kittens with tapered blazers and tilted caps. It was blunted wit, but startling for a commercial carrier. Caperton took note. Among other things, he consulted for a living. That morning, he'd been in meetings about a redo for a small chunk of lakefront.

They'd discussed the placement of a Dutch-designed information kiosk; one of the city-council guys kept calling it 'the koisk.'

'The koisk should be closer to the embankment,' the guy, a boy, bony in his dark suit, said.

'We can work on that,' a rival consultant Caperton had not known would be present said. 'The main thing is we're trying to tell a story here. A lakefront narrative.'

Were they supposed to make bids in the room together?

'My opinions are vaguely aligned with that,' Caperton said.

'But what colour will the koisk be?'

Caperton felt the surge of a strange desire to shelter this apprentice politician from future displays of idiocy, as you might a defective son, though Caperton had no children. He liked kids, just not what they represented. He wasn't exactly sure what that meant, but it sounded significant, even if Daphne had finally left him over it, had a baby by herself with some Princeton-rower sperm.

———————————————

Aloft in coach, Caperton found himself squeezed up against the trunk of a human sequoia. The man's white t-shirt stretched to near-transparency over his twitch-prone pecs. His hair shone aerosol gold. His cheek pulsed with each chew of a gum wad he occasionally spat into his palm and sculpted. He winked at Caperton, pressed the pink bolus flat, and slit a crude face in it with his thumbnail.

'I'm doing voodoo on the pilot.'

'A good time for it,' Caperton said.

'Don't be scared. The plane flies itself. I'll cure him before we land.'

'I'd appreciate that.'

'What brings you up into the sky today?'

'A personal matter.'

'Fuck, I should hope so. Can you imagine wasting a minute of your life on something that wasn't personal? Something that didn't mean anything to you? And, I mean, especially if you're helping other people. Like a mission of mercy. That should always be personal. Otherwise you're just doing it for the likes. What's your line of work?'

'It's tricky,' Caperton said. 'It's kind of conceptual marketing, kind of design. I'm a free-range cultural consultant. But my passion is public space.'

'Wow. Do you have all that bullshit on one business card?'

The man's enormous biceps jumped.

'Sorry,' he said. 'That comment was a little aggro of me. The juice does that sometimes.'

'The juice?'

'I don't hide it. In my field, I don't have to. We're entertainers.'

'What's your field?' Caperton asked.

'Dude, I'm a pro wrestler. What the fuck else would I be?'

'A bodybuilder?'

'Jesus, no! Those guys are pathetic narcissists. They were all abused by their fathers. Every one of them. Don't you know me? I'm the Rough Beast of Bethlehem. I wrestle on the Internet. You don't watch, I take it?'

'No,' Caperton said.

'You think it's stupid.'

'Not at all.'

'You think that, now that we're post-kayfabe, it's ultra-moronic, right?'

'Post-kayfabe?'

'Kayfabe was the code we followed. Don't break character. Pretend it's not staged. Now we wink at the audience and they wink back.'

'Oh, when did that go into effect?' Caperton said.

The Rough Beast snorted. 'You don't get it at all, buddy. It's not about wrestling. It's about stories. We're storytellers.'

Caperton studied him. 'Somebody at my job just said that.'

'It's true! You have to be able to tell the story to get people on board for anything. A soft drink, a suck sesh, elective surgery, gardening, even your thing – public space? I prefer private space, but that's cool. Anyway, nobody cares about anything if there isn't a story attached. Ask the team that wrote the Bible. Ask Vincent Allan Poe.'

'But doesn't it seem kind of creepy?' Caperton said. 'All of us just going around calling ourselves storytellers?'

The Rough Beast shrugged. 'Well, you can be negative. That's the easy way out.'

Caperton thought it might be the hard way out. The Beast slipped his gum into his mouth.

'Gardening?' Caperton said, after a moment, but by then the Beast had his earbuds in.

Stell met Caperton in front of his childhood house, in Nearmont. She leaned against the doorway the way his mother once did. They were not quite the same type, but ballpark, as his father would say. Larry preferred tall, semi-controlling women with light, wavy hair. Stell preferred to smoke pot, laugh, cook, yell at Larry, read good novels, and watch her shows. She'd proved a perfect stepmother, and she and Caperton flourished in their family roles, except for the deal with the refrigerator – or, rather, Stell's deal with Caperton rummaging freely in the refrigerator. 'Deal' was weak wording for it. 'Nearly unassuageable rage' seemed more accurate. Stell just thought it would be better if Caperton waited outside the kitchen area. She'd be more than happy to get him whatever he wanted. It would just be better, it really would, if he waited over there at the edge or even beyond the edge of the kitchen area.

Caperton harboured a secret ancestral claim to what his forebears had known as the icebox. There had been only so much depredation and madness an American child could endure in the past century. That's why the government had invented the after-school snack. But he supposed he'd evolved. This was Stell's house now, and, whatever her idiosyncrasies about the accessibility of chilled provisions, she'd kept his father's energy up for years, saved him from a fatal spiral when Caperton's mother died, even, or especially, if she'd been his mistress at the time.

For his part, Caperton's father called Stell the Bossman. Whenever she left the room he would twinkle his snow-blue eyes at Caperton and, his throat choked with affection, say, 'What a goddam cunt, huh?'

Larry had been married three times, cancered twice. Now the liver, as he put it, was negotiating a severance package. Larry had spent decades on the road, and Caperton used to picture a bawdy shadow life for his father, whiskey sours at a sleek, cushioned bar, a woman with his tie in her teeth. These were bitter visions, but he knew, guiltily, that the anger wasn't really for his mother's sake. He just didn't understand why the man seemed so antsy at home, as though he couldn't enjoy even a few moments of family life, drinking hot cocoa and overpraising young Caperton's tediously improvised puppet shows or the lumpy space soldiers he pinched without talent from bright clay. Why were there so few trips to the toy store, or the zoo, or the toy store at the zoo, or, better yet, the snack stand beside the toy store at the zoo?

'First World problems,' Daphne once told him.

'That's why they're so painful.'

Caperton had wanted to be, with his father, a team. But Larry had a team, his work buddies, gruff chums whose cruel whinnies carried through the house those Sundays they came to watch football or smoke cigars on the patio. Like Larry, these hard cases were not gangsters but grade-school-textbook salesmen. Larry worked his regions year-round, his returns heralded by the appearance of the exquisite red-and-gold Jade Dragon takeout cartons. Every business trip ended with egg rolls and spareribs and enough monosodium glutamate to goon them all into an animate diorama of menu item No. 14: Happy Family.

His father would debrief them, long, duck-sauced fingers curled around a frosted stein. He'd sing of the specialty foods of the nation – the Cincinnati chillies, avocado-and-sprout sandwiches, and spice-rubbed hams of the culinary mosaic – or describe the historic hotels he'd slept in, name the ones with the tastiest pillow mints, the fluffiest towels, the most impressive water pressure. Caperton had found receipts in his father's overcoat, though, and they all said Howard Johnson. Larry hardly mentioned the people he'd seen or what he and the other salesmen had done, unless they'd scored big on a sale. Many schools, he explained, still taught from textbooks that conjectured a moon shot. Once, he said, he told a school board in Delaware that he'd be delighted to inform Commander Neil Armstrong himself what passed for scientific knowledge in their district. Caperton and his mother whooped, and Larry grinned into his stein. A triumph for Enlightenment values, plus commission.

After Caperton's mother died, his father retired and built birdhouses for a while. He meant well, but to a grown Caperton these designs were rather Cabrini-Green-ish, huge and institutional, as though Larry meant to warehouse the local jays and sparrows in balsa-wood towers of utter marginalisation. It troubled Caperton to the point that he considered talking to his father about it, but then construction halted. Crises of the body beckoned. Lung inflammations, nano-strokes, mystery cysts, myeloma scares. Caperton raced home for it all. But Larry couldn't deliver, until, apparently, now.

Caperton kissed Stell and followed her into the house, past the foyer bench and ancient wall hooks. He saw the mauve sofa where he and his father watched movies while his mother died upstairs – Westerns and sports sagas, mostly. Larry loved the one about the ancient, pretty base-ball player who steps out of some Hooverville limbo to lead his club in a pennant race. Bad fuckers bribe him to tank the big game, but the hero jacks one, as Larry liked to say, into the stadium lights. Sparks shower down. The republic is renewed.

'In the book, he strikes out,' Caperton once told his father.

'I know. That's why it's a stupid book. Why go through all that trouble to make a great story and then give it an ending like that? That takes real bitterness.'

Caperton had said nothing, but thought there might be something brave about the bitterness.

'Your father's sleeping now,' Stell said. 'Would you like some coffee? Maybe a sandwich?'

He noticed a new strain in Stell's face. Her hands nipped at each other like little animals. Could he stop himself even if he wanted to?

'I can make one later,' Caperton said.

'I don't think that'll work. I can make one now.'

'I can make it. I'll just look around in the fridge.'

'I don't ... that can't ...'

'It's no problem,' Caperton said.

'Just let me make you a sandwich now. No big deal.'

'Exactly. I can make it, no biggie.'

'But you don't know what's there.'

'I can look.'

'No, honey, please don't do this. It's hard to see what's in the fridge. The bulb is out. But I know what's there. Tell me what you want.'

'I want a turkey-pastrami sandwich with capers and spicy pickles and sharp English mustard on a fresh-baked croissant.'

'What?'

'Stell, just let me look in the fridge. I have a right. I was looking in that fridge when you were just an old hippie in Jersey City.'

Stell stared at the carpet. She looked widowed already. Caperton agreed to let her make him a turkey on wheat, which she would store until he was ready.

'I just hope there's room in the fridge,' Stell said.

'Hope is what we have,' Caperton said, because he was a crumbum.

Caperton stood in his old bedroom, now Stell's study. Photographs of her family — nieces, cousins, a stern, tanned uncle — covered the bookshelves. Her people were much comelier than the dough-nosed Capertons. He recognised a few of his old textbooks behind the photographs, but most of the library was Stell's, an odd mix of self-help and hard science. He pulled out one on the human genome and flipped through it, pulled out another called 'Narrative Medicine: How Stories Save Lives.' Stell had a master's in this discipline. She counselled doctors not to be arrogant jerks, to listen to their patients, or clients, or consumers, or whatever doctors called the people they often helped and occasionally killed. She taught patients how to craft their personal tales. It seemed both noble and, perhaps, a lot of bullshit on one card.

Now a pain sliced along his upper torso. He'd felt it before, like being cinched in a hot metal belt. Sometimes the pangs brought him to his knees, left him breathless, but they always faded. Caperton wheezed and clung to a bookshelf for a moment. He was stressed, the doctor had said, because he was anxious. Or maybe the other way around.

A lakefront, he wished he'd said at the meeting, was a place where you could stroll and enjoy the sunshine and the lake. Wasn't that enough? Why bring history into it? History was slaughter and slaves. Stories were devices for deluding ourselves and others, like Larry's pillow mints.

Was this pretentious? Caperton had worried about being pretentious since college, when somebody told him he was pretentious. He knew he was just naïve. Why did he continue to struggle for perspective when others had moved on? A secret dunce gene? A genome? Maybe the scary belt that squeezed him was a warning: stop thinking your shallow thoughts.

Stay in the story, moron.

He pulled a faded red sneaker box from under the bed. Here resided all the junk, the objets d'crap of his years in this room: buttons, paper clips, lozenge tins, cassette tapes, rolling papers, a tiny airport brandy bottle, the watchband from his uncle's Seiko, guitar picks and toothpicks and a photograph of his mother leaning on the birch tree in the yard. Probably a box in Daphne's parents' house brimmed with similar detritus. A rabbit's-foot key chain, the fur dyed electric blue. A comic-book version of *The Waves*. Desiccated lip balm and a plastic ruby ring.

They'd met at an office party not that many years before, traded a few catchphrases from the sitcoms of their youth. That and the sex seemed enough. But then came the dumb baby question. People thought they could work on you. Wear you down. They assumed you didn't really mean what you said.

Caperton found a condom in the shoebox, the wrapper worn and crinkled, the expiration date three or four Presidents ago, a Herbert Walker rubber, a forgotten land mine that required defusing before some innocents got maimed, or had a baby too early, led stunted lives with little chance for either of them or their issue to someday stand in a room and listen to an elected official say 'koisk.'

Caperton unbent a paper clip and pricked at the wrapper. He noticed something gunked on the tip of the paper clip, like tar or bong resin. How could that shit stay gooey for so long? The universe was an unanswered question. Had Caperton read that? Heard it on public radio? He couldn't track what spoke through him anymore. He moaned and held the condom up to the window. Daylight poured through the constellation of holes.

Stell stuck her head in.

'He's up,' she said.

Larry sat in bed with a tablet in his lap. Caperton noticed the device first, then his father's freckled stick arms and ashy cheeks.

'I'm ordering tons of garbage. Stuff for the house. Gadgets. Why not? I should get some congressional shopping medal.'

'I'll make it my life's work that you get one,' Caperton said.

'What *is* your life's work, anyway?'

'Stell says it's serious this time.'

Larry looked down at the tablet, swiped the screen with a long, chapped finger.

'It's always been serious,' he said. 'Since you get born it's serious. I mean, I have a greater understanding now. Dying is natural. We're built to do it. We discuss this in my six-months-and-under group.'

'Your what?'

'It's online. No pity parties. Death is just a part of the story.'

'I thought it was the end of the story.'

'Mr Doom-and-Gloom.'

'Jesus, Dad, you're the one in bed. What do the doctors say?'

'Have you met my doctors? They have pimples. Peach fuzz. They're all virgins.'

'How do you know?'

'My tumours know.'

'OK,' Caperton said.

'The way you kids say OK,' Larry said. 'Sounds like it's not OK.'

'It's nice to be called a kid.'

'I'm indulging you,' Larry said. 'Sit down.'

Caperton took the rocker near the window.

'How long can you be here?' Larry said.

'I'll be back and forth. I'll be here.'

'I realise I was the boy who cried death. I'm sorry to put you out. But I think I need you. Or Stell will need you.'

'I'll be around,' Caperton said. 'I'll be there and back again.'

'Guess you've seen all of this before.'

'In this very room,' Caperton said.

'I know,' Larry said. 'In this very bed.'

The painting above the headboard was new, and Caperton couldn't quite tell what it depicted, with its fat swirls of white and grey. It was some kind of ship, or the spume of a whale, or a spiral-whipped wave in a storm.

Maybe it had been on the wall for a long time, but certainly not when his mother died. Or had it? He'd once been proud of the precision with which he recalled his mother's final weeks: the order of familial arrivals, their withered utterances, the last four things his mother ate (mashed potatoes, applesauce, cinnamon oatmeal, cherry ice cream, in that order), the exact position of the water pitcher on the walnut table. But now he couldn't remember if that painting had been there.

'You know,' Larry said, 'I had this English professor who used to talk about the death of the individual. "The death of the individual," he'd say. I had no idea if he was for it or against it. But at least now I know what he was talking about.'

'I don't think he was talking about this.'

'The hell you say,' Larry said.

Back in his room, Caperton checked up on the lakefront. There were no new developments, just as after all these meetings there would be no new development. It was all a joke. Most of his working hours he spent tracking down his pay cheques.

He composed a text to Daphne, which he still did sometimes, though she never responded, even when he lied and said that Gates Mandela McAdoo was a wonderful name for her child. Now he wrote, 'Here with Larry and Stell. Not good.' He erased 'Not good' and replaced it with 'More soon.' The moment he sent it an email zipped in from the airline, a survey about his flight. He was about to answer the questions when he remembered the purpose of his trip. Still, he'd rather not be rude. 'Flight was great,' he replied, 'but I'm dealing with some difficult personal matters.' Probably only robots would read the message, but sometimes it was crucial to clear the emotional desk.

He lay down on his old bed, a narrow, thin-mattressed cheapo he'd once cherished as a snuggle palace. He closed his eyes and had one of those mini-dreams he sometimes had before falling asleep. His teasers. This one featured the Rough Beast. They trudged through the rubble of a ruined city. Before them rose a bangled tower, a high, corroded structure made of pig iron, tiles, beach glass, and bottle caps. The Rough Beast paused after each step.

'Public or private?' he whispered. 'Public or private?'

Caperton flew at the Beast, bashed him to the ground.

'That's it, baby!' the Beast cried. 'Hurt my shit!'

Now there were different voices, and Caperton woke. A man who looked familiar but unplaceable stood just outside the open door.

'Hello,' he said. 'This must seem strange. But don't be alarmed. Stell told me to rouse you.'

Stell brought out tea and joined the man on the sofa in the living room. Caperton sat down on an ottoman. The man had stiff white hair, a velvet black unibrow. He jiggled Stell's hand in his lap.

'It's such a joy for me to see you again. I wish it were under better circumstances. Do you remember me?'

'You're Burt,' Caperton said. 'You used to come over with the other guys.'

'That's right. Last time I saw you, you were yay high.' Burt lifted his boot off the carpet.

'Really? That's very tiny. I must have been a barely viable foetus then.'

Burt chuckled, nudged Stell.

'Larry said he was a tough cookie. Your father loves you, you know.'

'I know.'

'Do you?' Burt said.

'Maybe you know better.'

'Your father's from a different generation, that's all. We weren't allowed to show our emotions.'

'I've met men your age who overcame that.'

'Outliers,' Burt said. 'Or possibly fags. I always liked you, you know. Even when you were a little kid and I could tell you were judging us.'

'Us?'

'The gang.'

Burt pulled Stell's knuckles to his lips.

'Hey, pal, my father's not dead yet.'

'Cool it, Omelette,' Burt said. 'Stell and I go back. I introduced your father to her. We're like family. Anyway, I hear you're a consultant.'

'Yes.'

'It's a very worthy path. I retired from the sales department about ten years after your father. Since then, I've taken up a new calling.'

'What's that?'

'Burt's a storyteller,' Stell said.

'No shit.'

'I must admit it's true,' Burt said. 'Every Saturday I go down to the library and tell stories to the children. I'm sure I bore the pants off them, but I get a thrill.'

'Tell me a story.'

'Well, I don't know if this is really a good time for –'

'Just tell me a story.'

Burt told Caperton a story. It had a boy in it, an eagle feather, a shiny blue turtle. There was an ogre in a cave. Rivers were crossed on flimsy ropes, wise witches sought for counsel, bandits hunted and rehabilitated. The blue turtle led the boy to a princess. The princess fought the ogre and saved the boy. Caperton soaked up every word and couldn't take his eyes off Burt's brow, which lifted at the close of the tale.

'Bravo,' Stell said.

'Pulled that one out of my butt,' Burt said.

'That's why you're a genius,' Stell said. 'Am I right?'

Caperton shrugged. 'I don't know. Seemed a little cheesy to me.'

'Helps if you're five,' Burt said. 'Not some snide turd turning forty.'

Caperton stood.

'You're right, Burt. What can I say? I'm feeling peckish.'

Stell shrieked. 'Please, don't go in there! What do you want? I'll get your sandwich! Or do you want something else? Just tell me what you want! Let me make it for you!'

Caperton opened the fridge and in the darkness saw what he wanted. What he could make. He scooped up a bag of bread, a tomato, a hard-boiled egg. Stell charged him, crumpled against his hip, wrapped up his knees. The egg flew away. Caperton slit the bread bag open with his thumbnail, balled up a soft slice of seven-grain and shoved it in his mouth. He bit into the tomato and seeds ran down his wrists, pulp splotched the wall.

'Stop!' Stell said. 'What are you doing?'

'I'm having an after-school snack,' Caperton snarled, and fisted up another bread ball, licked the tomato's bright wound.

'You're sick!' Stell said, and from her knees tried to shove him clear of the kitchen.

Caperton bent over her, whispered, 'Thanks for the medical narrative.'

He ripped open his shirt and crushed the mutilated tomato against his chest. Juice glistened in dark burls of hair. He thought that maybe he was about to make a serious declaration, or even try to laugh the whole thing off, when he felt a twinge, a test cinch for another spell of nervous woe. The Belt of Intermittent Sorrow, which he somehow now named the moment it went tight, squeezed him to the kitchen floor.

That night he texted Daphne: 'Can't sleep in this bed. It's crazy here. Creepy. Like a bad play. Or a bad production of a good play. How is little Gates? I'm sure you're a wonderful mother. Maybe if mine hadn't died I would have felt differently. Who knows? You know I'll always love you. More later. Talk soon.'

Minutes later Caperton heard his text tone: shod hooves on cobblestones.

'Let me introduce myself. My name is Miles and I'm the nanny. I was a Division II nose tackle not very long ago. If you keep texting Daphne I'll come to your house and feed you your phone. Daphne does not wish to receive messages from you, now or in the future. Good day.'

Good day?

Caperton shivered in his shoddy childhood cot. 'Let the sobbing begin', he texted to himself, and sank into hard slumber beneath his dank duvet.

The next morning Caperton stood beside a taxi in the driveway. Stell gathered him in for a hug.

'I'm sorry,' Caperton said, fingering the pierced condom in his pocket.

'Stop saying that. Just go see a doctor. And a therapist.'

'I will. I'll be back for the weekend. I'll be back and forth.'

'I know,' Stell said.

Burt stood on the lawn in cop shades.

Was he protecting Stell from her hair-trigger stepson? Standing vigil for his dying amigo?

Just before coming outside, Caperton had checked on his father. Larry had maybe taken a little bit of a bad turn. He looked pretty damn sick.

'Work beckons, huh?' Larry nodded at Caperton's coat.

'Afraid so. Be here Saturday.'

Caperton took his father's hand.

'Listen,' Caperton said. 'I realise I've been an idiot, Dad. All my pointless rage. I've wasted so much time trying to get a certain feeling back. But it's a child's feeling, and I can't have it anymore. But I love you. I really do. Know that. And let's not hold back. With the time we have, let's say everything to each other. That's all I want.'

Something like a ship's light, far away, began to glow, stately and forlorn, in Larry's eyes. He gripped his son's hand harder.

'I know you're strapped for time,' Larry said, his voice raspier in just the past day. 'But there's this new show on cable, you really should watch it. It's amazing.'

'A show?'

'No, really,' Larry said, strained upward, and coughed in Caperton's ear the name of the showrunner, and how this fellow had also created another hit series.

'The character arcs are ground-breaking,' Larry said. 'It's a golden age of cable television.'

'Sounds great.'

'I'd wait to watch it with you,' Larry said. 'But, well, you know ...'

'I'll be back,' Caperton said.

'And forth.' Larry said. 'I'm glad. I need you, son.'

Caperton was not surprised to see the Rough Beast in the terminal. The Internet wrestler sipped from a demitasse at a granite countertop near the gate. Caperton thought to approach him, but the quest for symmetry seemed a mistake. Besides, the Beast wouldn't remember a snide turd like him.

Caperton had two seats to himself on the plane. He wished he could relish the boon, but it made him anxious. A free seat meant that anybody could take it at any time, lumber up from the back rows looking for relief – a fatty, a talker, the ghost of his mother, Death itself, Burt.

Caperton took the aisle seat, the better to defend the window and, about twenty minutes into the flight, heard a loud grunt, felt a hard pinch on his earlobe.

'How are you, man?' the Beast said. 'What's the story?'

A pill from Stell had introduced Caperton to a new flippancy.

'The story, Mr Beast? It's ongoing. Arcing hard. It's an arcing savage, an astonishment machine.'

'Booyah! And how's your personal matter?'

'Everything's going to be OK, my man, within the context of nothing ever being OK.'

'Brother has been on a philosophical fact-finding mission, come back with the news.' The Beast proffered five, belly-high.

'Please,' a flight attendant said, approaching from business. 'No congregating.'

'Nobody's congregating,' the Beast said.

'We can't allow congregating for security reasons.'

'Just shooting the breeze here, sweetness. No box cutters.'

'Sir.'

'Maybe you're too young for that reference.'

'Please sit down.'

'OK, fine,' the Beast said, and walked back to his row.

When the plane landed, Caperton lifted his half-unzipped bag from under the seat and noticed a sandwich tucked under some socks. Pastrami and capers. On a croissant. Caperton chewed and waited for the plane to reach the gate. It would be an odd time now. Larry, the Fates willing, might hold on for a while. They would have a chance to grow close again. Caperton knew he would not run from this. Even if his father doubted him, he knew he would be there when it counted.

He checked his phone and saw the messages stack up in comforting fashion. Life might be looking down, but at least coms were up. It took just the briefest skim of his messages for all comfort to vanish. Now he could only ponder how strange it was that you could move at these outra-geous speeds through the air and know everything known and still control nothing. For example, during this one quick flight his father had died, and the bony young councilman, the Prince of Koisks, had kicked him off the project. Also, there was an email from the airline he'd just flown explaining how much they respected his time and offering consolation for his current difficulties. Worse than robots, really.

Caperton called the only person he could call. Daphne answered and told him to hold on. Another voice came on the line.

'This is Miles.'

'Jesus, I thought she made you up.'

'No, I'm very much an entity of your dimension. Somebody who could find you and stomp on your urethra in what we foolishly call real time. Did you not receive the text message?'

'I did,' Caperton said.

'But you thought calling was OK?'

'Did you say you were the nanny?'

'Goodbye, Mr –'

'No, Miles, please don't hang up. Just stay on the line for a minute. For sixty seconds. That's all. I'm having a bad moment. I don't need Daphne. You'll do fine. My father just died. Please just ... I just ...'

'Why don't you emulate your old man,' Miles said, hung up.

Caperton groaned, shook, curled up in his seats, and watched people stand and grope at the overhead bins. He heard the Beast barrel through the throng behind him. Here he loomed again.

'Caught the end of your call.'

'Yeah,' Caperton said.

'We'll be here awhile, waiting for all these people. Shove over.'

Caperton slid toward the window and the Rough Beast sat down. He patted Caperton's knee.

'Terrible about your pops. Mine went easy. Keeled over on his city snowplow up in Rochester. But that doesn't make it any better for you.'

'No.'

'It's OK. You're with me now. Everything will be OK. Cry for your father. What man doesn't cry for his father? Let it out.'

Caperton cooled his forehead on the window. The Beast stroked his back.

'They say it's a cycle, but there is no cycle. You get jerked in and reamed out. That's all.'

Caperton could not cry again. Also, he thought he might be onto a new phase. Lumped nullity. Drool drooped from his lip. He looked up and saw that the plane was empty.

'I'm sorry,' one of the flight attendants said. 'But it's time to leave.'

'We'll leave soon,' the Beast said. 'When it's time.'

'But it's time now.'

'No, it's not!' the Rough Beast shouted, cocked his hand for a karate chop. 'This man's in the middle of a fucking hinge moment! I'll waste you all!'

One of the flight attendants called security on her walkie-talkie. The others dashed for the door.

Caperton, who now felt a wider and more fiery belt of perhaps increasingly frequent sorrow begin to singe him, slid to his knees and crushed his face into the seat back. The underside of the locked and upright tray, cool and vaguely pebbled, was heaven on his skin.

SIX DAYS IN GLORIOUS VIENNA

Yoko Ogawa

[Translated by Stephen Snyder]

F ourteen tourists had signed up for 'Six Days in Glorious Vienna: Open Plan,' and since Kotoko and I were the only singles in the group, it was inevitable that we ended up rooming together at the hotel. Kotoko turned out to be a plump woman in her sixties who had been widowed some years earlier.

On our first night in Vienna, she kneeled politely on the bed and bowed.

'I'm afraid I snore,' she said. 'I hope it won't bother you.' And with that she climbed under the covers.

I'd thought women her age were chatty, but not Kotoko. When the rest of us had gathered at the airport or in the lobby of the hotel, talking excitedly about the trip, she had stood a bit apart, looking uncomfortable. She clutched the strap of a brown vinyl shoulder bag that was stuffed to the gills and eyed us uneasily, as though she'd wandered into our midst by mistake. Other than the fact that it was the first trip abroad for both of us, we seemed to have nothing in common.

Still, it didn't matter much. Since the tour was self-guided, and we would be on our own for the next six days, there was no need for us to get better acquainted, even if we were to be roommates. I hadn't come to Vienna to hear her go on about her grandchildren or badmouth her daughter-in-law; nor did I want her prying into my private life. I had been saving everything I'd earned at my tutoring job to celebrate my twentieth birthday with this trip.

As she had knelt there on the bed, Kotoko had looked a bit like a decorative object. Her face was round with folds of fat at the chin; her breasts hung down on her round belly. Generous layers of fat covered every part of her – eyelids, ears, shoulders, back, knees, fingers – each tracing its own distinctive curve, and there, next to the bed, lay the swollen bag, as if mimicking the shape of her body.

It was true that she snored, but so quietly that I was able to fall asleep almost immediately.

Kotoko knelt on the bed again the next morning as I was getting ready to go out. She seemed to be hesitating about something as she would take a map from her bag, sigh a bit, and then put on the cardigan she'd just taken off.

'Excuse me,' she murmured without looking up. 'Would you mind writing the name of the hotel?' she said, holding out the palm of her hand. 'I'm afraid of getting lost and not being able to find my way back. I know it sounds silly, but I can't read foreign words.' The springs of the mattress groaned as the bow made her round body even rounder.

'It's written right here,' I said, but she stopped me as I reached for the phone pad and held her hand up again.

'But I might lose the paper. If you write it here, I'm sure to have it.'

Her hand, too, was layered with fat, and the feeling as the tip of the pen buried itself in her palm was somehow satisfying. On it I wrote 'König von Ungarn' with a permanent marker. I had to admit that I wasn't exactly sure how to pronounce the complicated foreign name myself.

Kotoko studied her palm for a moment, tracing the pen marks with her finger, but then she began to squirm again, as though some new source of anxiety had occurred to her. She looked up and met my gaze, and then quickly looked down again. She seemed to be at considerable pains to let me know that she had something else to ask me but was finding it difficult to do so.

'Where are you going today?'

It was a simple question, and I asked it without thinking and without any real interest in the answer, but it proved to be the start of all my troubles.

Kotoko had come to Vienna with a single purpose: to visit an old lover who was hovering near death in the hospital wing of nursing home in the suburbs. The announcement startled me, since I had never imagined she would be uttering a phrase like 'old lover.'

I had originally intended to go with her as far as the streetcar terminal at Schottentor Station. She had explained that to get to the nursing home she would need to take the No. 38 streetcar from Schottentor to a stop called Grin-something or other.

'That's the No. 38 over there,' I told her. 'See, it's written in big numbers on the side. You take it and stay on till your stop – as simple as that.'

'Ahh ...' she murmured, seeming reluctant to let go of my arm, which was raised in the direction of the trolley. The vinyl of her handbag and the skin of her chest pressed against me.

'But what if I don't get off when I'm supposed to? I imagine the names of the stops will be written in alphabet letters, too. Of course they will, we're in Austria. I know I'm being such a baby. But how am I going to ask for directions to the nursing home? The truth is I have a weak heart and even standing here in a crowd like this is making it flutter ... But no, please don't worry about me. It happens all the time, so I'm used to it. But you see, I've brought along money for your trolley fare, too. This should be enough for the round trip, and I'd be happy for you to keep whatever's left over.'

Kotoko forced a wadded bill into my pocket. I took it out and found the image of Sigmund Freud, so wrinkled as to be barely recognisable, staring back from a fifty-schilling note. I did a quick – though pointless – calculation and realised that the sum would, indeed, be enough for the fare.

As we stood there, she clung closer and closer to me, and the No. 38 tram appeared ready to depart.

'We don't want to miss it,' I said. 'Let's go.'

Half amazed and half resigned, I climbed aboard with Kotoko. What was so wrong about spending a little of my time in Vienna with a widow with a bad heart who couldn't read the alphabet? Besides, I was sure I'd feel better helping her than leaving her to fend for herself. Or so I told myself as we sat on the streetcar.

Kotoko's expression was radiant now, but she clung resolutely to my arm, refusing to relax her vigilance. From time to time, she would reach into her bag and produce chewing gum or chocolate or rice crackers and offer them to me. Tools to curry my favour appeared one after the other: a bottle of water when we were thirsty, a comb when the wind blew, throat spray when I coughed. But as they did, I found myself silently planning my afternoon – a visit to St Stephen's Cathedral, a picture in front of the statue of Mozart, followed by a piece of Sachertorte at a café.

The story that Kotoko told en route of her long-ago love affair was a fairly simple one. Forty-five years previously, when she was nineteen, she had worked at a factory that produced ham, and when thirty-four-year-old Johan had come from Vienna to serve as technical manager, they had immediately fallen in love. As she put it, his pupils were like caramel candies, his golden hair like the softest dandelion fluff – and when, after ten months, Johan's time in Japan came to an end and he was headed home, he had promised to come back for her.

'But he never did,' I said.

'How did you know?' said Kotoko, he eyes wide with surprise.

'I suppose because it's a common enough story. And no doubt he had a wife back in Vienna.'

'You're young, but not much gets by you. How lucky for me to be rooming with someone so clever.' Kotoko nodded to herself and started rooting around in her bag again. I smiled, taking a bite of the chocolate bar she had given me. There was no trace of bitterness in her manner, despite the ancient betrayal.

'His wife died years ago and he's been in the nursing home for some time. But it appears he doesn't have much longer. He made a list of people he wanted contacted when the end was near, and my name was on it, along with the address of the ham factory. Mine was the very last name, apparently. They said they contacted me early since Japan is so far away.'

The tram stop was Grinzing, which was easy enough to find, but the route to the nursing home was long and complicated. Kotoko would never have found her way alone. We passed through a residential district, walked by a museum dedicated to Beethoven, and along a path by a stream. The building we were seeking appeared suddenly as we came to the entrance to a forest.

Tall, narrow windows were arranged on the plain, imposing façade at regular intervals. The carefully tended garden on the far side of the wrought iron gate merged into the forest beyond. Birds chirped in the trees.

For a woman who was about to meet her lover for the first time in forty-five years, Kotoko seemed surprisingly calm. In fact, as we approached the nursing home, her grip on my arm finally began to loosen and she fell back a step, hiding behind me as if to suggest she was just keeping me company.

'Here we are,' I said. Kotoko contented herself with a noncommittal sigh.

A receptionist led us along a winding corridor to a spacious ward facing an inner courtyard. Metal beds lined the walls in two neat rows, with stools for the visitors. I counted sixteen beds, each occupied by an elderly patient.

Though I had no experience with this sort of thing, I could see right away that the ward was reserved for those who were not long for this world. There was no life in their faces, and they were so emaciated that their bones were visible under the blankets. Most lay with their eyes closed, either sleeping or unconscious, and the few open eyes were little more than hollow cavities. There were several other visitors in the ward, but no one said a word. The only sounds were an occasional groan or hiccup or rattling of a throat.

I looked around the room. The patients were nearly indistinguishable to me. The subtle differences in hairstyle, the shape of an ear or thickness of the lips were swallowed up in the shadow of death. They were all cloaked in a shroud of old age that concealed their former appearance.

Kotoko went down one row and I the other, checking the nametag tied to the foot of each bed.

Kotoko let out a quiet exclamation when she found Johan. He was in the fifth bed in the row on the south side of the ward, resting quietly like the other patients. His blonde hair had been reduced to thin fuzz, leaving a scalp crusted with scabs. The eyes that had looked like caramels were hidden now under wrinkled lids.

We sat down on the stools and watched over him for a while. His blanket and pillow were clean and the floor around the bed was spotless. Sunlight shone through the window, illuminating every corner of the ward, and a light breeze blew from time to time. The poppies and daisies and violets in the beds outside looked fresh and alive, and bees flew among the petals gathering nectar. A resident of the nursing home walked slowly across the courtyard leaning on a cane.

'Why don't you try talking to him?' I said.

'But ...' Kotoko hesitated, fiddling with the strap on her bag. 'It would be a shame to wake him.'

'I doubt he'd be angry. It's the first time you've seen each other in forty-five years. He may just be resting.'

'I suppose you're right.' She cleared her throat a couple of times and then murmured his name. 'Johan.'

There was no response.

'You have to be louder than that,' I told her. 'He's an old man.'

'I know. I'll try again.'

This time her voice was a bit more assertive, but it did nothing to disturb his deep sleep.

'Why don't you try kissing him?'

'I couldn't possibly!' she said, flinching.

'He's Austrian,' I told her. 'That's how they greet each other. Besides, you must have kissed him when he was your boyfriend.'

'Well, I suppose, but that was a long time ago ...' Her eyes never left her lap.

'If you don't let him know you're here, what's the point of having spent the money to come all this way?'

'I know, but ...'

Perhaps because the bed was made for tall Europeans, Kotoko was forced to stand on the tips of her toes in order to reach Johan. Bracing her left hand on the pillow and her right close to his head, she stretched even further over the bed. Her breasts pressed into the railing, her calves trembled, but still she seemed uncertain. For his part, Johan remained oblivious to what was about to occur.

Finally making up her mind, she put her lips against his cheek – and though her posture was too painfully awkward to conjure up a long-lost romance, a kiss was, indeed, a kiss. A trace of her lipstick was visible on Johan's sunken cheek as proof.

She took a damp tissue out of her bag and wiped away the lipstick; turning the tissue over, she cleaned his mouth and around his eyes. Then, for the longest time, she sat next to him, folding and unfolding the tissue, as if reluctant to throw it away.

At noon, she treated me to lunch at the nursing home cafeteria, no doubt feeling that the change from the tram ticket was insufficient compensation.

'Now that I've found Johan at last, I'm starved,' she said. She ate a piece of boiled beef with a large portion of mashed potatoes, and, still not satisfied, had two helpings of ice cream for dessert.

'Why do you suppose he put your name on the list?' I asked her. 'After all, he hadn't heard from you in forty-five years.'

'Maybe he came across some old document with the address of the ham factory when he was packing and getting ready to move to the nursing home,' Kotoko answered, seeming strangely calm.

'Do you think he wants to ask for forgiveness?'

'I suppose he would have felt rather guilty.'

'After he left, did you go on waiting for him to come back for a long time?'

'For years,' she said. 'When no word came, I told myself all sorts of stories – his parents had locked him in the tower of their castle to keep him from me or he'd been in an automobile accident and had amnesia – but they were just stories.'

'You should have come to Vienna back then and forced the issue.'

'I could never have done something like that. Instead, I just stuffed myself with the new ham he'd taught us to make. But it never sold well and we stopped producing it soon afterward.' She ladled the melted ice cream from the bottom of the bowl and slurped it noisily from the spoon.

'He wasn't like that when I knew him,' she said, staring into the empty bowl.

'Of course not,' I said.

'He was stylish, very elegant, but with powerful arms – bigger than our hams – that could sweep me up as though I was light as a feather.'

The cafeteria was empty, perhaps because it was getting late. The tables were covered with white tablecloths and each one had a small vase with a single flower – apparently picked from the flowerbeds in the garden. Some of the residents were playing chess in the sunroom that connected to the cafeteria on the south side.

'In any case,' she said, 'I was happy just knowing that someone in a far-off place might be thinking about me, if only for a moment. That thought was a comfort on sleepless nights. I would picture that distant land and fall peacefully to sleep.'

She pressed her napkin to her mouth. Her lipstick was gone now.

'Here,' she said, sliding her hand across the table. 'Tomorrow's tram fare.' Another fifty-schilling note with a wrinkled picture of Freud.

In the end, I went with Kotoko to the nursing home the next day and the day after that. I never visited the Kunsthistorisches Museum or toured the Schönbrunn Palace or rode the little train in the Prater Park. I went nowhere at all but the nursing home. And all the while, Johan's condition seemed to deteriorate. But Kotoko sat quietly on the stool by his bed, slowly blending into the atmosphere of the sick room – as though she had been there all along.

Every so often I would go out to get some fresh air in the garden. Walking along in front of the terrace, I would look at the flowerbeds and then sit for a moment on the edge of the fountain. Sometimes I would even venture into the woods and linger for a long while, fascinated by the sunlight filtering through the trees. No one ever stopped to speak to me on these outings, and the elderly residents kept their eyes on the ground ahead of them as they walked. When I got back to the ward, Kotoko was where I had left her, with no sign that she had moved a muscle.

Every half hour or so, she would tap me on the shoulder. 'Is he still breathing?'

In response, I would put my cheek close to his mouth to feel the faint puff of breath and listen for the quiet gurgling deep in his throat.

'Yes, still breathing,' I would tell her, but she continued to study him with a dubious look on her face. She could easily have allayed her fears by checking for herself, but she apparently lacked the courage to do so, and a few minutes later the tap on my shoulder would come again.

Each time he made a sound – a burp or a cough or some other indeter-minate noise – or when his eyes seemed to move about under the lids, we would start and lean forward over the bed. Then it was necessary to check whether he was breathing all over again. And at some point in all this, it occurred to me that we were actually waiting for him to die.

When his hand pushed out from under the blanket, Kotoko would ever so warily take hold of his fingers. She would stroke his hair or straighten the collar of his pyjamas or moisten his lips with a piece of damp gauze. But she did all this with the greatest reticence, as though to announce by her manner that she had no right to do so and would instantly retire when some more appropriate person appeared to care for him.

Johan breathed his last on the afternoon of the day before we were due to leave Vienna. I have no idea what became of the other people who had been on his list, but the fact was that Kotoko and I were the only ones there at the end.

No doubt because the staff was so accustomed to the work, every-thing happened with amazing speed and efficiency. Once the doctor had confirmed that there was no pulse, each player performed his part seam-lessly. We stood aside and watched as they cleaned the body and then took it away to the chapel. Then a different attendant put clean sheets on the bed.

Several of the residents came to offer their condolences. They were warm and kind. Some of them wept as they praised the deceased and urged us to be brave. They embraced us, Kotoko first and then me. Though we were unable to understand a single word they said, their sympathy was abundantly clear.

As I stood enfolded by those old arms, feeling old hands on my back, the sadness slowly began to spread through me as well. Though I had no connection to the dead man and had never exchanged a single word with him, I could sense the pain that all those present were feeling. It bathed me like the waters from a chilly spring.

I took Kotoko's hand. The name of our hotel that I had written on her palm had faded and would soon vanish altogether.

When everything in the ward had been cleared away, the only remaining trace of Johan was the plate with his name attached to the foot of the bed. The new sheets were smooth, and any lingering body heat in the mattress had dissipated. A fresh, carefully fluffed pillow had replaced the old one.

The nameplate swung gently back and forth, though the air was still. I took hold of it – a simple label encased in plastic.

Joshua it read.

'Joshua,' I said aloud. 'That wasn't Johan, Kotoko. That was Joshua.'

Kotoko's mouth fell open and she blinked several times. She took the nametag from me and turned it over in her hands, rubbed it with her fingers. But that didn't change the fact that Johan was Joshua.

'But what are we going to do?' she said, breathing a quiet sigh.

'There's no need to do anything,' I said.

'And to think I even kissed him ...'

'Don't give it another thought. You did exactly the right thing.'

'But ...'

'Everyone needs someone to be with him at the end, no matter what his name is. You were simply being that someone.'

I glanced at the nametag on the neighbouring bed.

Johan.

There he was – as feeble as Joshua had been, with very little to distinguish them. Except that he was still alive. He was sleeping, the pupils like caramels concealed beneath nearly transparent eyelids. We stood looking back and forth between the real Johan and the empty bed, and then we pressed our palms together and said a prayer for Joshua who was now so very far away.

THE UNINTENDED

Gina Apostol

18. The insoluble puzzle at the heart of the labyrinth is not Magsalin's to bemoan

For the mystery writer, it is not enough to mourn the dead. One must also study the exit wounds, invite the coroner to tea, cloud the mind with ulterior motives, typically in triplicate. In addition, pay credit card bills for the grieving, if such bills are extant.

The translator and mystery writer Magsalin has undertaken (yes, no, pun) some of the above duties at previous incidents; but the insoluble puzzle at the heart of the labyrinth, the Icarian cry, is not hers to bemoan. That is up to the dead man's kin, who are, fortunately or not, also dead. It is said, for instance, that the writer Georges Perec's mother died in Auschwitz, his father of shrapnel wounds before the war even started. The writer Georges Perec had a wife. She is a widow. Her heart must be broken. (Magsalin cannot do that for her.)

For the mystery writer, there are the sheaves of paper, the umbrellas from James Smith and Sons (owned by the wife, shipped from Bloomsbury in London), the clippings of newsprint events of general interest, such as the Tunis-Marseille ship schedule, lottery numbers, and election results for mayor of the commune Ivry-Sur-Seine, 1979 (the winner is a communist). For the mystery writer, everything could be a clue, and a word has at least two meanings, both of them correct. And it is not right to jump to conclusions, especially when it becomes apparent that one's sorrow is misplaced, in this case.

First, the writer has been dead for some time. Second, she has read only two of his novels. Third, he does not figure at all, except as premonitory prompt, a standby ghost, in this story of disappearance Magsalin is about to foretell as she slips a horde of facts into her handbag (leather, from Cleo and Patek, aubergine with olive handles, always admired by salesladies): the writer's income tax returns, dental appointment cards, shipping receipts from James Smith and Sons Umbrella Shop of Bloomsbury, London, photographs bought from the Library of Congress, $3^{1}/_{2}$ x 7 note cards that slip out from envelopes, a stash of library books the writer thought he would have time to return.

19. Everything in the world is doubled

In Las Vegas in 1969, everything in the world is doubled – the chandeliers, the plush of the blackjack tables, the old women (in furs and mohair caps with rhinestone hatpins) swinging their sequin purses, the sheen of noiseless slot machines. Virginie is staring at an old woman clutching an empty pail in her hand, the name *The Sands* somewhat erased in a winding circle around the pail's dull tub. She stares because she and the woman are wearing the same Schreiner brooch: a pink rose. It is a coincidence. The woman's mouth opens in silent despair. But the only sound Virginie hears is the scratch of Luca's pen (it is a 1940s Esterbrook, a miniature in pale green, one of hers). Her husband is so young. This fact touches Virginie, though she is six years younger than Luca. Virginie's diplopia has the odd advantage of centring her focus only on the sound of Luca's writing. She sees double but hears nothing but scratch. Scratch scratch scratch scratch.

4. Chiara Brasi's trip

Chiara Brasi affirms to Magsalin that she is the daughter of the director of *The Unintended*.

Magsalin confesses she saw the film several times in her teens.

At one point, memorably, she recalls watching it frame by frame in a muggy class along Katipunan Avenue, a course called Locations/ Dislocations, about the phantasmal voids in Vietnam War movies shot in equally blighted areas that are not Vietnam. The disturbing web of contorted allusions, hidden historiographic anxiety, political ironies, and astounding art direction resident in a single frame, for instance, of a fissured bridge in the Philippines, in real life dynamited by the Japanese in 1943 and still unrepaired in 1976, and rebuilt specifically and re-exploded spectacularly in the film's faux-napalm scene against a mystic pristine river actually already polluted by local dynamite fishers – the movie, for what-ever reason, kept putting Magsalin to sleep, though she omits that detail before the filmmaker's daughter.

There was something both engrossing and pathetic about it, about reconstructing the trauma of whole countries through a movie's illusive palimpsest, and what was most disturbing, of course, was that, on one level, the professor's point was undeniably true, our identities are irremediably mediated, but that did not mean Magsalin had to keep thinking about it.

Chiara seems unconcerned, however, by the scholarly implications of her father's cult classic; at least she seems unburdened. She nods absently at Magsalin's squinting recall, as if she, Chiara, has heard it all before, as if she needs another Adderall. What she really needs, Chiara says, almost upsetting Magsalin's cup of chai, is someone to accompany her on a trip.

'Where to?' asks Magsalin.

'I need to get to Samar.'

20. Why Samar?

Luca pours out his dreams to her, and Virginie always restrains her own, as if hers should be checked so his can run free, though no one has estab-lished the rules. She knows it will be no honeymoon because he is still in the throes of thinking, a terrible condition, the way he renews his acquaintance with his demented plots: an epic about Rotarians; a love story involving Gus, the famous dying polar bear of Central Park Zoo (one of his weird obsessions); a musical about dwarves in space (a physicist's dream); an Italian soccer fantasy film with himself in a cameo, of course, as a deaf-mute goalie; a murder mystery set in Vietnam but in fact about pyromaniac grief, gruesome and disconsolate; an adaptation of *Tale of Genji* in a World War II Japanese internment camp (also a musical). He always has a jungle of ideas from which he zooms into his desire – his obdurate cathexis: the four-leaf clover she has missed. It is admirable how his desire just cuts through the brush, when Virginie can barely figure out which pin to wear: the pink Schreiner rose, one of her fabulous fakes, or her mother's choice, an antique pearl in an abstract coil.

The Colt .45 was invented to kill the Filipino *juramentados*, violent insurgents out of their minds, during the Philippine-American war. That much she is told. She has learned more than anyone will ever need to know about the Philippine-American war in the years she has been married to Luca. The genealogy of the genocidal Krag-Jørgenson rifle (Sweden, 1896), ignoble prop of a dirty war; the melancholy artistry of bamboo snares (Samar, 1899), useless prop of a hopeless war; the advent of stereoscopic photography (Underwood and Underwood Photographic Company, 1900), propaganda tool for the imperial wretchedness of this war. Luca keeps the gun on his desk as he researches, poring over maps he has ordered from the Library of Congress. As he shows her the trail they could take, using the gun to make his point, from the infernal streams of Samar's interior to the mountain passes above the Caves of Sohoton, she wonders if her husband has imbibed it, the spirit of his *juramentados*. Still, she knows she will go.

Virginie, too, has a sense of the wild, though it is not apparent in her outfits. She is dressed in brocade and gold. She glitters like a sunfish. She wears the metallics and embroidered dresses that she wore in the days she had first met him. Her mother, Chaya Sophia Chazanov of Sosnitza along the Dnieper, Cassandra Chase to immigration authorities, and now Madame Rubinson of Rubinson Fur Emporium on Park Avenue, had always favoured old-world props, lace and lamé. Madame Rubinson was a former set designer who, not quite by intention, married rich. It was Virginie's secret that she bore a sense of trauma that the world around her mocked – she was cosseted from birth, showered with toys after all; but she has this subliminal perception of a wound without root or reason, that not even she can see.

She had gone to the zoo that day in one of those bouts of ennui that took teenage girls like her, who had an excess of wit and indolence, into parts of the city that enthralled children and manic-depressives. It was

September, 1958. She lived only a few blocks from the animals, the hippos and the polar bears and the penguins, but she had never seen them up close. It was not proper, said her aunts, to do things in solitude: the devil is on the lookout for lonely minds. And zoos were for the vulgar. Every day after school, passing the zoo as a child, she would hear the chime of its hours, tinkling in a sunlit, dying fall, like the charmed suspiration of the endless tedium that lay ahead of her. That day, playing hooky, she found herself next to the sea lion tamer, studying as if magnetised the sleight of hand with which he fed the animals their mid-day, gleaming fish. The act's doubleness enthralled Virginie – the way she believed absolutely in the spectacle of beastly affection, at the same time that she saw the bait that fed it.

She needed to go out more.

In this way, she failed to see the filmmaker catching her figure, out of place in her sequined outfit and spotted leopard coat from Rubinson Fur Emporium. She had intruded onto his picture, but it was semi-neorealist anyway (i.e., done on the cheap). He was filming his pro-animal master-piece, tentatively called *Maniac in the Ark,* about an insane killer who turns out to be a zookeeper (of course) who wreaks mayhem to extort funds from the Mayor of New York to find a cure for his great love (Gus the Polar Bear, of course). No distributor bought it, yet Luca still thinks of the plot fondly. Luca caught her like this, a truant in his mise-en-scène of dubious enchantment, and when he asked her to sign away her right to privacy, asking also for her phone number, she did not see the symbolism – the tamer at play with a hungry beast. She took his bait.

The life of a filmmaker is one of scraps of plots sandwiched between the lack of means to fulfil them. The life of a woman in the fifties is one of scraps of plots sandwiched between the lack of means to fulfil them. It is hard for Virginie to grasp that she has agency, just as in those old films of femmes fatales dying in grisly circumstances (Garbo in *Camille*, or Garbo in any other role), the viewer starts shouting at the doomed woman who fails to grasp that she has agency – don't fall for that lousy count, you nincompoop! – and so she dies of consumption or jumps in front of that speeding train anyway. Eloping with a bearded *artiste* she meets at the zoo does not strike Virginie as a cinematic cliché. It seems like freedom. In the dark of the screening room, she watches the shreds and patches of the scene he has filmed. She clutches his hand in the scene of murder in the Arctic cages, as the killer raises his bloody axe. She screams. He tells her – look, it is just sleight of hand. All of your terror lies in the cut. No penguins were harmed in the filming of this movie. She does not look. But she keeps watching him rolling his film, feeding his gleaming reel.

He stops and starts and cuts and discards, including her scene with the sea lions (he says the metaphor is sublime but the lighting is not). And the power of that – the certainty of his director's vision – gives her *invidia*: a disease of empathy. It's that envy of the artist that arises in certain readers: a visceral connivance with his dreams matched only by the desire to kill him for fulfilling them.

21. Before the weeping and the cursing and the tantrums

Virginie's first trip with Luca to Las Vegas is that date in 1969. They are still childless. She hates leaving Manhattan but wishes to appreciate her husband's way of life. Luca prefers the Grand but she chooses the Hilton. There are lines of women in beehives and stilettos. It distresses and pleases her, to see herself as if in a mirror, to see so many women looking like her, all in a line to see a show. The rows of women give Virginie this rush, this thrill that comes over her in discordant places. The fact is, she is scared of crowds. She hides behind her husband's new fame, his monstrous vitality; in the photographs, she always strikes this sub-alar pose, like a puffin cub taking cover. She hates going to premieres. She discovers too late that she hates the movies, a detail that amuses her husband: the visual effects strain her nerves. She cannot help it. She imagines, as the train rushes straight at her, that she will fall with the hero into the abyss.

This neurological defect in Virginie draws her husband to her. Her sense that fantasy is never an illusion and that the purpose of art is hypnosis, a form of body snatching, arouses in Luca both tenderness and calculation. She is the ideal viewer for whom he makes his thrillers, but that does not mitigate the convenience of marrying a reliable investor.

It might be fun to see the shows, she says on the spur of the moment. Sure, Luca says, why not. Grist for the mill. Luca can write anywhere. But truth be told, he prefers the casinos. By the baccarat tables, he likes to spread out his 3 x 7 note cards, ruled. Security and waiters leave him alone. They are used to oddballs with money. He ponders a sequence then he shuffles, inserts a note card into a middle set, moves a top card to the second column, recording his rearrangements on a yellow legal pad, ruled. He's an orderly man and scratches his reconfigurations of the plot in a neat list of rejumbled numbers with corresponding new scenes. The arranging of movie scenes via numbered index cards is like playing solitaire with a set of laws that he is inventing. He is improvising, second-guessing. He can see the scenes coming together then he doesn't. The end is always elusive. His wife taps him on the shoulder.

I got the tickets, she says.

14. The dossier Magsalin receives

The sheets of paper Chiara Brasi had offered to Magsalin look like a script. Are there also drawings? Magsalin shakes out prints of Samar in 1901, ordered from the Library of Congress Prints and Photographs (the receipts fall out, too, from the envelope): index-card size pictures against yellowed boards – of banana groves, dead bodies in grey trenches, GIs in dress fatigues gazing down as if in regret at a charred battleground.

Each of the pictures is oddly doubled. Each index card is a set of thick, twinned prints, each identical print pasted, side-by-side, on stiff panels. All are roughly postcard-size.

Magsalin is familiar with the doubled photos, and they strike her cold.

They are late nineteenth-century pairs of stereo cards.

You look closely at the odd, twin pictures as if presented with one of those optical illusions that should come with a caption, *Find What's Missing!* But there is nothing missing to find: the two pictures on each stereo card are identical.

On the Smithsonian website, www.loc.gov, search 'Philippine insurrection,' and you come across them. Archived stereo pairs from the years 1899 to 1913, the bleak years of US imperial aggression before the surrender of the last Filipino forces to American occupation. You may as well just copy and paste the gist. *Soldiers wading across a shallow river; advancing through open country, et cetera. A group of men with crates of food on the beach, et cetera. A burned section of Manila. The burned palace of Aguinaldo. Firefighting measures. Artillery. Ducks swimming. Children wading. Soldier burying a dead 'insurgent.' Soldier showing off the barrel of his Colt .45. Et cetera.*

Et cetera. A history in ellipses, too repetitive to know. Not to mention the words in quotes and not. 'Insurgents' are in quotes. Insurrection is not. History is not fully annotated or adequately contemplated in online archives. This troubles translators, scholars, and passing memorabilia seekers looking for cheap thrills.

The puzzling duplication becomes mere trope. Photographic captions rebuke losers and winners alike. 'Soldiers,' for instance, refer only to white males. 'Burned' does not suggest who has done the burning. 'Firefighting measures' is a generous term, given the circumstances.

Magsalin looks with impatience at the familiar photos among Chiara Brasi's papers falling from the Manila envelope.

The passivity of a photographic record might be relieved only by the viewer the photographs produce. And even then, not all types of viewers are ideal. Photographs of a captured country shot through the lens of the captor possess layers of ambiguity too confusing to grasp:

there is the eye of the victim, the captured,
who may in turn be belligerent, bystander, blameless, blamed – at the
very least here, too, there are subtle shifts in pathetic balance;
there is the eye of the colonised viewing their captured history in
the distance created by time;
there is the eye of the captor, the soldier, who has just wounded the
captured;
there is the eye of the captor, in capital letters: the Coloniser who
has captured history's lens;
there is the eye of the citizens (belligerent, bystander, blameless, blamed) whose history has colonised the captured in the
distance created by time;
and there is the eye of the actual photographer: the one who
captured the captured and the captors in his camera's lens –
what the hell was *he* thinking?

15. The photographer at the heart of the script

The photographer at the heart of the script is a woman. The infamous photographer of the Philippine-American war abandoned a restrictive, Henry James-type *Washington Square* existence (similar to Chiara's own, except with more Chantilly lace) to become a bold witness of the turn of her century. She is a disturbing beauty with a touching look that her otherwise embarrassingly pampered life fails to obscure. Her name, whether classical allusion or personal cryptogram is still forthcoming – Chiara has not yet made up her mind.

Venus, or Verushka, or Virginia.

It is 1901.

She is not alone. The great American commercial photographer, Frances Benjamin Johnson, has already scooped the men of her day with her photos of Admiral George Dewey lounging on his battleship *Olympia*, docked in Amsterdam. Months before, the *Olympia* had fired salvos at Spain's pathetic ships on Manila Bay, thus claiming the new century for America. Frances Benjamin Johnson's photographs of arresting domesticity on a battleship are celebrated in *Ladies' Home Journal* and *Cosmopolitan* – Dewey with his lazy dog Bob, sailors dancing cheek to cheek on deck like foretold Jerome Robbins extras, pristine soldiers in dress whites on pristine white hammocks, and the admiral looking at photographs of himself, with the Victorian photographer in white Chantilly lace by his side.

It is easy to imagine Chiara Brasi reading Joseph Schott's book, *The Ordeal of Samar*, stumbling upon the idea of the photographer on the scene of the atrocities in the Philippines, in Samar. It is the photographer's lens, after all, that astounds the courtroom in the four courts-martial that troubled America in 1902: the trial of General Jacob 'Howling Wilderness' Smith; of his lieutenant, the daring Marine, Augustus Littleton 'Tony' Waller; of the passionate and vocal witness, Sergeant John Day; and of the water-cure innovator, Major Edwin Glenn (the rest of the Americans of Samar went untried). America is riveted to the scandal, as pictures of the dead in Samar are described in smuggled letters to the *New York Herald* and the *Springfield Republican*. Propriety bans the pictures' publication, but damage is done.

The pictures have no captions, but Chiara makes an effort: *Women cradling their naked children at their breasts. A woman's thighs spread open on cogon grass. A dead child sprawled in the middle of a road. A naked body with blasted head, sprayed against a bamboo fence.* The congressional hearings on the affairs of the Philippine islands, organised in January 1902 in the aftermath of the scandal, hold a moment of silence on seeing the photographs.

True, the photographer's fame is split.

Senator Albert J Beveridge, Republican of Indiana, calls the photographer a traitor to her class. Senator George Frisbie Hoar, Republican of

Massachusetts, nemesis of William McKinley, calls her a hero of her time.

Senator Hoar famously accuses his own party's president in the aftermath of the Samar trials: 'You have devastated provinces. You have slain uncounted thousands of the people you desire to benefit. You have established re-concentration camps. Your generals are coming home from their harvest bringing sheaves with them, in the shape of other thousands of sick and wounded and insane to drag out miserable lives, wrecked in body and mind. You make the American flag in the eyes of a numerous people the emblem of sacrilege in Christian churches, and of the burning of human dwellings, and of the horror of the water torture.'

Save for a few clauses of wishful thinking, his words were dudgeon enough:

'Your practical statesmanship has succeeded in converting a people who three years ago were ready to kiss the hem of the garment of the American and to welcome him as a liberator, who thronged after your men when they landed on those islands with benediction and gratitude, into sullen and irreconcilable enemies, possessed of a hatred which centuries can not eradicate.'

True that. Though the final point lasts only until 1944, when all will be forgotten.

It is easy for a reader to overlay this historical calamity with others, in which the notion of arriving as liberators turns out a delusion, or a lie.

And it is easy for Chiara to overlay montages of her own childhood with the heroine's: the baby among maids brought out for display at lunch parties on Fifth Avenue; the birthday girl whose abundance of presents includes her mother's monsoon weeping; objects of her desire in silent parade – rosewood stereographs and magic lanterns and praxinoscopes and stereo pairs from the photographic company with the aptly doubled name, Underwood & Underwood – her souvenir snapshots from hotels around the world – and an antique set of collectible prints captioned 'nature scenes': Mount Rushmore, waterfalls, black children, cockfights.

Her own aristocratic world can be seen as an easy stand-in, but in sepia wash. The movie's white-petticoated protagonist clutches the old Brownie camera that still remains Chiara's prized possession, given to her by her father Luca, her fourth birthday gift, in Manila.

The script, as Magsalin reads on, creates that vexing sense of vertigo in stories within stories within stories that begin too abruptly, *in medias res*.

The photographer's presence in Samar is a quandary for the military officers. The enterprise of the Americans on the islands is so precarious, perilous and uncertain, that the burden of the traveller's arrival in wind-driven bancas, rowed by two opportunists, a pair of local teenagers who hand off Virginia Chase's trunks to the porters with an exaggerated avidity that means she has overpaid them, gives the captain in Balangiga a premonition of the inadequacy of his new letters of command.

Who has jurisdiction in Samar if a mere slip of a woman in a billowing silk gown completely inappropriate to the weather and her situation flouts the general's orders in Tacloban and manages the journey across the strait and down the river anyway on her own steam, with her diplopia and diplomatic seals intact, a spiral of lace in her wake, a wavering tassel of white, complete with trunks full of cameras, and Zeiss lenses, and glass plates for her demoniacal, duplicating photographic prints?

13. The Thrilla in Manila

'OK,' says Magsalin, taking the envelope. 'I'll see what I can do. I know a few people who can help you.'

'Thank you,' Chiara says, in that shy, nasal voice that is so annoying. 'How do you get out of here?'

'Just follow the signs. There are detours for the exits. They're renovating, you know.'

'Are you leaving, too?'

Magsalin thinks she will take her up on it, on the forlorn implication in Chiara's little-girl voice that she would like some company, that she is scared of Manila and her impulsive clueless spiritual adventure to follow the path of her lost and problematic father and get to Samar – a Freudian notion of travel only people as rich and thoughtless as Chiara suddenly get in their heads and then stupidly follow through; and yes, Magsalin will lead her to the exit and get her safely through the mall and then onto Roxas Boulevard (formerly Admiral Dewey) straight down the length of the ancient Bay to the Manila Hotel.

'I want to take a spin around the mall,' Magsalin says. 'I'll hang around here a bit. So I'll see you tomorrow at your hotel.'

The waitress offers the cheque. Chiara pays with a credit card. The waitress shakes her head. Magsalin takes out her non-Hermès bag and pays with cash.

'Thanks,' Chiara says.

'No problem.'

'My father saw that fight, you know. Ringside. They used to watch all those shows in the States, in Las Vegas. Boxing. My mom preferred Elvis Presley.'

'They saw Ali-Frazier in Manila in 1975?'

Magsalin is not sure about the protocol, about when and how she can leave the filmmaker. Is she, Magsalin, the guest or is it Chiara?

'Yeah. The Thrilla in Manila. At the time we lived nearby in – let's see. I have it here in my notebook. Magallanes Village.'

'That's in Makati, not here in Quezon City.'

'Oh. The Internet was wrong.'

'Figures.'

'The Thrilla in Manila,' Chiara repeats, and then she gets up, just like that, leaving Magsalin and the pan de sal shop without any warning.

Bitch.

Chiara is in the dark hallway, and Magsalin has to follow behind. The filmmaker is blocking Magsalin's exit and gazing, as if mentally noting its pros and cons as a film location, at the boarded up spaces beyond Philippine Airlines, the scaffolding that might be a promised escalator or a remnant of someone's change of mind.

'Muhammad Ali Mall. What an interesting tribute.'

'Ali Mall,' Magsalin corrects, wondering if Chiara will ever budge from the door. 'That's what people call it. It's name is Ali Mall. Yeah, it's dumb.'

'Dumpy,' Chiara turns to face her, smiling, but not moving, 'but not dumb. I think it's sweet. I like tributes. I've read all the books about that fight, you know. I guess because I see it through the lens of my childhood. After my father finished *The Unintended*, you know, after Manila my parents separated. It was not his choice. It was my mother who filed for divorce. I lived with my mom. We kept moving. All over the place. New York. The south of France. She could not stay in one place for too long. Memory suffocated her, she said. She had dizzy spells. I kept missing my father. I think she did, too. For a while, we lived in hotels. She hated remembering places. Hotels were her way of erasing memory, maybe. She has this thing – about embracing the present. *One must embrace the present, Chiara – it is all we have!* The last time my mother, my father, and I were all together was in Manila. The Thrilla in Manila. I've watched that match over and over again, you know. On DVD. Round 6. When Ali says to Frazier –'

'They tol' me Joe Frazier was all washed up!'

'And Frazier goes –'

'They – told – you – wrong!'

'Hah!' Chiara claps her hands. 'You do a mean Frazier.'

'Thank you. Were you for Ali or Frazier?' Magsalin asks.

'I love Muhammad Ali.'

'Do you think he is real?'

'More real than I,' says Chiara. 'He's The Greatest.'

Magsalin smiles.

Just for that, Magsalin thinks, she'll do whatever this spoiled brat says.

'I am sorry about your parents,' Magsalin says.

'*De nada.* It is my life. When I think of the world around me –,' and Chiara's gaze does not wander, does not look at the world around her, 'how can I complain?'

'Myself, I liked Frazier,' says Magsalin.

'Really? But why?'

'Because he wasn't really an ugly motherfucker. He was no gorilla. Except Ali, the director, made him up.'

23. At the hotel in Hong Kong, unknown to her daughter, Virginie

At the hotel in Hong Kong, unknown to her daughter, Virginie sees visions. She is looking for ice. Down the hotel corridor she follows the curls of the carpet's tracks neatly along its moulting spirals – once, when she looks back, she is startled to see the snail-back humps of her former map disappearing at her glance. The carpet behind her has turned white, or fogged. It must be her dizziness (her vision is troubling, but she refuses to wear her glasses), a trick of her strained eyes. She shrugs the vanishing off. As she turns and weaves along the serpentine trail of the carpet's dragon-tail design, tottering along the amphisbaena spines in her insomniac stilettos (a woman who came of age in the fifties, Virginie has never worn flats: she grew up believing sneakers are a crime), Virginie follows the spiral toward the sign that says *ICE,* in Mandarin and English. She sees the man in his glittering suit, a spiral of lace in his wake, a wavering tassel of white, the singer in his fabulous garb, the one she had once seen in Las Vegas, so long ago. Virginie experiences no shock because after all she is in the Orient, which has the curious effect of disorienting her. He is filling up a silver bucket. Behind him, she waits in line.

16. Chiara meets the translator in Paco

Chiara in the taxi reads the email attachment from the translator. She barely registers Magsalin's pleasantries, how nice it was to meet!, etc. She reads online in the cursory way she was never taught at school – in school she had to annotate, then look up words in the *OED,* then give a synopsis of her incomprehension. School drove her nuts. Slow reading is an art, her teachers kept saying, but their faith was no insurance against her indifference. School gave her migraines: she kept being told to expand on her thoughts when she had none that merited expanding. Her brain seemed like a ball of hair in a bath drain, as miserably palpable as it was inert. She dropped out without regret to go on a drug trip occasionally punctuated by luxury tourism. The result was her first movie, *Stumbling into Slovenia*, a study of melancholia and apathy that became an indie sensation, though in truth all she wanted was to portray a certain patch of light on a beach in Ancona, against the Adriatic.

She scrolls through the attachment barely reading the words but taking in without question the insult she is meant to feel – the normal way one reads on the Internet. Temper tantrums are a hazard of fast reading. She begins typing furiously on her iPad as the taxi careens. After all, Chiara has a right to be angry, to be rude. The last hours of rest at the Manila Hotel have not erased her lightheaded feeling that this city wants her dead.

Punctuation is an ongoing online dilemma. Tacky exclamation marks provide rudiments of etiquette Chiara forgoes. She also scorns emoticons, stand-alone uses of colons with single parentheses, and illiterate shortcuts, such as *u* for *you.* She is an Internet prig in a world of online junkies. It is a black mark on her generation that the mindless adoption of the signifier *lol*, an insufficient proxy for the vagaries of the human voice, happened in her lifetime. She never uses it. Even with friends, she fails to sign off xoxoxo, as if her denial of trite, reciprocal affection were a mark of superiority. She never considers the signs of courtesy she has omitted in her texts and is not bothered by the affection she fails to convey.

She barely acknowledges the taxicab driver's bow as he pockets her tip. Her presence at midnight at the front door of Magsalin's home in the Paco district has the same substance as her online tone: unapologetic, admitting only of intentions relevant to herself.

If Chiara were not so tiny, wide-eyed, looking a bit troubled in her skewed, though still faintly perfumed tank top (you see, the maid catches Chiara's naked expression of distress despite the arrogant blue eyes' barely glancing at her, the servant, who could shut the door on her face), the late-comer would never have been welcomed into the Magsalin home – that is, the home of the three bachelor uncles from Magsalin's maternal line: Nemesio, Exequiel, and Ambrosio, drunkards all.

Midnight in Manila is no comfort for strangers. Servants in this section of Manila are justly wary of late-night knocks on the door. Corrupt barangay chairmen harass them for tong, doleful bandits pretend to be someone's long-lost nephew, serial drunks keep mistaking the same dark, shuttered home for their own. Chiara does not notice at first that the address Magsalin had scribbled on the napkin from the bake shop in Ali Mall is a haunted avenue in much too leafy, cobblestoned disrepair, full of deciduous shadows, aging tenements of purposeless nostalgia amid wild, howling cats, and the occult strains, somehow, of stupid disco music.

Chiara registers that the location has a disjoint familiarity, like a film set in which she has carefully restored elements of a childhood by dispatching minions to gather her recollections, so that her memory becomes oddly replete, though only reconstructed through the inspired empathy of others. Such is the communality of a film's endeavour that magic of this sort never disconcerts Chiara. Life for Chiara has always been the imminent confabulation of her desires with the world's potential to fulfil them. So while the street and its sounds have an eerie sense of a past coming back to bite her, Chiara also dismisses the eerie feeling. She steps into the foyer of the old mahogany home without even a thank you to the maid, who against her better judgment hurries away at the direc-tor's bidding to fetch the person she demands, Magsalin.

'I did not give you the manuscript in order for you to revise it,' Chiara begins without introduction.

'Pleased to see you again, too,' says Magsalin. She gestures Chiara to the rocking chair.

'I'm not here for pleasantries.'

'You are in someone else's home, Miss Brasi. My uncles, who are still awake and, I am warning you, will soon be out to meet you and make you join the karaoke, would be disappointed if I did not treat you like a guest. Please sit.'

Not looking at it, Chiara takes the ancient rocking chair, the one called a butaka, made for birthing. It creaks under her weight, but Chiara does not seem to hear the sound effect, a non sequitur in the night.

Now Magsalin is towering over the director, whose small figure is swallowed up in the enormous length of the antique butaka.

'I did not revise the manuscript,' begins Magsalin, knowing she must choose her words carefully, 'I presented a translation.'

'I did not ask for a translation,' says Chiara. 'I gave you the manuscript as a courtesy. It is the least I can do for the help you will give me.'

'I have not yet offered that help.'

'But you will. You will get me to Samar.'

'Yes, that is true. I have decided to help you get to Samar. But not without extracting my pound of flesh.'

'Co-authorship of my script?' snorts Chiara. 'That is unacceptable. You are only a reader, not an accomplice.'

'Permission to make of it as I wish, seeing as my perspective offers its own matter.'

'And desires that distort,' says Chiara.

'Possibilities and corrections,' murmurs Magsalin.

'Misunderstandings and corruptions,' retorts Chiara.

'A mirror, perhaps,' says Magsalin.

'A double-crossing agent,' snaps Chiara.

'Yes. The existence of readers is your cross to bear.'

17. In the last novel by Georges Perec

In the last novel by Georges Perec, a mystery of texts engenders the clues deciphering a murder of colonial proportions; that is, a writer dies. He dies in a vaguely political way, in the way in a colonised country only the political seems to have consequence. Otherwise, deaths are too cheap for witness. Does it matter, Magsalin wonders, if one day a world-famous director disappears in a derelict, tree-laden street in the Paco district of Manila, to the strains of Elvis Presley singing 'Suspicious Minds'?

And if anything happens to the protagonist, who would be to blame?

22. The monsoons of Manila

The monsoons of Manila give Virginie a thrill. Frogs from the garden leap onto her soaking carpet into the borrowed house's Chinese vases. The rain traps her in the sala. Catfish swim toward her shoes. Her baby daughter's Wellingtons come splashing down from the dusty ottoman while the feral cat, a castaway, casually invades the kitchen and observes. Virginie thinks a tadpole is tickling her wet toes, but she does not dare to look. The cat Misay is completely dry, like the dark-skinned maid in the corner cutting up the cantaloupe with utter calm. She is staring at Virginie's legs. 'Ma'am,' she says. An obscene dead cockroach, its genitalia splayed out for the world to see, is coming and going in waves, like an upturned boat with frail masts. Virginie looks down. She screams. The cat pounces. The baby claps, and the maid bustles about. The cat almost has the cockroach in its grasp, but the maid swipes at the cat, who runs off, and she sweeps the dumb flaccid bug easily into the dustbin, with a nonchalance that her mistress's embarrassment observes. It is odd that it is so sunny outside, Virginie thinks, when for all she knows the world has turned upside down. It is a sinking ship that was once a home. Her toes are cold.

23. The model for the svelte photographer

Virginie Brasi is a slim, disturbing beauty who, even in sleep upon a wicker butaka, cheeks checkered by abaca twine, or vigorously gardening in the tropics with her mouth open, red bandanna fluttering against monsoon winds that make wild commas of her hair while she tends her wilting camote, has a touching look that her otherwise embarrassingly pampered life fails to obscure. Maybe it is her posture – always a bit slouched, though not quite awkward – that makes her seem unaware of her power. She is inept rather than thoughtless, therefore her whims are pardonable – those dashes across the ocean, for instance, on suspicion of her husband's infidelity as he falls deeper into the abyss, the monstrosity of his enterprise in the jungles of the Philippines. Thrice she carried her baby, four-year-old

Chiara, wrapped in an Igorot blanket, onto a private, chartered plane. Chiara would find herself all alone in a hotel suite in Hong Kong, staring at the scarily erect arrangement of three cattleya orchids triplicated in the eerie mirrors, with her small curly head in triple counterpoint to the infinite trinity of her father's absence.

Those midnight migrations to grandiose and sterile rooms would haunt Chiara's childhood, though now her memories are blurred, and her mother, emerging in a white bathrobe and offering her a guava, Chiara's favourite fruit, taste acquired in the tropics, would look for all the world as if nothing were the matter, nothing mattered, though tomorrow she will cry herself to sleep in her daughter's arms.

Virginie's image in white bathrobe and silver heels haunts her daughter, though Virginie also looks vaguely and mistakenly like Gena Rowlands, or Mrs Robinson in *The Graduate* (an unfortunate, involuntary resemblance – but the cheap trick that pop culture plays on her daughter happens to the best of us). Virginie's image burns in Chiara's mind, a warning: her mother of the bedlam rests. She remembers her sleeping so deeply in that awkward rocking chair in Magallanes Village during that time of her childhood, in Makati, not Quezon City. If it were not for the occasional spasm of Virginie's slim foot dangling from the creaking butaka, the rocking chair made for birthing, for the optimism of creation – if it were not for that occasional twitch of Virginie's cold toes, little Chiara imagines her mother dead.

1. The story she wishes to tell

The story Magsalin wishes to tell is about loss. Any emblem will do: a dead Frenchman with an incomplete manuscript, an American obsessed with a Filipino war, a filmmaker's disappearance, his wife's sadness. This work is not only about writers who have slipped from this realm, their ideas in melancholy arrest, though their notebooks are tidy; later one might see the analogy to real-life grief, or at least the pathos of inadequate homage, if one likes symbols. Of course the story will involve several layers of meaning. Chapter numbers will scramble, like letters in abandoned acrostics. Points of view will multiply. Allusions, ditto. There will be blood, a kidnapping, or a solution to a crime forgotten by history. That is, Magsalin hopes so.

EXTREMADURA
(UNTIL NIGHT FALLS)

Kevin Barry

T he old dog is tied by a length of rope to a chain-link fence. Its hackles comb up a silent growl as I approach through the edges of the small white town and its eyes burn a high yellow like witch hazel oddly vivid in such a skinny and unkempt old dog. A dog that has known some weather, I'd say. There are no people anywhere to be seen – I am in the last slow mile after dusk and my calves are singing. There is a café up ahead but it is shuttered and dark. I have walked for many hours and in fact for almost fifteen years now. The dog eases into itself again as I come nearer and its flanks relax to this softer breathing and I crouch on my own hind legs by its side to converse for a while among the lights of our eyes.

It's as if I've known you for a long time, she says.

But when I lay my hand to her there is a shiver of nerves again as if she has known the cruelties, too. The town is not entirely quiet. Somewhere tinnily bleating behind shutters there is the sound of a soccer game on the radio or TV. I used to be afraid of the dogs but they got used to me. Ever the more so as I walk I take on the colours and feelings of the places through which I walk and I am no longer a surprise to these places. My once reddish hair has turned a kind of old-man's green tinge with the years and this is more of it. What the ramifications have been for my stomach you're as well not hearing. I have very little of the language, even after all this time but the solution to this is straightforward – I don't talk to people. This arrangement I have found satisfactory enough, as does the rest of humanity, apparently, or what's to be met of it on the clear blue mornings, on the endless afternoons. We are coming out of a very cold winter in Extremadura which is a place of witches or at least of stories about witches. To be passing the nights, I suppose. The dog has a good part of an Alsatian in her and random bits of mutt and sheepdog and wolf probably and she tells me of a thin life and a harsh one in this cold-hearted, in this love-starved town.

Go on? I says.

The lamps above us catch now and buzz for a moment as their circuits warm and also to mark the sombre hour there is the hollow doom of the church bells – they lay it on heavily enough around these places still. Footsteps as the bells fade out to echoes and there is a girl of about sixteen years of age and she does not see me at all but mouths the words of a popular song, a song that is current, I believe it is a Gaga, I know it well enough myself from the cafés and the concourses – all the years I have doled out in that same old (it seems to me) estación de autobuses that exists at the edge of all these towns, I use them not for the buses but for sleeping – and she moves swaying down the road in a cloud of distraction (if sleep is what you could call it!) and she hums as she goes and she is not a pretty girl exactly but neither plain and what she has in truth is a very beautiful carriage – buenas tardes? She turns in surprise over the shoulder but there is not a glimmer, really, she just blinks and moves on, and the dog simpers and stretches; now there is the chug of a moto as it troubles its lungs to mount a rise in the road and a shutter is pulled inwards with a hard sharp creaking and the sound of the soccer game loudens; all across the silver hills in the east the cold spring night lovelessly descends. February is an awful fucking month just about everywhere. There is a waft of sweet paprika and burnt garlic from a kitchen somewhere. Still there is no life at the café. Whatever is going on with that place. Far away in the north my very old parents must be waiting for me or for word of me, at least; they are waiting for me still at the bottom of the dripping boreen framed by the witchy haw and the whitethorn. It's what keeps them going, I'd say.

I don't know what people take me for as I pass along the edges of the roads. What money I have is by now so comically eked out and in such tiny dribs that my clothes are not good at all and as certain as the weeping callouses on the balls of my feet is the need for new boots or for a pair of good trainers at least. I sleep generally where I fall. In doorways sometimes or if the weather's foul in the cheapest hostals run always by spidery old women in black or in the bus concourses, under the benches, or in the lee of buildings, or on the black sand beaches in the south if the winter is especially long and hard and I've turned down the road myself. At one time *southerned* was a very common word and *southerning* a practice. For the better of the lungs and so forth. Sometimes I'm not sure what century I've mistaken this one for and I wonder would I be better off elsewhere. Sometimes I feel as if my engines are powered on nothing at all but the lights of the cold stars that will emerge above us now. I can get by on almost nothing and it is conceivable that I might become very, very old myself and as spidery.

The summers don't present much of a problem. You can always find cool places. The moto comes into the line of our vision, its engine turns off for the decline of the road and it coasts and a teenage boy steers and parks it beneath a tree across the way from me. He steps off and looks across and nods and lights a cigarette and he looks down along the road after the singing girl and she senses his glance and turns a look back to him – her thick black hair moves – and their glances catch for a moment but as quickly she turns from him and is gone; an old man appears as though from the dust and sits on a half-collapsed bench by a white wall that it seems clear to me was at one time bullet-riddled. Now we all watch each other closely and the sense of this is companionable enough. A heavy-set middle-aged man appears in just a flimsy yellow t-shirt that reads Telefonica Movistar – it's all go – and he crosses the road to the boy with the moto – he mustn't feel the cold – and he talks to him and they look down calmly together at the workings of the bike, each of them with their hands on their hips and their cigarettes at a loose dangle from their mouths, and they squint through the smoke at the little moto and its failing organs and the man reaches for it, turns the key, revs the handle, listens with his head inclined at an expert's careful angle, and lets it dies again and shakes his head. Not long for the road by the looks of things. I crouch on my hind legs with the dog whose snout rests in the curve of my shoulder now and she whispers to me that the girl is named Mercedes and is wanted by not a few of the young louts around this place with big hands on them – these are country people – and she has already in fact given it to one or two of them. On Saturdays. The clocks must have stopped for them. Awful to be sixteen or eighteen and already your finest hour has gambolled past you like a grinning lamb and your moto is fucked also. The sky makes a lurid note of the day's ending – there are hot flushes of pink and vermillion that would shame a cardinal. The chain link fence encases nothing but a crooked rectangle of dirt and dead tyres and stones – old chicken ground maybe – and it has an air of trapped misery.

And more than that you're as well not to know, the dog says.

Dogs, I find, are much the same everywhere. Much of a muchness, as my father would say. They know everything about us and they love us all the same. My father when he wanted the sound of the television up or down would say highern it or lowern it. One time in Ronda I nearly fucked myself into the gorge there altogether. A thousand foot fall would have settled the question decisively. But I thought that might be a bit loud. I am not by nature a man who has that kind of show in him. No extravagances, please.

The old man calls across to the pair by the moto. It is a weak scratchy call like an injured bird would make. The pair by the moto ignore him utterly. Another shutter opens. Another TV bleats. The sky pales again as quickly as it coloured. As if somebody has had a Jesuitical word. That ours beneath this vaulted roof might be an austere church. There was a time when I tried to fill the sky with words. Morning and fucking night I was at it. In my innocence, or arrogance – the idea that I might succeed. But I walked out of that life and entered this one.

The teenage boy kicks the back wheel of the fucked moto; the middle-aged man in the t-shirt laughs to make his belly rise and fall. A hunting bird moves across the acres of the sky in the last thin light of the day and a breeze comes up the road with quick news – a tree shakes out its bare branches and moves. There is a rancid olive oil on the air over the odour of stale dog. I'm sorry but there is no pretty way to say it. I wonder if I was to make off with you altogether? I could slip this rope from you as easy as anything.

I'd love to go, she says, and yet I'd not go. Do you know that kind of way?

Oh, I do. I'd love to go home again but I will not go.

Imagine coming up the boreen in Roscommon with my tale of the lost years and my rucksack of woes and the little gaunt tragic sunburnt face on me? Wouldn't they love to see it coming. I do believe they're back there still – I believe they're alive and that I'd know somehow if they weren't. I stepped onto a train that night in Madrid and out of my life. Love? Don't mention it.

They must whisper their love to Mercedes as night falls. A hand cupped neatly to the shape of her groin. The question mark of it. The old man gets up from the bench and walks like a clockwork scarecrow by the side of the road. I stand again to stretch out my bones. If I looked hard enough, I'd find a café open someplace among these white-walled streets and hidden turns – I could have coffee with hot milk. But I have nearly had my fill of the cafés. There is only so much of that business you can take. And there is the danger always of the cerveza and the brandy. There are only so many times you can climb over that wall.

I rise onto the tips of my toes and look along the darkening sky and road and here she comes again, Mercedes, and still she jaws vaguely on her song – buenas tardes? Again she ignores me and it is as if she cannot see me even. She carries beneath her arm a carton of table wine – *tinto* is one of the words I have, and never too far from the tip of my tongue – and a jar of Nutella and in a blue plastic bag a frozen octopus. This will mean a grocer open down the road someplace and a stick of bread for me. Tentacles and spindles and bulbous sacs – I need to dig into myself harder lately for the words of things. The dog is up beside me and she sniffs at the air after Mercedes and the evening falls away from us quickly. I'll need to decide soon where to lie down tonight. The animal must choose its lair. The first stars burn coldly on the plain and I am so many miles from home. I reach out a last time for you. Your warm skinny flank and the way that you sigh and move closer to me just once more just this last time. I fix a finger under the rough collar of rope and work it to loosen it and you settle in this moment that much closer to me.

A moto runs its troubled lungs; the young girl's step recedes; the old man's falters.

The man in the yellow t-shirt passes along and he says hello to the dog and he looks right through me. This is no place for me tonight, I decide – I would rather not their shelter. I'll move on again and maybe tonight I'll keep moving all the way through until the sunlight wakes the yellow of the yellow of the fields of rapeseed and in truth I am still drinking some of the time because I have not yet drank her all the way out of my mind and I still have this broken heart.

HOLY ISLAND

Ross Raisin

She lies inside the warm belly of the dune and looks out over the furred complex of sandhills, at the sea. The sun, in, out, of the swift clouds is on her back. She closes her eyes, allowing herself the pleasure of it. The sea presses against the island. Waves crash and suck at the shingle beach below the dunes. The warmth, the rhythm of the water, lull her – but she returns her eyes sharply to the sea, scanning the bare horizon, willing herself to remain vigilant.

The following day is colder. A wind is through the dunes. At the crest of the sand slope tiny white flowers quiver in the marram grass. A bank of raincloud a few miles out is moving over the sea, advancing on the island. For an instant she thinks that she sees something. A dark speck. She keeps her eyes focused for a long time on the same patch of water, but it does not appear again.

There is a low rumbling behind her. She moves to the other side of the dune and lowers herself by the earthy spyhole at the top, from which vantage point she can see the top of the quarry and the roofs of the scattered colony of cottages that is growing up beside it. She waits, her forearms pulsing against the sand. There are voices. The whinny of a horse. She creeps closer to the spyhole, watching the opening a short distance away where the wagonway on its raised embankment emerges from the sand hills.

The usual two men appear, at the head of a convoy: behind follow a grey horse, harnessed to a dumpy wheeled tub rolling along the tracks of the wagonway; a boy; a second, larger, chestnut horse; another tub, then two more men at the rear. As their course curves closer to her she can see the heaped chalky stone inside the first tub and the faint white smoke above it when the tub judders over the track joints. She tries to listen to the conversation of the front men, but she can pick out only the odd word. Rain. Castle. They are Scottish, she thinks. Their boots, clothing, faces are smeared white. The hooves of the horses too are whitened, and as they pass directly beneath her she notices the white prints on their stomachs, which she knows, as she observes the boy moving between the animals, patting, stroking, are his. Every few steps the boy turns to glance at the men behind. When the one she presumes to be the foreman, because his clothes are not stained, quickens his pace to join the men at the front, the boy slips from his pocket a halved apple and feeds it to the grey horse. Then, without taking his eyes off the foreman, he drops back and repeats the action for the chestnut.

The procession travels past her, towards the south shore and the kilns below the castle. It begins, lightly, to rain. Before she has pulled her shawl fully over her head it is a downpour. Craters plug the sand around her face. She scrambles to her knees, watching the men rush for the saddlebags strapped to each horse, to take out covers that they pull over the tubs of limestone. She waits until they are a good distance ahead before she gets to her feet, runs out from the dune, jumps the tracks and is away over the brown exposed farmland across the island for home.

The fire is going in the kitchen. Her mother crouches beside it, pressing a spoon against the dry salted cod that is roasting in a pan on the hearth girdle. She has changed into dry clothes but her hair is still wet, clung to the rain-raw skin of her neck.

'Will you see on the butts, Elfrida?'

The girl gets up from the table, where she is binding lats for a crab pot, and goes out the back. Rain pours from the roof down a channel into the water butt. It is almost full; she shunts it aside and slides into its place a second, empty, butt. When she is back inside she sits again at the table to continue working at the crab pot, watching her mother by the hearth.

'They are come in their numbers, the limers,' the girl says.

Her mother does not look around from the fire. They fall again to silence. There is only the sound of the rain, the minute crackle of fish skin.

'More cottages is gone up. I seen them from the dunes up by the Head.'

Her mother stands up. She goes to the corner of the room and bends to inspect the weather glass. The level in the jar has dropped, the water drawn up into the small upturned bottle that floats inside.

'They have you interested.'

'They are getten a lot, is all,' the girl says, but she lowers her face so that it does not show in the light of the candle that she is working from. Her mother comes to join her at the table. She takes up two lats and begins, quickly, skilfully, to bind them. There is a rash on the back of one hand, another on the exposed part of her chest, and Elfrida knows that she has been at the harbour all day, sitting in front of the herring houses, viewing the passage onto the sea.

They complete the base of the pot, eat, clear away, and her mother goes up the stair. She goes out to check on the butt and finds that the rain, which has been easing with the approach of evening, has stopped.

She leaves the cottage and walks through the village to the path up onto the Heugh. When she is at the top she lays a blanket over a large stone, a few steps from the cliff edge, and sits down. From here, even in the ebbing light of the sun she can see for miles around. To the west the wet amber gleam of the mudflats stretches away to the mainland. Below her – a sheer rock fall to the shingle beach and the harbour, on the other side of which the Needles tower above Black Law. Hope surges inside her chest at the sight of them; the urgent belief that they must be visible still from the sea.

She looks out at the open water. A wind that she can see but not feel batters the Farnes, foams over the concealed ridges of rock that lie just below the surface. Last summer, there had been storm after storm. The herring shoal, as it migrated down the coast, had been unpredictable and the island cobles, her father's amongst them, had drifted farther and farther out to sea in search of it. They had provisioned for three nights. By the sixth night her mother ceased her vigil by the harbour. After eight nights her father returned, with the other survivors: the sixty-three men out of ninety who had set out.

A shifting breeze brings the smell of smoke from the village, snugged into the corner of the island behind her. The weather has been kinder this summer, she reminds herself. The men have set out better provisioned – her father with seven days of squeezed corned beef and onion sandwiches, water, tea. She recites her usual blessing, pulls her shawl tight to her chest against the strengthening wind. By tomorrow the excursion will have entered its second week. She trains her sight on the black throat of the harbour passage onto the sea. An awareness of duty, and her mother, holds it there, or tries to – but her eye is drawn back to the land at the side of the passage where the castle, massed against the darkening sky, rises above the six glowing orange rims of the lime kilns. Since they were lit the previous week they have burned all day and all night, and before long they are the only thing remaining in the gloom, except for the intermittent flare of the lighthouse on Outer Farne.

She watches the convoy roll out of the sand hills and she shrinks back as they pass below her. Once they have gone ahead she is pulled by guilt to squint a final time at the sea, before she comes out of the dune.

There are no hills or long grass so she follows stealthily on the shingle alongside the wagonway, wind and spray lashing her cheek until she is close to the south shore. Through the gap between two large boulders she can see a great deal of activity beneath the castle. Men are coming in and out of the access tunnels at the base of the kilns. A schooner is moored at the staithes by the foreshore – a pulley-wheel in its rigging winching down a basket of coal to where three men stand on the rocks ready to reach and guide it. She looks for the quarrymen, and spots them stationed by the track up to the kiln tops. She watches the boy, stroking the chestnut horse's neck, until the foreman appears from an access tunnel, at the head of a small group. There is some calling out which she cannot understand,

and her gut hollows at the sudden thought of her father – his opinion of these migrants; these landsmen.

Ropes are tied to one of the tubs. Some of the men move to the front of the tub and take up the ropes, wrapping them around their waists; others form a ruck behind the tub, bracing their hands against it. At the foreman's command they begin to heave it up the slope to the kiln tops – and it does move, slowly, but some of the men start to slip in the mud, losing their footing sliding with the tub back to the bottom.

The foreman claps his hands and two men move towards the horses. The boy shakes his head. He stands between the horses, gripping their reins. The foreman says something to him and points to the tracks up the slope. Again the boy shakes his head. More men advance and there is a short struggle as the boy is restrained while the chestnut horse is tethered to two ropes.

The new combination of horse and men ascends steadily. When they near the top the boy breaks from where he is detained and runs to the slope. ''Tis over hot for her,' he shouts – he is Scottish, she comprehends, pressing her forehead to the stone gap. There is a commotion, but the boy indicates with his hands that he does not intend to stop the operation. He runs easily up the muddy slope and positions himself by the horse's head, talking into its ear, cupping a hand over its eyes.

As the horse reaches the level ground at the top she notices the heat haze above the pots, the air rising and glistening over the castle ramparts. The horse starts stamping, arching its neck. The boy unties it from the ropes while the men, shielding their faces with their hands, turn around and put their backs against the tub to drive it towards the lip of the first pot. It tilts, tips, and limestone cascades down the chamber. There is a dull crash, sparks jumping above the pot, but her eyes move to the horse, and the boy, his mouth against the animal's neck, soothing, stroking, guiding it gently back from the pot.

She is woken early by the sound of feet outside. Voices. There is a loud knocking at their door. A moment later there is another at the next door, then the next, repeating, echoing down the street. She gets out of bed and goes into the kitchen where she finds her mother, dressed, pulling on her boots. Her face is bright, desperate.

'They are home, Elfrida.'

Other people are hurrying down the street: wives, mothers, sisters, sleep-dazed children. An old man is coming out of a doorway, through which the embers of a fire breath slowly in the dark. She stays in step with her mother, who is almost running now: she is making a noise, a thin repeated moan, that shocks Elfrida, embarrasses her. Her mother, though, seems oblivious to her presence – her eyes are set on the pink horizon of sea and then the harbour that is coming into view as they hurry with the others down towards it.

The tops of coble sails show above the barnacled roofs of the herring houses. Blood is thundering at her temples. She counts the sails – realising, before they reach the back of the throng of women, that they are not all there. Half, at most. She scours the sheds along the harbour where men are hauling in carts and shattered remnants of wood but she cannot see her father so she looks to the cobles, bobbing and broken on the water, and cannot find his own. Some of the women are crying. Two have their arms around their men, sobbing into their chests. Another woman is on her knees, trembling, alone. Elfrida wants to take her mother's hand, but her mother's hands are bunched into tight red corals of knuckle and she knows that she cannot go to her.

A fisherman, a friend of her father, is at the water's edge, addressing the crowd. Behind him, half a dozen men stand motionless, looking down at their boots submerged underneath the green skin of water.

'No shelter, nothing,' the man is saying, 'and thereckly the entire sea is boiling and we cannot see an arm's length.' The men in the water remain silent as he relates the story and it occurs to her that they have rehearsed this; they have agreed on these words to say to the stricken congregation of women.

'We are pulling buckets, and all we are thinking is to get left the storm but when it is passed we are someway a clean distance off where we were, and it is only us, these cobles that you see here.'

'Did you not go back?' one woman shouts.

'Ay, of course. But nothing. Nothing.'

'They are swep away?'

He lowers his face, shaking his head. 'I couldna tell you. I don't know.'

Her mother begins to walk away. Elfrida turns instinctively to go with her; but there is nothing that she can say. She does not move. She watches her mother's even progress away from the harbour. Through the clouds a weak blanket of light is thrown upon the crumbled remains of the priory as she passes below it, onto the village lane, out of sight.

All afternoon her mother has kept to her room. She came out for the short silent meal that they have recently finished and now she is in there again. Elfrida watches the passage by Castle Point merge into the rocks and the black sea beyond. Two seals playing in the harbour are perceptible now only from the occasional oiled flash of fur as they jump and slip about each other. She urges herself to feel more of her mother's pain, but it will not come – she feels instead a blank, a blackness; and the constant sidling desire to turn her sight to the six molten rings.

Three figures are walking up the shore below her. She steps to the edge. When they are almost level they look up, all three, to where she stands. She is afraid, exhilarated, but she stays rooted to her position. They look away, then continue down the shingle until they are beyond the rocks at the corner of the island. She waits, her shoulders stiff with cold, until the black spots of their heads come into view again on the other side of the rocks, walking on and gradually receding into the dark sheet of the mudflats. An uprising of seabirds launches, some way ahead, at their approach. A moment later she listens to the passing thunder of wings, follows and loses the flock in the night sky.

The curing begins the following morning. Elfrida and her mother make the walk down to the harbour in long boots, oilskin jackets and shawls wrapped across their chests. The same gathering of women is outside the herring houses, hair pinned above pale faces, waiting by the silver blaze of fish that is piled inside a line of carts, already stinking in the sun.

Mrs Allan, who used to teach Elfrida in the school, arranges them into threesomes. She comes up to Elfrida and her mother and signals for another woman, May, whose man is returned, to join them. As she calls the names Mrs Allan places her hand on her mother's shoulder. Elfrida sees the fingers squeeze; sees her mother clasp Mrs Allan's elbow in return, and she is hurt by this fleeting gesture, left out, a child.

They file through the doorways of the two upscuttled boats, into the dark stale workspace. Some of the taller women drag in the carts and pour the herring into the long, brine-filled troughs that cross the length of the room. Elfrida binds May's then her mother's hands with strips of flour sack-cloth to protect them from any slip of the gutting knife. She can feel her mother's breath on her face as she ties the strips fast with thread, running it round and round her sturdy, unflinching hands, stroking secretly over her fingers with each circuit.

The teams take up their formations along the troughs and are immediately to work, with no explanation or preparation, straight into the fast rhythm that will continue into the evening. Elfrida starts pricking on, scraping the scales from the herring and cutting off the heads into a basket. She slides each completed fish to her mother and May, who gut and separate the cleaned fish into a bucket, ready for packing. A sunset of blood deepens over the cloth on her mother's hands, working beside her own. Blood pools in the trough, drips to the floor. All around them the room is silent but for the sound of scraping and gutting. Sliced necks. The soft patter of piling heads. There is the wet stink of guts. The basket between her feet filling with eyes. Through the bright doorway the men are at work: some folding drift nets and torn sails, for the women; some sitting and tending to the bust hulls of their cobles, which have been lifted and lined up on wooden blocks along the side of the harbour, like casualties.

Elfrida, carefully, regards her mother. She studies the side of her face for any sign of what she is thinking, but there is nothing. She is intent only on her task, the quick skilful dance of the fish and the gutting knife in her hands.

They break, late in the afternoon. Each woman is allotted a single herring, which they take home to fry and eat with bread, onions, a meal that will become as inevitable over the coming days as the thick clag of oil in their hair and the briny cuts on their fingers.

When Elfrida and her mother have eaten, Elfrida, left alone, clears the plates and, with the time that remains before the evening shift, goes up to the Heugh. The air is warm and still. The sun has lowered behind the Needles, and for a tiny moment two brilliant halos flame around them. At the throat of the harbour a porpoise breaks the surface – it goes back under and she traces its course, anticipating where it will come up again.

'Alright.'

She startles. He stays, unmoving, at the top of the path.

'Sorry.' He points to a rock close to her own and walks towards it. She finds that she cannot respond, even to move her head.

He sits down on the rock.

'A view, that.'

They both look down at the drop.

'I seen ye, up a height here.' She does not know if he is looking at her. 'Ye the harbour pilot eh?' he says, and she is at once fearful that they have been talking about her, the quarrymen, laughing at her. But when she glimpses across at him he is staring at the cap on his lap, his hands fisting, unfisting inside it. Four miles over the sea the castle at Bamburgh is backlit, then gone.

'Speak English? Where ye from?'

'Here.'

'I'm from Dundee. Working for Nicoll's, burning the lime. I stay next the quarry.' He stands abruptly. 'Ye can see it from here.' He points, as if it is new to her, as if she does not know by heart every dune and pool and plant of the place.

'I am away to work,' she says, getting up.

He does not understand, so she nods in the direction of the herring houses. 'Curing.'

He continues watching her. She feels herself colouring and wonders if he can tell through the dusk.

'Good night,' she says, and begins the descent towards the village.

She can hear her mother's voice inside the cottage as she nears it, coming back to pick up her oilskin. Assuming that she is praying she waits on the step until she has finished, but there is a succession of ratcheting sobs, words, muttered and broken in between. She moves back from the step and walks alone down to the curing sheds.

When her mother arrives, a short time later, she hands Elfrida her oilskin, without comment, and Elfrida does not look at her face; nor, fearful of what she might detect there, does she let her mother look into hers.

The morning is grey and soft. A fine mizzle dampens their faces as they hasten towards the bustle and laughter that is audible before the edge of the village. On the approach to the sheds they see that a new group of women, a dozen or so, have arrived. They stand apart from the islanders, in yellow aprons, talking. Herring girls, from the mainland. They are looking out at something. Elfrida views with them, surveying the kiln tops, the wagonway, flushing with unexpected relief when it dawns on her that they are looking at the castle.

'Shake your feathers, you lot, come on now.' Mrs Allan claps her hands and the crew of silent island women watch the newcomers, all of whom are young, some not much older than Elfrida, go inside the first shed.

A team of three is stationed to one side of her at the trough. She tries, without attracting their attention, or her mother's, to follow their conversation – rapid, Scottish – about Berwick, the poor state of their dormitories above the curing sheds there; the relief of decent rooms now, above the pubs, where there is not the constant reek of fish. Or men, one of them says, quietly, though Elfrida senses that May and her mother hear it too.

Their work is quicker, more precise, than the island women. From last season she knows that they will have been moving down the coastline since the spring, trailing the migrating shoal, stopping at each of the fishing towns along the way – accumulating money, stories, adventures, moving on. Their four teams finish the first gutting almost simultaneously. They sort their fish into piles of three sizes, then each of the packers climbs with a simple easy motion into their barrel to arrange the first layer. Many of the island women slow or stop to observe. In very short time they have the layer flush and clamber out, pour salt into the barrel, then press it down with the tamp stick – except for one girl, whose team, Elfrida suspects in mockery of the island women, lower her by her ankles into the barrel to tamp down the layer of salt with her hands.

He comes at the same time, as the sun is burning into the back of Bamburgh Castle. He nods in greeting and sits on the same rock. For some time, neither of them speak. When she gives a cautious glance over she sees that he is stroking a thumb over a long red weal on the centre of his palm.

'Tide is running,' he says.

She looks at the thickening membrane of water over the flats. An ancient excitement – altered tonight, new – runs through her: the knowledge that the island will soon be cut off, freed, taken by the black swarming sea.

'Ye ever get left this place?' he asks.

'Ay, of course.'

They fall silent again. Her mind turns to Berwick. The tight busy streets. The herring girls, laughing in their dormitories. She wonders if he has seen them; if he knows that they are on the island.

The last time that she was on the mainland was in the winter, with her father. He had been in need of new netting and had borrowed a horse and cart from the Arms' landlord in agreement that he would pick up the pub's supplies for the week. She can remember his quiet carefulness with the horse; her own determination not to disappoint him. And, strongly, the same sensation of being adrift that she has known each time she has been away from the island. The strange threatening absence when the noise of the sea is not all around her – even while it echoes still inside her body, soft and insistent as the blood in her veins.

She pictures with sudden clarity his coble, wrecked, wood and boxes and floating sandwiches. A need to be home grips her. She gets up, barely letting herself look at the boy while she mumbles a goodbye and walks away.

The next evening he has something for her. Nestled inside his cap, which he carries with slow reverence up the path and across the cliff top towards her, is an egg.

'Where d'you get this?' she asks.

'Ahint the quarry.'

'It is took'd off a nest?'

He smiles. 'Clam the rocks for it.'

'It's a Cuddy Duck. You'll have to put it back.'

He gapes up at her, baffled, disappointed. 'This is all I took. There was more.'

'They are not for taking.'

She is surprised at the force of her own words. They both look at the perfect green shell, spruttled all over with thin white streaks, like a prize gooseberry. She imagines showing it to her mother. Here, look, I have been given an egg. This is what I have been doing, thinking, with my time while you are praying and hoping and grieving alone. Small tufts of down are still clung to the shell. 'You must put it back,' she says again, and leaves him there, cradling his cap.

While they work that evening, rain begins to tap on the roof. She is not onto the next fish before it becomes loud enough that they have to shout above it. The herring girls rush to the doorway to look outside at the steaming harbour. Her mother, though, does not look up once from her work, her eyes remaining fixed on the slice and twist and purple slurp of entrails onto the table.

Mrs Allan lets her go early, when she has come to the end of her batch. She goes outside into the rain, but instead of following the path home she starts to walk in the opposite direction, following the edge of the harbour, past a bait pile of shellfish taller than herself, then along the foreshore past the schooner moored at the staithes and − shielding her momentarily from the rain − the castle ramparts, until she comes to the kilns. She pauses, listening to the chemical fizz of water hitting the roasting lime, then continues on to Castle Point.

Through the misted dark she cannot see farther than her fingertips reaching towards the sea. She shivers at the caress of water running down her neck. Her face feels bruised with cold, but she stays there, refusing to yield. Diffused for an instant through the sea fog is the minute brightening of the lighthouse. She lets out a cry, a howl, which immediately disappears.

The rain persists through the night and into the morning. Inside the shed the air hangs with damp. The herring girls are quieter than usual, and

Elfrida grows certain that they can sense the anxious mood of the island women. Her body aches. She knows it is likely that she will fall ill. She scrapes and slides and discards the tornbellies, staring into the bucket of eyes, trying to concentrate.

Before lunch the wind picks up and a belt of clear sky moves in from the sea. Excitement speeds through her at the sight of it, which she suppresses, knowing, however she tries to convince herself otherwise, what it is for.

———————————————

He is there, waiting for her. Straight away he tells her that he has returned the egg: he did it at night during the rain and almost slipped to his death the rocks got that slick. She says that she is pleased. He smiles, studying his feet.

'Are ye working the morning?'

She shakes her head. It is a Sunday.

'Will ye meet me?'

'Where?'

'Anyplace. Here. Show me the island?'

———————————————

She tells her mother that she will be gone for the morning, and has planned an explanation that she is taking out over the flats with a small party collecting ragworms for the start of the cod season, but her mother does not ask, so she leaves her in the kitchen, kneeling at the hearth.

He is ready on the Heugh, a cloth sack over his shoulder. Her skin goes cold when he comes towards her, but he stops a few paces away.

'We'll be off, then?' he says.

She steps carefully onto the steep stony path, charged with an aware-ness of him behind, following her. At the bottom he comes alongside and they walk together onto the beach. To their left the tide is full out and the flats lie bare beneath a thin haze. They skirt around a soft wet heave of seaweed: brown, dark green, seamed here and there with red, then yellow, like a forest at the turn of the season. He does not appear uneasy

at their silence, she thinks. They slow to watch a curlew toying with a crab
– tossing it into the air then monitoring it scuttle brokenly away before
going again in chase of it.

They enter the sandhills. They rise along ridges where marram grass
brushes against their legs, then dip into the hollowed shelter of the dunes,
which are warm already in the sunlight. He lets her go ahead of him to pass
through a narrow gully – and they come upon a pond. A small tree grows at
the centre of it, directly from the water.

'I've no been down here before.'

She does not know how to reply, so smiles, but he quickens ahead and
she judges that he has recognised where he is – the quarry visible now away
to one side.

'You'll have the sea thereaway just now,' she says. And as they come over
the lip of the next dune it is there, shimmering and unending before them.

'We'll sit down here eh?' To her surprise he pulls from his sack a rough
woollen rug, dusted with white patches. He lays it down on the bank
facing the sea and she waits for him to sit down – but he gestures for her
to go first so she lowers herself at one side of the rug, and is relieved when
he settles down at the other.

'I've pieces,' he says. She cannot help letting out a small laugh when he
takes out two unwrapped sandwiches, uncut, a brown filling seeping from
the middle.

She shakes her head. 'Thank you.'

He takes a large bite from his sandwich, gazing at the sea. 'That
Berwick?' He points, chewing, to the huddled smudge of town far away
on the mainland.

'It is.'

'Dundee's too far to see,' he says, staring north, intently enough that
he is not distracted by the doleful signal of a seal, screaming from the
rocky peninsula beyond the beach where an eccentric party of seals and
spread-winged shags are enjoying the sun together.

'Yer family work the herring catch eh?'

'Depends the season.'

'Yer da, he a fisherman?'

She turns her face from him. Her throat is constricting. A small noise
escapes her and she knows that here, now, she is going to cry. She laughs

weakly, as the tears come, because it is happening in front of him. She fights to control herself but he is moving closer to her and as she sees his face, gentle, unembarrassed, she lets herself place her head against his chest. His shirt smells of something animal; horses, she realises.

'I'd heard tell about the fleet. I'd no thought – just no thought, sorry.'

She stays against him for a moment. When she pulls away he is mindful not to look at her while she wipes her face.

He goes into his sack. 'Here.' He produces an earthenware mug, full of blackberries. 'These is off the bushes by the wagonway.' He hesitates, then offers the mug, grinning. 'I'm allowed to take these eh?'

She smiles, picking a couple out. 'Them that wants them is welcome.'

A sudden rush of noise from behind makes them both start. A dense flock of knots – twenty thousand or more – appears over their heads. He twists, grabbing his sack, and holds it above her. For several breaths the dune is in shadow – and then the flock passes, the sun once more on her face. She watches the dark cloud of birds speeding to sea, a long tendril at the back swirling and thinning, splitting from the main body, then absorbed again into its mass. He stays where he is, close to her. He is stroking the red mark on his palm, and she sees that there are other cuts and scabs on his knuckles.

He notices her looking. 'Hands is battered. See.' He holds them out. 'And see this.' He pulls up the sleeve of his shirt to reveal a long raw blister up the inside of his forearm. It is recent. Damp. 'Burned it. All that rain. Makes the quicklime terrible jumpy.'

She puts out her own hands. 'I've keens too. Bealings on all the finger ends.' She shows him the swellings where brine and salt has got into the tiny cuts from the scaling knife. He takes one of her hands, carefully cupping it in his own, to inspect more closely.

'Working hand, that.'

He trails a finger lightly over her cuts. She closes her eyes – but opens them again at the thought of her mother. She gets to her feet, saying quietly that she is needed. He gives a small nod before she scales the dune side. Only when she is at the top and turns round to take him in does she see the people on the beach below, coming down from the quarry cottages, some pointing, waving, to sea – where a distant scattering of cobles, nine, ten, not enough, is sailing towards the island.

THE PLACE FOR ME

E.C. Osondu

Whenever Tochi's elder brother visited from London their house became one long party that did not stop until his departure, right up to the moment his flight was called. Lots of Star and Gulder beer was consumed. Chicken Pepper Soup was made the way his brother preferred it – clear and light and spiced with habanero peppers and scented leaves. And of course the girls, a different girl each day, sometimes two. Tochi often wondered what it was about living abroad that made his brother go at life with such gusto.

At their house his brother would stand on the balcony wearing only a pair of shorts with a towel around his neck because he was perpetually sweating. He said it was the change in the weather, but that bottle of beer followed bottle of beer could not have helped. He would look up, raise his hands and say, 'Ah freedom! So this is me enjoying my life here. This country is sweet, I tell you. Life in London is great – the only trouble is that white people don't know how to enjoy themselves. They don't know how to have fun. Breathe in their air over there, so sterile. Smells of nothing.'

And he would breathe in the air noisily.

'Do you know how many things I can smell here?' he would say. 'I can smell the aroma of akara frying. I can smell tomato stew. I can smell the bread from the bakery. I can even smell the sawdust from the sawmill. This life. Give me another beer. Let me enjoy myself *jare*.'

He would be drinking and he would pause, tell Tochi to increase the volume of the music playing on the sound system and he would break into a jig.

'Won't you dance? Ah I will dance, oh. If I lived here I would be dancing every day.'

Tochi wanted to ask him if he was not living in the same London where the latest dance moves they watched on TV originated from. Eventually, he did.

'Have I not told you that they don't have the secret of enjoyment the way we do here? They dance over there but their dancing has no spirit.'

'What about the ones we see on TV dancing?' Tochi asked.

'Those ones are dancing for money. They are performing. Putting on a show. Do you see them dance with reckless abandon the way we do here? Besides, they only dance with their feet. Here we dance with our entire body.'

And he danced his way to the bathroom.

His brother's old friends from high school visited. His brother complimented them. He told them he envied their lifestyle at home. He said he would come back in a second if he could get their kind of jobs.

'But you make money over there,' they told him. 'You make hard currency. Iron money. Pounds and euros, not this weak naira.'

'Over there people make money with one hand and the government takes it back with their two hands. Tax, tax, tax. Everything is bills and tax. You see this our house, you see this balcony, if this house was in London you'd be paying taxes because your house is overlooking the street.'

'But what about the girls? The pretty white girls we see on television and in the movies?'

'Forget them. When you are in a relationship with them you are always looking over your shoulder. Watching your back. Sleeping with one eye open.'

'But they are not materialistic and demanding like our girls.'

'Yeah right,' his brother said and he laughed.

'Wait until they kill you for the insurance money and then you'll know who is more materialistic.'

Tochi listened to these conversations nervously. They made him a bit uncomfortable because there was something he had been meaning to ask his brother. For days he could not find the courage. It was not until his brother was packing his bags for the return journey that Tochi eventually found the courage to ask if he could join him abroad in London.

'To stay here and go to school is what I believe is best for you,' his brother said.

'But I have already gone to school.'

'Go to school some more. Get a master's degree or even a doctorate. I'll sponsor you.'

'But there are no jobs here.'

'And you think there are jobs in London?'

'It must be better than here.'

His brother laughed. It was not his usual deep-throated laughter. This laugh was totally lacking in humour.

'Let me tell you something. If you cannot swim the Lagos lagoon there is no way you can swim the river Thames. I see all my friends here; they work in banks, they own their own companies. They wear suits, they have drivers, maids, houseboys. They come back from work; they go to the club to drink beer and eat *suya*. They are happy. Such opportunities rarely exist for us outside of here.'

'But look at you, you are successful.'

Once again, the dry laughter. He shook his head.

'You do not understand.'

'Make me understand.'

'Here's the difference – no job is considered too low over there.'

'You know I am a hard worker.'

'Seven, eight years ago before I left I was like you. Let me just say this. I will not stop you. If you step into the city of London at any time my door is open.'

Getting the visa was not difficult. Through a contact his name was included on the list of healthcare workers attending a mental health conference at the university of London. He became a psychiatrist at the university teaching hospital. He had his letter of invitation and was prepared for the interview. The young interviewer asked him a couple of routine questions and just when he thought it was over she paused.

'Tell me, why have you never attended any international conferences before now?'

'I have never been invited before now.'

'Really?'

'Yes, and I only go where I am invited.'

His response made her smile. She told him to return in a couple of days for his visa.

Three months later Tochi arrived London. After he had cleared immigration, he walked casually to a Thomas Cook to change the twenty-pound note in his pocket so he could buy a train ticket. He did not want to join the long lines at the ticket windows. He was coming from a place where long lines or lines in general were a dreaded thing. He handed the note to the clerk. The clerk held it up to the light. Brought it down. Held it up again and seemed to sniff it.

'This is your money innit?'

'Yes it is.'

'And whereabouts did you get it from?'

'I bought at a Bureau de Change in my country, at the airport.'

'No worries. Please step forward towards me,' she said politely.

He stepped forward. She made a call. In the next minute a man in a dark uniform appeared by his side.

'Come with me, please,' the officer said.

He began to sweat beneath his heavy wool coat.

'This is a counterfeit pound note,' the officer said to him in the airport police station. 'I am going to keep it and it will be destroyed at a future date. You may go.'

He had shown them the receipt from the Bureau de Change from which he had purchased the currency, he sensed that was what had saved him. He was exhausted but buoyed up by the fact that he would soon be seeing his brother. He soon arrived at his brother's council flat in Peckham.

But the brother he was seeing in London was the opposite of the brother who visited home. This one slept through the day and left for work dressed in a well-made suit at night.

Who wore a dapper suit to work at night? Tochi wondered what type of job his brother did.

His brother encouraged him to familiarise himself with the city.

'Get to know London. Some people live here for thirty years and don't even know where Soho is. Tourists visit here for two days and they go to Soho every day. Get to know your way around.'

He bought him an expensive ticket with which he could ride the bus or tube. He rode the double-decker. There he listened to fellow Nigerians as they conversed with themselves in their native dialects like they were on a Lagos Molue bus.

He loved the names of the bus stops. They were like mini-stories in and of themselves; Elephant and Castle, Bird in Bush, Bricklayers Arms.

He got an occasional casual cleaning gig with a Ghanaian. The Ghanaian taught him the tricks of the trade.

'Clean a little bit. Make the work last. You are paid hourly. If you want to sleep, turn on the vacuum cleaner on high, leave it running and go sit on the toilet seat and sleep. When your supervisor is coming he will hear the sound of the vacuum cleaner and think you are busy and turn back.'

He kept what he earned. His brother bought all the foodstuff they needed. There were so many Nigerians living in Peckham that one could live in Peckham as if one lived in Lagos. You could conduct all your business using a local Nigerian language.

Then one day his brother bought him a nice navy blue suit and a powder blue TM Lewin shirt and a dark pair of brogues and told him to shave, take a bath, use an aftershave and cologne and get ready to go to work with him.

They drove over the bridge that separated Peckham from the city, went past the football stadium, and into the city centre. Just after Trafalgar square his brother brought the car to a stop in front of a Gentlemen's Club. Tochi began walking towards the entrance his brother stopped him.

'Where do you think you are going?'

'I thought we were going inside.'

'To do what?'

'To watch the dancing girls.'

'Don't be silly. You are here to watch me, not the girls.'

He sat back in the car and began to watch his brother. As soon as the club began to empty out he approached a man who looked a little drunk and friendly.

'Do you want company mate?'

The man gave his brother a strange look.

'What kind of company?'

'Girls, any kind of girls you want – white, black, blonde, redheads. I have them all.'

'Where?'

'In my place not too far from here. Get in the car. I'll take you there.'

The man got in the car a little nervously. He sat in front while his brother drove.

His brother tried to reassure the man that he was safe.

'You'll be safe and comfortable where I'm taking you to. If for any reason you feel uncomfortable just let me know and I'll drop you off at your hotel or wherever.'

'Is this some kind of brothel?' the man asked.

'Not a brothel, mate. We'll soon be there. Nice cosy place with friendly girls. You can relax. If you don't like it I'll take you back for free, like I mentioned earlier.'

Then his brother was on the cellphone.

'Yes, a friend and my younger brother I had earlier mentioned to you.'

They parked on a side street. The buildings looked like office buildings. His brother rang the bell. A girl let them in. At first he thought she was a black girl. Later he would see that she was just darkly tanned. She was Eastern European but liked black guys and was trying hard to make her skin darker.

In the large sitting room of the flat were lots of girls. Some were dressed in lingerie. A few wore swimsuits. Some sat in the large kitchen drinking coffee and smoking.

The girl who answered the door was attending to the man they had brought in. She was rubbing his shoulders and asking him to feel at home, look around and pick any of the girls hanging around to be with. Another guy, apparently the owner of the place, was typing on a laptop as an Indian guy read numbers off a credit card to him.

The man they came in with was guzzling a cold can of Heineken's beer. A girl was sitting on his lap. She was touching his face and telling him in accented English to make himself at home that she was not about to eat him up unless he wanted to be eaten. The man laughed. The girl laughed. Soon the man gave some money to the girl who handed the money over to the dark-tanned girl. The girl who was earlier sitting on the man's lap took the man's hand and led him into a bedroom. They shut the door. His brother tapped him on the shoulder.

'Time to go,' his brother said.

They drove to another Gentleman's Club. Again his brother waited. Again the patrons streamed out and he homed in on one. They chatted. He got the man into the car and drove him to the flat.

By the time his brother brought in his last customer it was almost 4am.

The guy on the computer was still feeding in numbers with the Indian guy standing beside him.

'These are no good. Bring new ones tomorrow,' he said to the Indian.

The dark-tanned girl came into the kitchen where they were sitting and handed his brother some pound notes. His brother took it and pocketed it immediately.

'Aren't you even gonna count the cash?' the tanned girl asked.

His brother smiled.

'No need to count, I know you are not gonna cheat me, Eva.'

'I don't cheat. It is you Africans that like to cheat. Like my ex, your good buddy Ade. Never satisfied with one woman.'

His brother only smiled. He made Tochi a cup of coffee and made one for himself. 'Now, you have seen everything. This is my job. This will soon be your job. You will study me. This is your school. You must never pick some nationalities. Slightly tipsy men are good but not totally drunk men. You must be careful so you don't pick an undercover cop. Usually, the men are mostly tourists who have been at the strip club. They are aroused. They want to be with women. We bring them here to the girls. They have a good time with the girls. They pay good money. We get a cut. Nothing complicated about it. Leave the girls alone. I know it is tempting but keep it strictly business.'

At night the next day, Tochi wore his suit and began to get ready to head out to the gentlemen's clubs. He looked out into the London night. Back home the night descended suddenly without warning and covered everywhere with impenetrable inkiness. Here the night was grey – gauzy, even – but like the night at home it still hid much.

THE RAPE ESSAY
(OR MUTILATED PAGES)

Suzanne Scanlon

'Well yes of course I'd read it, but you know it's hard –'

'You dated him anyway!'

'I mean how could I –'

'There's a blog about that –'

'Something so cartoonish could not have been *real,* you know?'

'A Twitter maybe, something.'

'Or very real.'

'Surreal. That way. That he was just what – I mean, worse – than the men he wrote about.'

'The one who sleeps with the Hippie Chick?'

'Or the two guys having that sick conversation –'

'Today's modern woman blah blah –'

'Something about the way it was like how – women, ha! – were totally hosed, you know, by wanting to be independent and also wanting to be totally overcome and undone and ravished in love, by a man. Like blissed out and destroyed, obliterated.'

'Yeah.'

'Well that was actually smart. I mean that's why he gave me it that day, before we –'

'Very.'

'Do you think –'

'It's like this book I'm reading where this –'

'But regardless, it is condescending for a man to come to such a conclusion – like, he's trying to undo through intellectual analysis the very women he's seducing.'

'Where she talks about um how you can't desire what you have – how it's like hide and seek and you can't seek what isn't hidden –'

'The most cynical –'

'But I mean maybe there's something to it. Also.'

'But smart. Yeah. I know.'

'I know you know. I'm just saying. I'm just saying.'

'Yeah.'

Maybe the story begins here: Harold just beyond the doorframe; you see him, don't you? He holds a sweatshirt: grey and torn, with the insignia of a Jesuit boy's school in the Bronx: XAVIER. Esther's sweatshirt, a gift from a boy she'd met in asylum. That's what Harold liked: that it belonged to a boy, a boy from asylum, another boy, and that the boy must have liked Esther very much, to give it to her. And now, he, Harold, is the one who got it, and got her, too.

Not that the boy in asylum ever got Esther, of course. But maybe that was better, leaving it there, in the realm of desire. Or not even desire.

Back to the moment, the beginning: here's Harold, in the doorway, wearing tennis shorts. His elegant legs, which taper at the knee.

'This is what makes legs sexy,' a girlfriend once advised Esther. They were in high school.

'Without that taper, you have fat legs.'

Esther considered her own legs.

'My mom said these were the legs of an obese person.'

'You can't have everything,' the friend consoled.

Or was it later, the beginning, or maybe this was the end, that day in class, when Harold held up his copy of the essay, to make his point. With his left hand, gesturing to the page, saying,

'This was originally published alongside *a very unattractive photo of the author.*'

The beginning might be later, too, like the time Harold took a pair of sweat-pants that had been given to her by a boyfriend she'd had when they met.

'I fed them to my dogs,' he told her, of the sweatpants, and it seemed to be a joke, hyperbolic.

Still, Esther loved it, the way Harold wished to possess her, this violence of competition. She'd never been loved that way before, violently, madly; and even though, later, she decided it was not love, she'd never, anyway, had love performed that way before this, which was what mattered sometimes, above all, or in the moment of it: the performance of love.

If Esther were asked now to describe Harold – in one line, retrospectively – she would say: Harold wore shorts. Or: Harold was aware of the beauty of his legs.

'To be concerned with fame is much like a preoccupation with sexual appeal: one day it pleases you, soon enough, it destroys you.'

'…'

'You become consumed with trying to keep it. Like everything else, it becomes something to lose. The prospect of losing it terrifies you.'

'…'

'So what you have to do is not get attached to anything; it's all here to be lost, just as we are.'

If you worship money and things, if they are where you tap real meaning in life, then you will never have enough, never feel you have enough. It's the truth.

Worship your body and beauty and sexual allure and you will always feel ugly.
And when time and age start showing, you will die a million deaths before they
finally grieve you.

Esther holds back the curtain covering the small window at the top
of the door. Harold is no longer in shadow; he is complete, in colour, lips
pursed and head bowed.

'Did you get my email?' Harold asks.

'I don't want it.'

'...'

'My dad would be mad if I lost –'

'It's not really me, mine, I don't care.'

'It's important to him.'

———————————

So a boy named Brian, incidental here but maybe not? had given Esther the
Xavier sweatshirt years earlier, just after he was admitted to the adolescent
program. This was late in Esther's stay. Suddenly, there were so many kids
on the ward; it changed everything. Brian carried a bible, wrote notes he'd
sign with bible verses. St Francis Xavier School in the Bronx, on Haight
Street.

Esther didn't want to be a mental patient anymore, not this way – not
in front of so many children. Little eyes on her: it forced her to grow up.
Eyes that did not gaze, but needed. *Be not afraid. 1 Peter 3:4* Something
had to make her want to leave that place, why not the transformation of
long-term asylum into short-term high school respite? *Babies are famous
to themselves*, Harold said. She'd sung the biblical line as a child. The idea
of it: Jesus, a Savior, holding you. Nothing to fear. This was how the gaze
worked. She became supplicant. She wanted to believe. This, too, was why
she loved Harold; he also wanted to believe. He didn't believe, but he
wanted to.

If Brian believed, why was he in a mental hospital?

'Do the Jesuits look askance?' she asked one day, thinking of James Joyce.

'Not at all.'

'I don't think fervour sits well.'

'They only mind when I speak of the visions.'

'...'

'When I'm lucky. Occasionally. I have to prepare, to be ready –'

'What happens?'

'A bird flying over, around and around in circles; he comes closer and closer and then – right into my heart.'

Brian closed his eyes, put his hand to his chest, a lowered salute.

'...'

'Another time, spiders, bleeding, but others – Saint Dymphna, for example.'

'The patron saint of nervous illness.'

'She was, in fact, molested,' Esther told Brian; she'd loved *Lives of the Saints* as a girl. 'I mean, that's the irony, right? She was abused like so many women here on this psych ward but really she'd been raped, desired by her own father, then ran away.'

'I didn't know.'

'He cut her eyes out.'

Esther's aunt sent a prayer card of Dymphna to the asylum; Esther threw it in the trash immediately.

'So why is she the saint of mental illness? Why not the saint of women traumatised by wacked-out patriarchal violence?'

Brian listened, nodded, but didn't register the story as Esther did. He told her it was usually a male saint or apostle appeared to him, anyway. *This is where mental illness gets interesting*, Esther wanted to say, but stopped herself. She did like Brian, even if he lacked specifics; that fatal flaw of the faithful. He went on about Jesus coming to him, laying hands; treacly imagery from her own, tired girlhood. Next it was Francis of Assisi, a hallmark version of goodness and love.

But back to the real story here, which is about Harold, and now that we've discovered where it begins, let's get to the point. There is a point! I promise. For example, here's Esther, out of bed now, in jean shorts, no bra, carrying the big book to the door. It's Harold's book. Harold won't walk through the entranceway, she notices, a new boundary. She hates boundaries. *Boundaries are for maps*, a woman protested, in a play she had seen some weeks earlier. That's how she felt. Maps. Keep your boundaries for your maps.

But not really. She liked boundaries sometimes. She liked them when Brian was around.

———————————————

Here's what Esther wrote of the moment later, in her notebook:

I said fuck you but not out loud and only in retrospect. I wanted to be back in bed. You could see that and yet. You needed it. Something about your father. I said I will give you something. And I got your book, a big book, which I never wanted, with an essay you insisted I read, an essay I of course read, an essay about rape, an essay written by one of my favorite writers ever, a writer you would only call 'weird' which fine so what or was it 'scary'? No 'scary' was how the other prof, my default-prof, described Kathy Acker: 'Scary'.

Some background: back when they still liked each other, when boundaries were for maps, maybe, but certainly not for student-professor relationships, Harold appeared at Esther's door one afternoon; he carried a big book.

'You have to read this,' he told Esther, of the book, but not the book itself but just one particular essay within the book, an essay written by a female writer Esther admired. In the essay, which Harold wanted Esther to read, the writer argued – or so it seemed to Esther – that *date rape* was a reductive, problematic term; women, the writer suggested, were less often the victims they wished to be considered.

Or so it had been in her experience.

The writer of the rape essay was the first to articulate for Esther what it was to be woman right now. Not in this rape essay but in her fiction, which Esther admired, where the writer wrote sharply, smartly about women doing stupid, dark, destructive things: fucking men they feared or despised, for example.

Esther sat down to read 'The Rape Essay' as she came to call it, though that was not the title. She ignored the implications of Harold gifting her this way, but acknowledged the gesture as ritualised courtship, which Harold took seriously. She hadn't expected how essential this phase would be for Harold: the opening of car doors, for example.

The problem, the admired writer argued in this essay, was that many women allowed themselves to get to a risky, dangerous place – flirting, drunk, physically involved – because of the erotic charge – and yet, these very women wish to call it 'rape' when it ends violently or forcibly or merely regrettably.

Esther and Harold had bonded over asylum stories. 'War stories,' he called them, but it was also intellectual inquiry; she found it exciting. Sparring as flirtation.

'It reminds me of, like, Bill Cosby.' She tells him later, by phone.

He groaned.

'Didn't he like blame black people for not being, you know –'

'If you think you can compare what it is to be a privileged white woman to what it is to be black in this country, under the hold of systemic racism.'

'That's not what I –'

'The juggernaut of 20th-century feminism.'

Esther re-read the essay in bed that night, and again the next: what the woman argued was for a more nuanced understanding of relationships between men and women. Sometimes women got what they wanted but didn't want. *Be careful what you ask for*, as a particularly simpering asylum keeper would say to Esther and the others.

Back in the doorway, things are still rising: Harold, esteemed and brilliant, appears helpless, shy; lacks the energy or bravado of his first appearance in her *genkan*.

It was hard to believe that this was the man she'd been hating with such intense feeling all week. It was easier to hate people who weren't bodies, who didn't have faces.

———————————

'It's true that some of us are, well, complicit in ways we don't want to acknowledge. In our own joy and suffering. It's not possible *not to be.*'

'That doesn't mean that –'

'Rape still happens.'

'I read the essay –'

———————————

He doesn't move.

You burn with hunger for food that does not exist.

———————————

Q. Why was the t-shirt special?

A. It was from the American Philosophical Association.

Q. What did it say?

A. On the front it read 'The statement on the back of this shirt is true.'

Q. And on the back?

A. 'The statement on the front of this shirt is false.'

———————————

The large book fell open first to another essay in the book, which contained one of Harold's essays. It fell open to the page, she discovered, where Harold had mutilated some text, taken scissors to pages, cut entire paragraph-sections.

You are like me, but worse, she thought.

You have been snared by the delusion that envy has a reciprocal.

'Was he a cutter?'

'Not really, but.'

'Same thing?'

'For sure.'

It's funny how easy it was for her, Esther, to imagine that to be Harold was more satisfying than it actually was. To be Harold was, in fact, excruciating. Or so his mutilated pages revealed.

This could be the climax: a few days after dropping off the book, he invites her to take a ride in his new Volvo. On the way to the Super Kroger, he spoke of his work.

Did he bring it up, or did she?

It's hard to say. She told him she hadn't read his big book. Which was true.

Was reading it required?

He said that was good. He said it was a relief. He said he much preferred hanging out with people who hadn't read his books.

She said, *But I loved the others, and that one story*.

Which?

That was the story of my life! she told him.

Did your family read it? she asked.

My mom and sister I think.

Not sure.

Really?

They don't talk about it.

Why did they speak of it?

She closed her eyes, thought: *I want to sleep with you because I want to be you*. Or, as the poet wrote: *I want to sleep with what I want to become*.

That wasn't it.

He wanted her to know: *I am nothing.* Nothing. And the fact of you desiring me because I am something has me wishing only to make you feel that nothingness, too, as I do.

She'd read something in the paper.

I don't read it.

You were mentioned.

I don't read it. The Japanese woman, she called me a misogynist.

He was parked in front of her house now, just across from a park. He looked at her.

That really hurt.

She didn't ask.

Why didn't she ask?

Maybe we are all misogynists, then.

They both knew what the Japanese lady meant.

Esther could no longer say how many men had given her books to read, or told her to see a certain movie or listen to certain music. But how many of those men held the authority of Harold?

Harold did not care for or about her at all. He never had. The simple truth was perhaps obvious to everyone from the beginning – but had not been to Esther.

'It would be, as your professor, an act of love to maintain boundaries,' the doctor asserted. 'That's what parents do, what professionals must do, too. To do otherwise is selfish.'

To his co-professor, to fellow students, to the many other women who had been objects of Harold's attractions, this was not news.

'Abusive, too.'

'It sounds simple but it's profound: the ability to love in this way, from a distance, through restraint.'

Rang cherries was Harold's phrase for that shock of recognition. The essay was contained in the large book Harold held in his arms; the book also contained an essay written by Harold, though he did not mention it.

> *It was funny how you used the word date. We both laughed. It was funny how you opened doors for me. It was funny that when I commented on the insistent opening of doors you said that your mother had taught you. To open doors. It was funny that I knew then that I would teach my son the same thing.*

They laughed, Esther thinks now, because they both understood the absurdity of the charade. There is nothing more attractive than shared secret knowledge with another human being – secret knowledge that will lead the two of you to a shared space.

Socrates: *the best learning takes place in bed.*

Harold's joke that wasn't a joke.

'Sometimes,' Esther confides in Harold, 'sometimes I need so badly to write the book that is in my body, yet feel unable to write it – and this gap makes me want to die.'

Harold told her she must write, no matter how afraid.

'You write as if saving your life,' he tells her.

'It will kill you but you have no choice.'

'That's when it matters, when you have no choice.'

The truth will set you free. But not until it is finished with you.

Years later, people say to Esther – *You are brave* – and it will chafe.

What does it mean to be brave when you don't have a choice?

The older you get, Harold told her, the more you *feel* that line of Heidegger – *that to be fully alive means to feel yourself in decay, moving toward death.*

So, is there a resolution? Maybe it was the night Harold told Esther he admired the rape essay but otherwise found the writer herself *scary*.

'How so?'

'Just scary. That was my impression.'

In the box with the notebook she'd kept while knowing Harold were papers she'd saved from college. One was a paper she'd written in asylum, in response to an assignment for a course titled Skepticism and Affirmation, taught by Maire Jaanus, the striking Estonian who had been married to Edward Said. This she only learned later, reading Said's obituary in the *New York Times*.

'In the future, perhaps we will all attend college while living in a mental hospital,' she joked.

'It made me sad to read of this woman and scholar so essential to my undergraduate education, to my inchoate intellectual identity – now rendered a mere footnote in the obituary of a great man.'

'And later my default prof called Kathy Acker *scary*.'

'This made an impression on you?'

'It seemed that women could very easily be scary – and these were women I most admired – women I wanted to be.'

'I began to understand how terrified I was of these women, and how I wished to become them – at once.'

'Perhaps it is that some of us need to write and others shouldn't be writing.'

'The world is divided into two kinds of people.'

Toward the end of The Rape Essay, the writer Harold described as 'scary' wrote:

A few years ago I invited to dinner at my home a man I'd known casually for two years. We'd had dinner and comradely drinks a few times. I didn't have any intention of becoming sexual with him, but after dinner we slowly got drunk and were soon floundering on the couch. I was ambivalent not only because I was drunk but because I realised that although part of me was up for it, the rest of me was not. So I began to say no. He parried each 'no' with charming banter and became more aggressive. I went along with it for a time because I was amused and even somewhat seduced by the sweet, junior-high spirit of his manner. But at some point I began to be alarmed, and then he did and said some things that turned my alarm into fright. I don't remember the exact sequence of words or events, but I do remember taking one of his hands in both of mine, looking him in the eyes, and saying, 'If this comes to a fight you would win, but it would be very ugly for both of us. Is that really what you want?'

She came outside, sat next to him on the porch. He noticed a scar on her thigh, visible in the midday light. From a far off boulevard, she heard the lone squeal of an ambulance.

'You know I wanted to see you because I saw you the other day in Stevenson –'

'What?'

'I was getting off the elevator and you were in the –'

'I didn't see you.'

'I said Hi, and you looked at me, like – like I was a piece of excrement.'

Esther told Harold she did not recall seeing him that day, but it was possible. They were silent for a while. She found a ladybug on her arm, flicked it away.

'My doctor says it is sexual harassment.'

'Well, I don't – we could have a fight about it, and I'm not sure who would win.'

She stared ahead.

'Yes, you would win, but it would be very ugly for both of us. *Is that really what you want?*'

'There's nothing to win.'

He didn't say anything, just looked ahead: his lips pursed, eyes narrowed, a long frozen stare of gratitude, sadness, anger or nothing at all.

FINISHING LINES

Sara Baume

I.

've often thought that pigeons resemble tiny, shaved-headed men in high collars with their arms shoved down inside their shirts, the sleeves tied behind their backs. I know this is ridiculous; how can a bird possibly look like a man? But it's the picture that lights up in my head every time I see a pigeon, inescapably.

Since I was a child, my mother's uncle has kept homing pigeons. He lived four doors down the terrace from my parents and me. Almost every evening I'd call to his house on my way home from school, and he'd allow me to measure the un-popped kernels of corn into the feed trays, to choose a bird for him to lift. Then he'd hold her in his lap, his fist encircling her wings, gripping them still for me to extend a finger and stroke her plumage, very gently, very slow.

These days only my great-uncle and I live in the same terrace, four doors apart. My mother and father are both gone from this town which has, in recent years, become more of a suburb. It has an apartment block and a multistory car park; there are more traffic lights than trees, more supermarkets than churches. Now my great-uncle has lung disease and coughs at the end of every sentence and sometimes at the beginning and in the middle too. Now he wears a red button. *HOME CARE PERSONAL ALARM SYSTEM* it said on the box it came in, but my great-uncle calls it his rocket launcher, and he never presses it; I know because mine is the number it will phone first if ever he tries to launch his rocket.

I live here in my mother's house with my boyfriend, who doesn't like it when I call him my boyfriend; he thinks it makes us sound slipshod, unserious, liable to be rent apart at any moment, as if we aren't soldered by stronger stuff. We are soldered by our baby. She was born with so much hair, more than my boyfriend, more than my great-uncle, more than all the tiny men-pigeons I have ever found myself imagining. When I brush her hair, I try not to picture it sloshing around the pools of fluid inside me. Even though she has been born for nine months, has now been out of me for as much time as she was in; even though my boyfriend and I gave her a noble and beautiful name, we have yet to call her by it or cut her hair; we refer to her only as 'the baby'.

2.

Two weeks ago, four of my great-uncle's pigeons were taken to St Malo for a cross-channel race. He never transports his own birds, and so has never seen them liberated along with all of the others, like a battery of feathered missiles, I imagine, like ash-coloured fireworks. My great-uncle only ever waits at home for them to come back to him. Three returned roughly when they were expected but there was no trace of the fourth until he received a phone call from a woman in Bethnal Green, a stranger. Then I took out my old school atlas and opened it across his kitchen table. He showed me Brittany and I turned the page and showed him London, and my great-uncle shook his head and said he couldn't make any sense of that. But it must be my bird, he said, how else could the woman have called my number?

For years, I believed that the way a homing pigeon navigates has something to do with ley lines, with Feng Shui, with water divining, but this isn't so. There are particles of iron in the tops of their beaks, microscopic magnets which keep them aligned to the north. When they are far away, they smell the air, they listen to the sound waves: my great-uncle has explained this to me, though in different words. And once they're closer to home again, they identify features in the landscape. A pigeon can race from six months of age right the way up to ten years, and in most cases, he says, an older bird is better. The strength and speed of youth is no match for the experience and fidelity that comes with age.

My great-uncle said he could not fly himself, because of what it did to his ears, and he couldn't sail either, because of what it did to his stomach. But I knew these weren't the real reasons; the real reason was because he was old and afraid. Think of all the people who've been born since me, I've heard him say, think of all the things they know which I don't. He told me that he would pay for the trip if I arranged it, that he did not care about the cost, but it had to be as soon as possible; this was the important part.

I am to go by bus and plane, to return by train and boat. He gives me a carrying case which looks like a cat box and has another, smaller box inside which doesn't have any air-holes, which rattles when it slides. Then he gives me instructions: for handling, for feeding, for calming down when in distress, and he gives me the name of the fourth bird, the lost and found bird, as if she might answer to it. Her name is Martha.

What about the baby, my boyfriend says. Because he earns a better wage than me, my boyfriend is the one who works full-time. He is an engineer. But he takes a half day every Friday and spends long hours every weekend watching the TV channel which shows nothing but sport. I'll only be gone for one night, I say; you can look after her. I am annoyed with the baby because of something she has done to me; a small act of violence. Three mornings ago, as I bounced her on my hip and tried to single-handedly butter toast, she fastened her puny fist onto my earring, and pulled, hard. It was such a bizarre moment. My instinct to protect myself collided with my instinct to protect her; I dropped the butter knife and raised my free hand to slap her off, but stopped myself just in time. Instead, I blew hard into her face. I blew because this was something the family dog had been frightened of when I was a child, was the only way he could be made to surrender whatever forbidden thing he had clasped between his teeth. He'd flatten his ears and squint his eyes but open his mouth and back away. Something made me assume the baby would react as an animal would, and I was right. As soon as I blew in her face, she let go of my earring, and started to bawl.

3.

I try to carry the cat box onto the bus, but the driver says it is too big and makes me put it in the luggage hold. It's a non-descript day in February; on every dual carriageway the sky is white as it always is, the grass is green as it ought to be. Whenever I take a long trip, which is seldom since the baby, I try to make the time pass by looking intently at the changing landscape; at each new, yet similar, segment as it arrives into and departs from my field of vision. Once, in secondary school, my biology class was taken on a field trip to a nature reserve where we were each given a small wooden square and instructed to toss it randomly into the air and chase it to where it fell. Then we had to get down on the ground and analyse everything we found in the plot of earth inside its frame, which at first looked like nothing but grass, yet on closer inspection became weeds, seed-heads, pine needles, three different species of tiny fly, and a woodlouse. Now, looking out the bus window, I try to see beyond the white and green, to single out the unexpected. I remember how my school friends were jealous of the plentitude of my squared-off plot of earth, of my woodlouse. I remember how our teacher said that plentitude was a reflection not of the plot itself, but of the person who analysed it.

From a seat somewhere behind me comes the sound of a computer game, its unmelodious yet cheerful tune. I wonder if there's a child back there; everyone I am able to see is an adult who is attempting to sleep, as if to defy the arduousness of remaining conscious throughout this suspended period of time, this journey. After a while, I try to sleep too, but every time the bus stops, I wake against my will, like a doll with tipping eyelids. At every stop, I look out at people lingering on the footpath below the bus, saying hello or goodbye to their loved ones; they are people not watching and not waiting for me, not wishing I would wave. And this suddenly makes me miss my boyfriend, miss the baby, makes me finger my wounded ear. Though the hole was stretched beyond its limit, the lobe was not torn open, and I didn't go to the doctor even though it bled and throbbed more than I thought such a useless wattle of flesh could. What still bothers me about the whole thing – what bothers me most – is how, for all the time the baby was pulling, I was mewling in distress, and she did not respond to this at all, even though I know she must be able to understand the meaning of someone crying out in pain, as every animal does.

The last thing I see before I finally fall asleep is the speck of a very high aeroplane, small as a stain in a fingernail, one of those ones which is meant to indicate that your body is deficient in calcium or zinc, or something else I can't remember. And when my eyelids tip open again, the bus has arrived at Terminal Two.

4.

Again, my cat box is rejected by officialdom; I have to bring it to Oversize Luggage, to watch as a gigantic kitchen appliance encases it in super-strength cling-film. I find I have forgotten all the inane little protocols of flying. Before I am allowed through the security gates, I have to stand over the designated bins, throw away a perfectly good pair of tweezers, choke down a carton of pineapple juice. I have not boarded an aeroplane since I gave birth, and this makes me assume that the airport police will not frisk me. I've been frisked for almost every flight I've ever taken, but something makes me expect that I am no longer ineffably suspicious by virtue of having become a mother. The plastic archway doesn't bleep, but the airport policewoman still draws me aside and invites me to raise my arms, to outstretch them as if I am pretending to be the aeroplane. As she runs her gloves up and down my body, I sing the soft, burring sound of an engine inside my head.

On board, I read the duty-free brochure from cover to cover; I pay full attention to the attendant who performs the safety announcement; I even study the In-Case-of-Emergency leaflet. I'm going to be the only one who survives this flight, I think. Then I look out my window and see the wing. I always end up in a seat where I can see the wing when I am flying; I always spend the entire flight watching for some part of my part of it to break off.

I've never understood how a building can be one hundred floors high, how a tunnel can travel beneath an estuary; I cannot picture what sort of crane-like machine it was that built the first crane, nor how an aeroplane is able to lift into the sky, and hold there, and climb and continue to climb for thousands of vertical miles, and finally to land again at its destination without any part of either wing breaking off. I am a social worker by profession; my domain is strictly human, and so, what I find most strange and fascinating is the way in which people, in which we, every single day, place our trust, our lives, in contraptions we don't fully comprehend. Even though my boyfriend could easily explain all of these things, cement up the cracks in my perception, I never ask.

I look out the window as we fly, past the obtrusive wing. The movement of the wind and the rebound of the sun, their conspired optical illusion, makes it seem as if great swatches of grass have been cast in silver. How evenly shaped and neatly spaced the landscape seems. It makes me think about a project I did with a little girl as part of an art therapy session: together we made a garden on a tray with pebbles for paving slabs, moss for lawn, a tin-foil pond and matchbox shed. From the plane, the landscape is too placid and perfect to seem real; it seems instead like the set of a miniature railway, an architectural model, a garden on a tray. The little girl came into care that day because her mum had been evicted and needed some time alone in which to condense the contents of an apartment to the size of a single room in a B&B.

You don't have to get up very high to meet the edges of this island. Soon all its even shapes and neat spaces have bled together into green and blue, into shadows of cloud on the surface of the sea.

As we begin to descend, my ears swell up with air. They have never hurt like this on a flight before; it is as though they are acting in sympathy with my great-uncle. For a while, the noise grows ferociously loud, until it seems impossible that I am the only passenger who can hear it, that it is still only inside me, until, at last, my ears burst, clear. I look around at my fellow passengers, see that they are all, again, either asleep or gazing directionlessly, distracted by their own swollen, blaring silence, stupefied by the in-flight air conditioning, the sculpted foam, the poetry of remaining still and the world remaining still but something in-between you moving, uncontrollably. Now we come down over the monstrously tall buildings of London city, drop below the birds in flight, the ones who flap and flap and never seem to get anywhere, the ones who glide and seem to get incredibly far with almost no effort, now we land with all the landed ones.

I won't be flying back again because Martha would not be able to tolerate it; ascending beyond the point at which her wings could ever reach alone inside the hold of a hollering machine would be too much for an already disorientated bird to bear. Her beak-magnets would be misbalanced beyond realignment, my great-uncle explained, in different words, and I am enthralled by the peculiarity of this, of the bird who cannot fly, either by its own aeronautics, or by ours.

5.

I am to follow the directions in my phone, to go first to collect my great-uncle's pigeon, then to the flat of my friend where I'll be staying the night. I have not visited London since I was a student, and I'd forgotten how much of the city is papered with advertisement panels, making it feel as if I'm walking through the pop-up pages of a magazine. There are a lot more squirrels than I remember, at least one in every tree I pass, and sometimes in the bins too, all of them grey, and there are even more pigeons, on every footpath, windowsill, phone wire or on no fixed thing at all, just treading air. There are so many pigeons in London, I suddenly realise how absurd it is to have come all of this way to retrieve a single, particular one. By the time I find the right address in Bethnal Green, I'm tired, thirsty, too hot from tramping around, from the streets and buildings and underground trains all crawling with moving bodies. I want to tell the woman who phoned my great-uncle that she should never have removed the band around its ankle; that she should have disregarded his pigeon like all of the others, but, of course, I only thank her and accept her tea.

I expect Martha to be somehow less pigeon-like, more special. I want her to be a bird-of-paradise pigeon, but she is grey like all the others.

My friend's flat is in a Victorian terrace in New Cross, on the top floor. It's terribly clean, and I hope she hasn't cleaned for me. I always feel enormously guilty when my friends tidy up on my behalf, because cleanliness is not something I have ever noticed or appreciated in the way that other people seem to. My friend is single and childless, so we don't talk very much about my boyfriend and the baby. Over the dinner she has prepared for us and glasses and glasses of wine late into the night, I'm happy to talk about the fine points of her life and feelings towards them. Only once it's very late and I'm very drunk do I find myself chattering about homing pigeons, telling her the things I've learned from my great-uncle over the years. They're the only bird able to recognise themselves in a mirror, I tell her. They mate for life, and when a squab is born, it takes three days for its heart to start beating, four for its eyes to open. The homing pigeon is a domestic species; her spirit of adventure has been selectively bred away, and so as soon as she finds herself removed from her nest box, I say, she'll fly up to a thousand miles just for the quotidian privilege of sleeping there again. My friend seems genuinely interested, or at least, convincingly pretends to be; she fusses over Martha, wanting to know if I'm quite sure she is OK, not injured in any way, or excessively fatigued, dehydrated, hungry.

At first my friend says she thought that homing pigeons were extinct, and I explain that she's thinking of the passenger pigeon; the last one died in Cincinnati Zoo in 1914 and now her sawdust-stuffed skin is on display in the National Museum of Natural History in Washington, and people make pilgrimages to see her. She is called Martha, I tell my friend, and this pigeon is her namesake. Now she wants to know how they're trained, and I tell her that some breeders believe the best way is just to be nice to their birds, to build a bond strong enough for them to attempt to fly back to their treasured home and treasured human whatever the conditions: over channels, through storms, across the paths of peregrine falcons. But my great-uncle uses a different method, I tell my friend, the one he believes to be the most effective. My great-uncle only races hens, and each hen is first allowed to pick a mate and raise young, in order that, even after they're weaned, she retains a powerful attachment to the nest box where they were raised, and then, only after she has returned intact from a race does my great-uncle grant her access to her box and mate, her promised land. He trains his birds by means of deprivation and reward, I tell her, and my friend says, isn't that kind of cruel? And I agree; it is.

A couple of times over the course of the long evening, my friend suddenly stops speaking in the middle of a sentence. Her eyes widen and she holds a hand up to hush me, but after several seconds, she waves her upheld hand and says, never mind me, I'm sorry, it's nothing. Just before we go to bed – she in her room, I on the futon – she explains that she has seen a mouse, and though she hasn't been able to find any of its traces, though it hasn't stolen any food or nibbled any wires, it still bothers her because she is afraid of things which scuttle, of things with naked tails. Now she tells me how, one night she attacked the flat with duct tape, sealing up every fissure and gap, every skirting board. If I happen to hear a mouse-like sound during the night, or see a mouse-like thing, my friend says, I have to promise to tell her. She is not absolutely sure she's sealed it in instead of out.

I don't fall asleep straight away; I lie on the futon feeling red-wine sick, studying the indeterminate shapes of someone else's room in the dark, the unfamiliar shafts of light. I listen for the mouse, but all I can hear is the traffic passing, the pigeon shuffling and muttering in her cat box. I can't sleep and now the drunkenness subsides and I start to miss my boyfriend again, to miss my baby, and I realise that this must be exactly how Martha feels.

6.

Martha seems perkier in the morning, but I feel abysmal, as though I have been beaten-up, poisoned, water-boarded. I haven't drunk so much alcohol in a long time, not since before I learned that I was pregnant, and the hangover renders me vulnerable to all the slightest things which are wrong with my body: my earlobe throbs and my lower back begins to ache; I feel a cold sore coming. My friend says she'll walk me to the train station; already I've forgotten the way.

Before we part, my friend and I agree to make that pilgrimage together some day, to Washington, to go and visit the original Martha. Standing on the platform with my bag and cat box after she has gone, I watch a man outside the station, down in the street below. He is wearing fluorescent yellow and trying to lift the cover off a manhole. He has a long metal gadget hooked into one of its dents but he is struggling to angle it properly; the cover repeatedly rises up about ten or twelve inches before clanging back down again, and each time it does, it pulls him down a fraction after it, causes him to stumble. For as long as it takes for my train to arrive, I watch the fluorescent man battling against this contraption invented and cast in iron and set into the street by other fluorescent men just like him.

I have to take three different trains before I arrive at the ferry port, and every time I'm out again in the open air, amongst the free pigeons, and then at the quay side, I think about the feathered missiles, the ash-coloured fireworks; I think about liberating Martha. But I know, of course, this would be pointless. On the ferry, I find us a quiet corner on the topmost deck, an empty bench in the shelter of the funnel. I place her down beside me and watch her tiny man's bald head through the window of her cat box, the way her tiny man's arms are hidden and bound. I extend my finger through the bars and stroke her grey plumage, clammy with salt and rain and spew.

Before I left for London, my great-uncle told me that he wasn't going to race pigeons any more. The rules have changed too much, not just because of bird flu but because of pylons, masts, satellites. Nowadays, the air is full of radio waves and phone signals; it interferes with the earth's magnetic field, with ley lines, with Feng Shui, with water diviners, with the tiny particles of iron inside a homing pigeon's beak, my great-uncle told me – in different words. It was the only race in the world – he said, in these words exactly – with a single starting gate but a thousand different finishing lines. Now it's just like any other race; now it's just like all the other races.

ANIMAL HEART

Niven Govinden

L ighter than he ever felt; in transit he's free of the bulk that's plagued him all his life. Through his weightlessness he understands how inconsequential he is as a form; one of a million sycamores scattered by the wind. His learning comes from nature: the animals that are bred and killed on his father's farm; how one creature is replaced by another. Death, not of one's choosing, but determined by others. He no longer has a voice, his throat raw from the pain he's been made to express. Hoarseness too, from his captors. The fourth man, who stands at the bottom of the tower, who enjoyed his work more than the others, shouting now until his voice reduces to a whistle. Let this be the last time this bastard speaks to anyone. Let his vigour and greed rob him of that which his deems so precious: his righteous tone. Both his fear and hatred are finite: the length of time it will take him to hit the ground. He understands distance like never before; and how, in his case, the pull of both death and gravity are intertwined. The month before he butchered a goat with his father to celebrate the birth of his sister's child. The two of them had stood apace from the animal, untethered in the yard, watching it gorge on a final meal of scraps; to their minds, oblivious to its fate. He watched his father's movements:

how he managed to be both fast and gentle as he crept towards the beast and scooped it up into his arms; the width of his palm as he stroked its head upwards from eyes to crown, firm and slow; words passing from his lips that he was unable to hear; soothing the animal the way he too had been soothed as a child. He understood in those five swift steps from the kitchen to the barn door, where the cutlass was waiting, that parenthood was itself a lie: its kindness could no longer be believed if soft words could belie violence so readily. When, at the top of the tower, one of his captors had said 'We will get you something to drink soon. Pepsi,' he knew then what he was in for. He did not need the blindfold removed to see the truth marked on their faces. He gives thanks that his family are not here; that the party he chose to visit was in another town that took half a day to travel to. He is proud that he withheld his name, and that he was unable to identify the others (nor they him, if they too were similarly rounded up on leaving). He is proud that he has cried and screamed, and uttered noises that made them uncomfortable; naturally effeminate notes that made them beat him more. He is still learning how the world works, no more so than in these past days; learning on his feet; aware that he too can instil a fear of his own; that it remains in his power to do all that he can to make them afraid. 'Fifteen is nothing. If you are old enough to dance with these men, you are old enough for the punishment,' the fourth man said as he was pushed up the tower steps to the balustrade. The shouts from below – cheers, screams, prayers; it no longer matters – recede into the distance as he travels; deafened by the rushing air and his heartbeat that races alongside. It is only now that he sees his body as a machine; how he has been engineered by something greater than physiology; stream-lined and functional despite his defects. That only through levity, he is so capable. The mark he will leave. Flails. Flies. Falls.

DISTANT SONG

Kristín Ómarsdóttir

[Translated by Lytton Smith]

H ere she is, walking the streets because she's bored. She's called Lilja, and she's bored even though she has a beautiful name. This street has looked the same way for years: for dog years and cat years (and girl years). Pink houses, gray concrete, pavement slabs, meadowgrass, blue sky. Boredom costs less than elation; elation is pricey and only offers prosperity in the right moment. Lilja doesn't take risks; she has found her equilibrium. She looks at the clock, bored, looks at the clock, bored, looks at the clock. She's never met a more boring person than her, she doesn't know whether she's able to get rid of herself and enjoy someone else's company. Because of this, she thanks her friend when they meet in the square.

'Humpf, I'm sooooooo bored,' she interjects.

He stares at her: she's wearing a light green, polka-dot summer suit. She stares at him: he's wearing striped summer gear with a yellow sixpence similar to a sun-crown on his head, the son of a powerless sun king whose name isn't recorded, not here nor anywhere, save for on a tombstone which stands among all the others in an anonymous garden.

'Not nearly as much as me. I'm dying', he says.

They walk off. The sun shines in the empty sky; it makes no difference.

Isn't it going to shine tomorrow just the way it shone yesterday? That means you can rely on its appearing in timely fashion each morning. They head into a garden together. Doing so might possibly lead to an inconsequential alteration, a detour on the way to their lunch spot via the fragrant park, given that boredom is bad enough to kill – and even allowing that flowers aren't fragrant, except for in books.

'Listen to the birds: do you hear the bird?' Lilja asks. 'I've never heard this kind of birdsong before.'

'I concur,' answers the nameless sun king's son, 'I've never heard this bird. What's the bird called?'

They peer around. On top of the tree branches a red bird sings.

'This species went extinct a long time back,' he opines, 'I've read learned articles about it in scientific journals.'

Lilja points: 'But look at that one! It's green and sings like a rabbit born in the wrong body, and I read about it in this book I had when I was little; it ended its miserable life in the woods as a meal in a fine palace.'

She claps her hands and jumps up high. How fun to recall children's stories as the sun approaches midday.

'The Queen had never tasted such a delicious meal', she continues, laughing because she's proud of the memory. It's warily that he observes his friend's unexpected delight; if it continues along such lines, rejoicing excessively at the wonders of nature, it could endanger her mental health and put their security at risk.

'This species of bird was also killed off a long time back,' explains the wary friend once he's scrutinised the trees more closely; he points to the bench: 'Then take a look at the tortoise resting under the bench! Such tortoises haven't been seen anywhere in the world for decades. Yes, and do you see that flower?'

He points to flowers which resemble a bridal bouquet.

'Never seen it,' she concludes.

'Never seen it,' he agrees.

'Except in books,' she adds.

'Except in books,' he adds.

'What is going on?' she asks.

'What is going on?' he asks.

'Smell that,' she asks. 'Oh, I'm dizzy.'

'I'm getting a headache,' he answers, and sneezes.

'It gives me icy chills, even though it's spring, and doesn't lessen the boredom despite the brief pleasure; it's all confused and, what's more, I can't be bothered to be a part of such puzzles. Let's leave this ghost-garden.'

He repeats her words and, silently, counts himself lucky: he recognises his girlfriend again.

'Let's leave the ghost-garden before we become part of the ghostworld. Lilja, my dearest, might we be dead?' he continues, questioningly.

'An extinct and obsolete species?' she adds, just as questioningly.

They take to their heels along a broad gravel path that runs through the middle of the garden, beginning by the south gate, or what here passes for a southerly direction, and ending at the northern gate. They draw breath and examine each other intimately. The speckled summer suit is just the same as before. The striped summer clothes just the same. The sixpence as yellow as before. The twitching in her eyes is still there. They convince themselves they aren't dead and they aren't an extinct species. She pinches him; he complains. He pinches her; she complains. They are awake and their breath reminds them a heart beats in their breast.

'Oof, we survived without being stamped out or killed, but I have to admit: we almost didn't make it, Lilja.'

'But we aren't surviving boredom, are we?'

'No.' He shakes his head.

'Oof, this puzzle exhausts my mind, and I've still got to go to work for four hours this afternoon,' she says, blowing her nose into a yellow handkerchief she got as a summer present.

'It's better to live bored than to be dead,' he says, and his reassuring words have their desired effect. They continue their journey and go into another, muted garden.

'It's good to be in here because we can't hear chirping,' Lilja asserts. 'This is a good place for boring folk like us,' and he concurs; he is of the same mind. They each take the other's hand and walk along a broad gravel path through the garden to the north. Their shadows indicate the path to them like a manual or a compass needle. On either side rise statues of kings, queens, working folk, slaves, angels, horses, goats, dogs, birds and snakes. So quiet is this museum made of stones, soundless, soothing, peaceful, and it ennobles the wretched mind. The midday sun sidles into the napes of their necks but doesn't blind them in the eyes or wipe them flat, just lovingly warms their shoulders and their palpating hearts. At the end of the garden they come to the north gate; from there, it's a short distance to a nice lunch spot.

They sit down, tuck white serviettes into their necks, order fresh mussels that are safe to eat because they were grown in a pool where parasites are destroyed without ruining the fine taste and salt, or the texture when teeth bite into the seasoft pebbles. The sensation approaches utter bliss.

'I'm almost starting to miss the boredom given how glorious this food is. We'd best be careful,' she says, her admonishing tone tinged with humour.

'Squeeze more lemon on the dish', the sun king's son suggests, 'and it makes the dish better still.'

'I don't want it to be too good because I'm afraid of utter bliss.'

'There's nothing to fear, Lilja, it'll pass; you'll be bored again come four, latest. What do you say we meet up after work, compare notes, go into a music store and listen to beautiful sounds to lift us up before the sly evening tedium takes over?'

'It's a deal,' says Lilja.

They seal their pact, palms together.

'Can't we avoid the garden of extinct organisms on the way back?' asks Lilja once they've paid for their meal with winning smiles: they live in a city which has done away with cash, in which payments are made through physical gestures.

'I'll keep an eye out for that,' says her friend, full of confidence in himself, for confidence means an advance, a tax reduction. He takes her by her arm and guides her through the garden which is ornamented with statues.

There's a statue of a naked man leading a horse. Following him, statues of two naked women, stopped in their traces; one holds a baby, the other leads a goat.

There's a statue of a naked man leading a cow. Following him, statues of two naked women, stopped in their traces; one holds a baby, the other holds a goose.

There's a statue of a military commander riding a horse. An officer, with a winged helmet on his head.

There's a seated statue of a naked woman, and in her lap and tiptoeing along her shoulders, birds; one bird examines (eyelessly) the world from the top of her head as she reads a book.

There's a kneeling statue of a boy; he cradles a bird in his palms.

At the boy's feet lies a statue of a girl with a knife in her heart; the pool of blood is the same color as the stone.

There's a statue of a naked man leading a donkey. Following him, statues of two naked women, stopped in their traces, one holding three children and the other two travel bags; their donkey is laden with parcels and luggage.

And a lion statue tears apart a wolf.

Standing there is a statue of a hunter and a young boy; he's holding a dead goose, and a retriever stands at their feet with a fox in his mouth.

And there's also a statue of a naked man holding a globe; around his neck a snake hangs. The man's hair blows as though there's a wind.

'Are we statues or are we extinct or are we an obsolete species?' Lilja asks her friend, who has a consuming passion for questions of a philosophical nature. She leans her head against his shoulder, feeling like they're both statues: although they seem to be walking, in reality they are motionless, and it's the world that's going past, the park passing them by until they reach the south gate.

'Examining the situation more closely, we probably intend to be all of them at once,' he replies, having first stroked his chin as a way to think ponderously.

'You have to choose, whether you'd rather be a statue or an obsolete species,' she demands.

'An obsolete species in the kingdom of heaven,' Lilja herself responds once she has waited so long for an answer that she's about forgotten her question. 'It's got so that things are more exciting in the kingdom of heaven than in the world of the living, though it's rather crowded there and there's barely room for any more extinct creatures – it's totally jammed, yeah? – that's why men keep inventing new drugs to postpone the arrival of more people, see, due to the bottleneck that's formed on the divine side. But it's not possible to delay arrival indefinitely: everyone dies, unless something's discovered, an injection for eternal life. Those pitiful extinct animals that cannot reincarnate: they gallop around in heaven like I'm here in this city.'

He lifts the locks of hair that hide her eyes from him.

'When you think this way, it leaves me even more bored than this morning and I get so sad I cannot be bothered to drag my feet along the ground,' he admits frankly, smiling such a beautiful smile that the funds in his bank account swell enough to possibly cause an abnormal swelling of the economy.

'You don't need to drag your feet along the ground,' answers Lilja, unabashed, 'the earth moves for you and takes you where you want to go.'

They stand in the square, half of which is hidden from the sun, though the main part of the square reveals a set of balmy circular tables with chairs and sunshades for tired and thirsty passers to sit under and rest their weary bones, satisfy their thirst, send loved ones the following message: *I am less bored because I have you to think about and to look forward to kissing on the cheek when next we meet, and though we never meet, I've still got you to think about.*

They say goodbye to each other with a kiss on the cheek and promise to meet at the end of the workday, at five, in the music store. They each point at the same time to the music store which stands beside the soap shop on the shady side of the square. When they have broken themselves away from each other, they wave goodbye. She has put yellow gloves on. For his part, he's put on sunglasses. She works in an office, designing tech that let you communicate with your subconscious, in the adjoining street to the left. He works in an office which builds dreams, in the adjoining street to the right.

They put on their headphones and listen to beautiful songs in the music store. She closes her eyes, and when she closes her eyes, he closes his eyes.

'I'm less bored with my eyes closed,' he thinks, and she thinks the same, while the music envelops them.

It seems to her that that the notes lift her up. It seems to him that the notes lift him up and back down when the silence comes. They descend to earth. They smile beautifully at each other – a bonus, a bonus, clink, clink, the clinking of a moneybox – smile, smile, smile – she takes his hand and he takes her hand. The moment becomes impatient waiting for them. Until finally they take off the headphones and hang them back on the pock-marked wall of the booth where headphones wait for customers to listen to music. The husband and wife who run the store smile at them even though they've not bought anything.

'I feel I owe you my good fortune when you smile at me the way you did when the music ended,' says Lilja.

'Then we're quits,' he says, 'because I felt the same when you smiled at me when the music ended.'

'Let's go home,' she wishes.

'Let's go home,' he wishes.

They each take the other by the hand and walk home along a long sidewalk beside the equally long street. Cars drive in the opposite direction from their direction home. The sun sets and causes long shadows that stamp the sidewalk behind them like a bungee rope which wants to drag them back to the square – but they won't let it, the shadows have no say over their lives, their homeward steps are purposeful – clink, clink – and on the horizon a fine block of flats rises, friend and beacon, and the shadow of the flats offers them a welcome home after their long walk along a noisy street, the traffic swelling a noise like irons dragged in a monotonous direction.

'That was a long walk and I wasn't really bored at all,' says Lilja, once they're standing by the gray wall and yellow door that leads them, via physical gestures, inside.

'Same here,' says her friend, 'I am less dissatisfied in myself than I've been for a long time. Home is best.'

'Home is best,' repeats Lilja.

Clink, clink.

They lie under a white duvet, she in a check night-dress, he in vertically-striped pyjamas, staring up at the ceiling, which is white, and sits under the roof, lacking clouds, sun, moon or stars; it's not been forgotten that the ceiling was painted recently.

'I miss the birds we heard and saw in the park today, in the garden of extinct species,' whispers Lilja.

'I do, too,' he admits, 'and, worse still, I feel I can't remember how they sang. Do you remember the color of the turtle?'

She shakes her head. No. 'Can't remember anything, except that when we walked through that mysterious garden it really got on my nerves, but now I miss the birds. Will we find them again?'

'Probably not,' her friend answers, morosely.

'We should look in the morning, before we go to lunch.'

'But we'd just be sadder and more bored by the sensation,' he warns.

'I expect it to be that way, I can't get enough of it, I want to bore myself exponentially each and every day so that on the way home we arrive eventually at a settlement, the harmony spoken about in books.'

'I don't entirely follow you, Lilja,' he admits frankly, sensing that the discussion could result in poverty, could lead to their exclusion from this fine block of flats.

'Hopefully we can't find the garden tomorrow because then we will experience regret mixed with boredom, and as a result I'm sure the green potato soup I'm going to have at the lunch spot will taste better still.'

'I think the mixture 'boredom + regret' will sit poorly in the soul,' he says, trying to protect the stability of their lives and their livelihood.

'Boredom gets new dimensions from regret and the longing for the song of extinct birds. Listen, try to listen to your soul now.'

She begs.

He lends ears to his quiet soul.

Listen, listen.

The soul is soundless, no chirps come from it.

She lends ears to her own soul.

Listen, listen.

This is an expensive joke, their bank balances shrink, falling in value as the situation continues.

She hears something that could be called longing – she believes – for the singing of extinct species of bird, for flowers that resemble veils, a snoring turtle, the breaking sound when the sole of a shoe steps on a nest.

'Lilja,' says the son of the nameless sun king, giving up the search for the sound of his soul, giving up getting lost in the silence of his soul, like a spirit in the desert, 'don't be offended, my best and only friend, but I think you might lose your mind if you keep continuing on.'

He takes her hand under the duvet because he wants to look after her and provide her security. The moon casts a beam through the window which they forgot to blind and the light twinkles on the duvet like the feet of extinct dance-maidens.

'If I lose my mind, I'll die and go to heaven with the extinct organisms. There I'll come upon birds and seals, tigers and lions and a polar bear who will eat me, and thus I will end up reincarnated on an earth that has turned into a desert. I will look for you and not find you.'

'Why won't you find me?' he asks, alarmed.

'Because you'll have drowned in the swimming pool which is run by cannibals.'

'Lilja, my dear, my sourest lemon in this city, I think I should call the doctor, you are losing your mind: if you continue in this delirious babble we will be cast out from this block of flats and end up destitute on the street, dressed like wretches. I feel it deep inside; I feel it deep inside. I am sensitive and attuned to my environment, or else I would not have achieved so much in my job.'

'I reckon Noah must have followed the extinct animals to heaven,' Lilja ponders to herself, and watches her friend run out and grab the phone with a frantic grasp; he dials. He has legs reminiscent of a bird, a torso reminiscent of a bear, the head could be on a flower. She thinks. The man on the phone answers:

'State Department for Extinction, who is calling so late at night?'

He throws the phone up towards the ceiling. Their lives plummet in value.

BIG ISLAND, SMALL ISLAND

Francesca Marciano

The swallows keep darting back and forth across the roof like shooting arrows. I think they must be playing a game – a kind of hide-and-seek – because they don't seem to get tired of it. I am not used to seeing birds fly through airports. It's quite a stretch to call this thatched roof standing on pillars an airport and I'm worried about the size of the plane we are about to board. If this is the size of the airport of the Big Island and we are going to the Small Island, how big can the next plane be?

I look around at my fellow passengers. We are not more than ten and that worries me too. There are large men clad in white *kanzus* (I'm already using the local language thanks to the *Teach Yourself Swahili* booklet I bought in Dar es Salaam) and *kofia,* which I just learned is what their finely stitched cap is called. Judging from their potbellies and thick gold watches they seem rather affluent. A couple of them have small-sized wives sitting next to them, wrapped in the black cape they call *buibui*. The men talk loudly, mostly among themselves or on old-fashioned Nokias – only a few have smartphones – whereas the wives don't flinch. They are as still as pillars of salt surrounded by hefty bundles and boxes. I can see baskets brimming with mangoes, cartons containing some household appliances, an electric fan, a kettle, a DVD player. They must've been shopping on the mainland; I didn't see any shopping opportunities for such items as kettles or fans on the Big Island. Just a few gift shops and a desolate, half-empty supermarket. A crackling voice on the intercom speaks in Swahili, and the man next to me shakes his head with disdain.

'Delay,' he says, meeting my eyes.

'How much?'

'One hour.'

It could be worse, I think, so I pull out my book.

I've been to Africa before – to Egypt and Morocco – but never south of the Sahara and never to such a remote place. During my travels I rarely ever mix with the locals, sealed as I am in my work bubble, always surrounded by colleagues. We end up spending most of our time inside conference rooms, in line at those ghastly buffet lunches, or in our anonymous hotel rooms watching the news. Since I've been on this particular detour I've been feeling more vulnerable but also more adventurous. I think I'm beginning to get the hang of traveling solo. For instance, whenever I am the only white person within a contained space, I find that reading is the best thing to turn to. It's actually an act of courtesy, I realised; it allows people to stare and even point at me if they need to – usually it's the women who find something ridiculous about my clothes and tend to giggle with hands over their mouths. My reading gives them total freedom to examine me without creating unnecessary embarrassment.

'Are you Italian?' a voice asks me in English.

I lift my eyes from the book. Sitting across from me is a man in his early fifties. He's clearly been looking at the cover of my book. He must have just sat down; I hadn't noticed him earlier. He wears a white linen shirt, nicely tailored cotton trousers in a shade of ochre, Ray-Bans and soft loafers without socks. This last detail, more than anything, tells me he must be Italian as well. Those are expensive car shoes, the kind Mr Agnelli made famous. Only Italian men wear loafers without socks with their ankles showing this much beneath the trousers.

'Sì,' I say, and I shake the hand he's already holding out.

I am not sure whether to be relieved or disturbed by this chance encounter. He lights a Marlboro and begins to chat amiably in Italian, ignoring my desire to read on.

His name is Carlo Tescari, he's been living in Tanzania for the last ten years. He's built a couple of luxury safari camps near Ngorongoro. Before that he lived in Kenya, where he built more luxury camps and sold them for a fortune. Twenty-five years in East Africa, he says, as though it's a record of some kind. Funny, because he looks as if someone had just lifted him from the Via Roma in Capri and landed him in this tiny airport on the Big Island, on his way to another, smaller island not many people have ever heard of.

'Are you with the NGO?' he asks me.

'No.'

'Just visiting?'

'Yes.'

'There are no hotels, you know. Not even a guest house.'

'I'm staying at a friend's place.'

'Are you?' He looks at me with a hint of suspicion. 'Is it an African friend?'

'No. An old friend from Italy. He has been living there for fifteen years.'

'Is this the man who works for that NGO?'

'Yes. That's him.'

'I thought so. Someone at the embassy in Dar suggested I see him to get some advice. I've got his contacts somewhere.'

He opens his leather briefcase and flicks through his documents.

'Here it is. Andrea Nelli, right? I spoke to him last week on the phone, he's expecting me. Well, that's quite a coincidence, isn't it?'

I nod, politely.

'Then I'll come along with you to his place. We can share the cab. If you don't mind.'

'No, I don't,' I say, even though I do, actually.

'I just need to ask him a few questions, it's not going to take long. He's the only *mzungu* that lives on the island, other than Jeffrey Stone. I'm staying at Jeffrey's, I know Jeff from Nairobi. He's the local veterinarian and hates it there. Apparently your friend has been on the island for, what did you say, fifteen years?'

'More or less, yes.'

'Jeffrey has been there only three months and he's desperate to leave. Not much company.'

'No?'

'No. And it's a dry island. No booze. The death of an Englishman. Very traditional Muslim community.'

That, I'm aware of. Andrea has instructed me over the phone 'long sleeves and no bathing suits. You can swim in a dress if you *really* have to.'

Carlo Tescari seems eager to extract more details about my host.

'What's he like? He wasn't very forthcoming on the phone.'

'I haven't seen him in ages. Since he moved out here.'

'I see.'

He takes a good look at me.

'So is this a happy reunion?'

'Yes.'

'A sort of "Dr Livingstone, I presume" moment.' He chuckles, then adds, 'I hear your friend has become very local.'

'I wouldn't be surprised, given that there are only locals, as you say. Except for your unhappy vet, of course.'

He grins, showing a crown of teeth so white they might even be false.

It troubles me, to arrive at Andrea's house in the company of this man. I had envisaged a completely different scene when I decided to track him down a couple of weeks ago. And now, after such a long journey, I am nearly at his doorstep, about to show up with exactly the kind of person he will loathe.

––––––––––––––––––––

This part of the journey, from the Big Island to the Small Island, was a last-minute diversion from my original itinerary. I'd been invited to attend a conference in Dar es Salaam on ecosystem disturbances and the management of protected forests. It was only once I was on the plane to Tanzania, while perusing the map of East Africa, that I realised how close I'd be to the place where Andrea had disappeared. Not exactly close-close, but certainly closer than I'd been in all this time, when it seemed he had vanished somewhere unreachable and exotic, never to be found again. None of us – not any of his friends – had ever heard of this tiny island in the Indian Ocean, which at the time of his disappearance was mentioned only in passing in guidebooks; later, when we'd all become expert Internet surfers, all I could find online in relation to the island were a couple of blurred photos of the ruin of a mosque, as though no travel writer had ever cared to explore it.

I'm a biologist with a doctorate in agriculture and food sciences and my specialty is biodiversity in Central European forests. At the conference in Dar I spoke at length to a sleepy audience on the effects of atmospheric pollution on lichens. Afterward, in the half-empty conference room, a mix of scientists from different parts of the world exchanged mild comments about my talk over watery coffee and stale biscuits. Before I could say anything they had already switched subjects, and were discussing the heat, the malfunctioning of the air-conditioning in their rooms and the poor reception on their phones. Once in my hotel room, instead of giving in to my resentment, I decided I still had a chance to give this exhausting trip a more significant purpose. To finally get hold of an ex-lover I hadn't heard from in ages seemed a much more rewarding task than introducing rare species of lichens to my colleagues. I Googled all the local airlines till I found a connection that could take me to the island where Andrea supposedly still lived. From Dar I'd have to fly to the Big Island and from there the only way to the Small Island would then be to get on a rusty ferry that takes a day and a half. The Indian Ocean tends to be choppy——at least that's what I read on Trip Advisor – so I opted for a twelve-seater plane. Before I bought the tickets I Googled Andrea's name in various combinations with the island name till I found a number for an NGO. Someone picked up the phone after the first ring. It was him. I gasped.

'Andrea? You are not going to believe this. It's Stella.'

'Hi, Stella, where are you?'

He sounded wholly unfazed.

'I'm in Dar es Salaam. Not too far from you.'

'What are you doing in that horrible city?'

'I am a speaker at an international conference on biodiversity.'

'Sounds like you got your Ph.D after all.'

'I did.'

Silence. I thought maybe the line had been cut off. Then I heard him clear his throat.

'Come see me. I haven't spoken Italian in so long.'

'I was thinking I actually might do that. I could come for three or four days. If that would be OK ... I mean, if you are not too busy.'

'Just come.'

There was another pause. I then tried a more familiar tone.

'Andrea? It's wonderful to hear your voice again. It's been such a long time. How are you?'

'I'll tell you when I see you.'

Naturally Carlo Tescari sits next to me during the short flight on our tiny plane and continues with his entire life story and his future business plans. Apparently our shared nationality gives him the right to treat me like an old friend and there is very little I can do to fend him off. So I learn the real purpose of his trip. On the east side of the island where the main village is situated, the coast is just mangroves and muddy shores. But on the northwest side, beaches as white and as soft as talcum powder stretch for miles and miles. He surveyed the coastline from a Cessna a couple of months back. He opens the briefcase and shows me a map. On a half-moon-shaped cove he plans to scatter a few thatch-roofed huts (he calls them *bandas*), with a larger common area built in natural materials and to be exquisitely designed by a Dutch architect. A minimalist, ecological, yet stylish and highly comfortable retreat for people seeking complete privacy in the wilderness. Of course he'll need to bring a road and water, but he doesn't think it'll be that hard.

'Building the road is going to be the most work of all, but I think I can get some politicians involved,' he says. 'Hopefully your friend can give me some advice as how to oil the right people.'

From the sky the landing strip looks like a narrow slit cutting through the dense foliage. I close my eyes and hold my breath till we touch ground. The ride in an ancient blue taxi corroded by rust is just as bumpy as our landing; the roads on the island are packed dirt scarred by large ruts. It's baking hot, the earth is a deep vermilion and there's a film of orange dust shrouding the trees lining the way. I keep my eyes on the window, looking straight ahead, while Carlo Tescari goes on and on about the difficulty of dealing with old-fashioned Muslim politicians who don't welcome foreigners.

As we approach the town, an ugly tower looms over the tops of the trees. Its concrete structure is covered in blackish mould, the plaster is flaking, the window frames have rusted badly and have come off in places. Strings of faded laundry adorn the squared balconies of apartments that look as though they were intended for the Russian working class. The tower – designed in the seventies by an architect in Leningrad? A gift from the Communist party to the president of this corrupted republic? – is rotting away in the sticky weather. We keep on driving, past the town on a winding road snaking through coconut and banana trees, random patches of vegetable gardens, ugly cinder-block houses. Women carry yellow plastic buckets on their heads sloshing with water. I intercept their corrugated brows and suspicious looks as they peek at the white people inside the car without smiling.

So this is where he has been all these years, while we, his friends, fell in love with other people, moved to different cities, got our degrees and found jobs. Some of us had children, some of us died in car accidents, some overdosed, some became famous, others did nothing with their lives.

In the beginning, when he first left, we often wondered why Andrea had stopped answering our letters. Then, as the years went by, we ceased to think about him, as though it were pointless to keep track of his existence: he'd simply gone too far and had fallen off the radar. If we mentioned his name, it was always only to say how lucky he was, to be living in such an exotic place, to have fled from our pasty, predictable, urban lives.

Funny, how we assumed the island he'd escaped to should be a setting out of a Graham Greene story: we pictured a small colonial town on the edge of a harbour in a lush, tropical landscape, its narrow streets winding through a lane of wooden buildings with lacy balconies, latticed verandas, with a touch of romantic decay.

He's waiting for us on the porch of the house – another no-frills cinder-block box with a blue door and small windows – standing erect, with arms crossed, in an assertive posture that demands respect. He's wearing a starched white *kanzu* and a *kofia* and, because of his dark hair and tanned skin, he doesn't look that much different from the local businessmen I flew in with. He's put on some weight and grown a short beard. He's quite stocky, actually, and his curls are gone, though his green eyes flicker for a moment when he sees me and that flash of mutual recognition gives me a jolt in the stomach. I feel a light resistance from him, a rigidity, when I fling myself into his arms. He moves his face slightly to the side, so that I miss his cheek and end up kissing air. He steps backward and smiles shyly.

'Hey, Stella,' is all he says.

'I can't believe I finally got hold of you!' I almost shout, unable to repress my enthusiasm.

'Wait a minute, let me deal with him first,' he says calmly, almost dreamily, lifting his chin toward Tescari, who has stayed behind, talking to the taxi driver, possibly telling him to wait for him.

It's disappointing, of course, that joy for this reunion should be put on hold and mitigated by the presence of a stranger.

Tescari sprints onto the porch baring his white teeth. He offers his hand.

'So very pleased to meet you at last. I can't stand communicating via email or phone; one has to be able to look people in the eyes when talking business, don't you think?'

I catch a flash of surprise in his eyes as he takes in the white *kanzu* and *kofia*.

Andrea doesn't answer, he simply shows us into a small room, empty save for a green couch sheathed in plastic, a makeshift bookcase with a few paperbacks, and a sisal mat on the cement floor. On the bare walls hangs but a single picture, Arabic calligraphy. Tescari takes in the ambiance, then throws me a reproachful glance, as if I have lured him into a trap. Andrea shows him the couch.

'Please sit down.'

Andrea instead sits on the floor, folding his legs in lotus position. Tescari slides uncomfortably onto the very edge of the couch, as though he wants to avoid contamination, and the plastic cover makes a screeching, embarrassing sound under him. He opens his briefcase and pulls out the drawings. I stand, as I've not been asked to sit down yet, glad to keep a distance from the position that Tescari has been given on the couch.

There is a moment of uncomfortable silence. Andrea and Tescari stare at each other as if neither one wants to be the first to speak. Then Andrea makes a gesture with his hand, signalling that Tescari should begin.

Tescari fumbles through his documents, then unfolds a large drawing.

'As I told you on the phone, I have investors in Europe that are extremely keen on this project. They are ready to come in as soon as I let them know the permits have been secured. Here, take a look at the plans.'

Tescari hands the drawing down to Andrea, who takes a cursory look at it and says nothing. I hear a noise in the next room. Someone is splashing water on the cement floor.

'We're planning to fly the clients down from Dar to make it easier for them to reach the camp. All we need is a landing strip for a Cessna, that's not a problem, but we'll have to build a road to carry building materials and so on.'

Tescari taps his shirt pocket.

'Can I smoke?'

'No. You can go outside if you wish.'

Tescari leaves the pack of cigarettes in his pocket.

'How far is the beach from the main road? From the plane we couldn't see, the foliage was too thick. And how about water? Do you have any idea how deep one has to dig?'

Andrea doesn't answer. Just sits there with his legs in a knot. Tescari is puzzled but decides to ignore the awkward silence.

'You are the first person I am talking to, here. I will see the Ministry of Land and Forests as well, of course. But before I do I wanted to have a clearer picture of the technical aspects. I was told you're the best person to talk to since you know everybody on the island.'

Tescari watches as Andrea folds the map shut.

'I've lived in East Africa long enough,' Tescari says. 'I know it can be tricky to start a project like this if you are an outsider. That's why I came to see you first. To get a sense of –'

Andrea hands the plan back to him. He speaks, slowly, enunciating each word distinctly. His tone is steady, unwavering.

'You can rest assured you will not get any permit, nor any help, to build this resort. The people on this island are not interested in facilitating this kind of project so that you and your investors can stash your clients' dollars in a Swiss account. If anything, I will do everything in my power to prevent this from happening.'

There's a moment of silence. Tescari clears his throat.

'I'm afraid there's a misunderstanding. We are going to hire locals. Everyone will profit from this venture,' he says. 'By which what I really mean is that it will give jobs to lots of people. I'm sure that you, more than anyone here, realise that this island needs some –'

Andrea raises his palm to stop him.

'This is a traditional island. We won't allow foreign speculators to wreck our customs and offend our values. We don't want half-naked tourists on our beaches smoking and drinking. The people here don't need jobs, we grow our own food and catch our fish, and this is the way the island has lived for centuries.' Andrea's voice is quiet, unperturbed. 'We don't need you. Is that clear enough? Now you can go. Please.'

And he stands up, gesturing toward the door with a sweep of his arm.

Tescari shoots up, holding his folded plans to his chest, stunned. He turns toward me. 'This man is crazy.'

'Please go. I see your taxi is still waiting for you,' Andrea insists, standing by the door.

'Crazy,' Tescari says to me, a finger to his temple. 'Honestly, if I were you I wouldn't stay here.'

And then he's out the door.

I hear the engine start and the taxi pulls away. It is a relief and yet part of me feels abandoned.

'Wow,' I say.

I'm waiting for Andrea to remark, waiting for him to erupt in a roaring laugh and utter something outrageous. For him to undo the monastic posture, get out of the starched *kanzu* and declare that what he just said was a joke, a performance he played on the Italian with loafers.

Instead he keeps very still and suddenly I feel uneasy.

'What are you?' I ask.

'What do you mean?'

'What are you here, anyway. Are you some kind of mullah?' I say, with a nervous laugh.

Andrea strokes his short beard and thinks for a moment. He doesn't get that my question is meant to be humorous.

'No. Although I did convert to Islam years ago.'

'Oh. I see,' I say, as though that explains everything.

We stare at each other uneasily. I look around the empty room and I wonder many things at once: whether he has a guest room for me or I am to sleep on the screeching plastic couch, whether he might in fact have gone crazy or even be under medication, whether coming here was a terrible mistake. It has nothing to do with his converting to Islam. It's that he just seems so much slower. Numbed.

'That guy,' he says, 'isn't the first one to show up here with a plan. I've told them all to fuck off. One by one.'

Here he gains a bit of speed. He's more animated and that feels reassuring.

'I know how their plans work. They build what they call an *eco-friendly self-sustainable* camp in the wilderness for a pittance, so that for five hundred dollars a night millionaires can take a crap under the stars. Then, slowly but very, very surely they declare the beach off-limits, they deny access to the local fishermen because their clients need their 'privacy.' As though this has been their land for generations. Over my dead body they'll get in here.'

'Absolutely!' I cheer. I'm relieved: he's sounding like himself at last.

It's only now that I realise that since I first arrived Andrea still hasn't really looked at me. And I cannot tell whether he's happy to see me or not.

His body used to be lean and taut. Hip bones, ribs and knee-caps showing under baggy jeans and faded t-shirts. Long hands and nimble fingers that touched things gently. I loved his feet too. Once I told him, 'You have the hands and feet of a dancer,' because there was a special gracefulness in the way he moved in space. He never brushed his hair, which was a tangle of light brown curls, often shading his eyes – those green, bright eyes that changed with the weather – and I suspect he didn't wash it often. Whenever we'd be all together – me, our friends – discussing something we'd read, whether it was politics, literature, ethics, he'd sit back while we made our loud arguments. His silence made us edgy, we felt observed and judged. We wanted him to level with us, so we'd turn to him and say, How about you, Andrea, let's hear what you think, and often what he said was just the opposite of what we'd so fervently maintained till then. He always seemed to come at things from another perspective, and what we had thought was right suddenly seemed wrong, what we thought was daring seemed banal.

We all wanted to be a this and a that: a writer, a photographer, an actor, an architect, a political activist, whereas he didn't seem to strive to be anything. He was good with his hands, he knew how to fix things and work with wood, he worshipped his motorcycle and spent hours adjusting and calibrating its mechanisms. We were aware that he knew a lot – more than us – that he loved to read and the books he chose were unusual and difficult, as though he had already read and digested what we were reading and was way ahead of us. He read essays, literary criticism, obscure play-wrights and poets, but he never lectured, never quoted from them. I think he found it pathetic, the way we showed off, always keen to sound wittier, more well read, more up-to-date.

We never met his parents and knew very little of his background. He was an only child and apparently his father was a strange man who drank too much and didn't seem to have a real job. His mother had left the family when Andrea was a teenager and he didn't like to talk about her. Once he said he thought Freud had given all of us an alibi to whine.

At a time when we all strived to be reckless, he was the most fear-less with drugs, though he never seemed high, only more concentrated, sharper. We made love the first time under a shower, while tripping on LSD. I still remember how the yellow mosaic of the bathroom glimmered, and how I was convinced I was inside an Egyptian palace, shimmering with gold and sunshine. I don't remember whose apartment it was, and why I was alone under the shower – the sprinkling water felt like a cascade of yellow diamonds – but suddenly there he was, smiling, getting out of his clothes, entering the magic circle of gold with me.

I was already in love with him by then and I wasn't the only one. We all fought to get his attention, to spend time alone with him – men and women alike – and some of us fought harder to become his lover. There were jealousies and treacheries, though he never used the power we had given him to manipulate us.

One day he announced he was going away. Someone he knew had

offered him a place as a volunteer to teach English to children in Africa. He mentioned the name of the island, a name so difficult to pronounce that it became impossible to remember.

The last time I saw him it was on a winter day on the street right below my apartment. He had come around to say goodbye right before getting on the plane. He must have buzzed the intercom and I had come down. I was living by the Via dei Riari then, in a small studio at the end of the street, at the foot of the Gianicolo Hill, and I remember the feeling of sorrow clinging to my clothes as I walked out on the street. It was drizzling and cold and he wasn't wearing a coat or a jacket; all he had on was a thick black turtleneck and his old leather gloves. I also remember how he was leaning against a brick wall next to his motorcycle and how the wind ruffled his hair.

He has a wife.

She must have been the one throwing water on the floor. She is only a girl – a very thin, very young girl like so many I saw along the island road with sloshing buckets balancing on their heads – who looks frightened to see me. She wears a threadbare *kanga* wrapped around her waist and another one with the same pattern over her shoulders. As she advances, she pulls its edge over her hair, which is braided in thick cornrows, as though she needs extra protection. Andrea speaks quickly to her in Swahili, and she whispers something inaudible. She lowers her eyes to the floor as she stands before me like a schoolgirl in front of the principal.

'This is Farida,' Andrea says. 'She hasn't met many Western women.'

I stretch out my hand and she hesitates before moving hers tentatively toward mine. I rush to grab it. It's limp, and still wet from the washing.

'Hello, Farida, very nice to meet you,' I say in English.

I realise my voice has taken the hideous inflection I sometimes can't help myself from having when talking to Africans. I tend to stretch all my vowels, in an unconscious effort to imitate their accent.

'Women don't shake hands here,' Andrea warns me.

'Right. Sorry.'

'Don't be sorry, foreigners don't always know.'

Farida has beautiful eyes with long, curled eyelashes and her skin looks soft, flawless. She must be eighteen at the most. Her pupils dilate with apprehension, so I let go of her hand.

'She doesn't speak any English,' he says.

Farida whispers something to him, he nods, releasing her, and she rushes off, back where she's been hiding.

He shows me where I am to sleep. It's a small room in the back, behind the kitchen, with a Spartan four-poster bed and a mosquito net. He stands by the door for a moment and I feel his eyes on me for the first time. I look at him and again, for a split second, I feel that flicker of recognition, a tiny leap of the heart, as though we both know what the other one is thinking. Snippets of the past are hovering between us. I am about to say something – I am not sure yet as to what – but I need to say something that will shorten the distance, make us close again. He cuts me off before I open my mouth.

'I'm going to the mosque for prayer, then we'll have dinner. You must be hungry.'

***

It's beginning to get dark outside when he comes back. I hear more water splashing, this time from the plastic bucket he showed me in the bathroom we are meant to share. When he knocks at my door to call me for dinner he has changed into a pair of cargo pants and a faded t-shirt. We sit on the mat under a bright fluorescent light and Farida brings out our dinner. Andrea scoops up rice, fish in coconut sauce, thinly cut greens mixed with sweet potatoes and chapati from warm aluminum pots covered by lids, while Farida retreats again to the back room. He hands me a full plate and begins to eat skillfully with his fingers, using the chapati to gather the food and mop up the sauce. I take a moment to study his technique. No food reaches past his first knuckle, I observe. A trick I'm unable to imitate.

'Would you like a spoon?' he asks.

'That would be great, actually.'

He says something in the direction of the kitchen, and after a moment Farida reappears with a spoon, then departs again.

The food is not bad but it is bland. I am disappointed; I was counting on some delicious surprises coming out of that kitchen. Instead it's an unhappy sort of food, without zest, like one finds in hospitals or schools. And the buzzing light overhead washes everything in a deathly pallor.

'Isn't Farida eating with us?' I ask.

'No. She eats later.'

'Why?'

'It's just the way it is.'

'Women eat later?'

'Yes.'

'That's absurd.'

'Relax, Stella. It's OK.'

He throws an amused glance at me.

'And trust me, she much prefers it that way when there are guests.'

'Why? Am I that scary?'

He smiles. 'It's very likely she thinks you are.'

There is tenderness in his voice when he speaks of her. I see now how protective he is of her and that he won't let me intimidate her more than is necessary. I am the stranger here.

'So,' I say, suddenly eager, as if it's time to get down to business, 'where is your office?'

'Which office?'

'The NGO you work for.'

'This is the office. Right here.'

I look around. There is no trace of a desk, file cabinets, papers. Only an antiquated telephone sitting on the bookshelf.

'We've lost a few big donors because of the recession, like everyone else, and we had to get rid of staff. I'm alone right now. In fact, there's not much activity at the moment.'

He explains how for the past five years he's been working for this NGO that offers microloans to women. He was hired, he says, because of his expertise with the local culture. He says all this with an ironic tinge. I tell him I've heard a lot about micro-credit and how very successful it's proved in developing countries. He says that yes, it is a good template, but it needs to be adapted from place to place. Here on the island, he says, the idea is to give the women two goats each to start with, so they can slowly build a herd and sell the milk. They can also get chickens, for eggs.

Theoretically within a few months they should be able to repay the loan and start saving some capital.

'Why theoretically?' I ask.

'Stuff happens all the time. Either it's the animals that die of mysterious diseases, or they're stolen by neighbours. Or the husbands take the money and use it for whatever they need. So actually most of the women have failed to repay the loans.'

'That's disappointing.'

He nods and keeps eating in silence. Somehow I had expected him to feel more passionate about this project. That he'd find it a rather noble task to devote one's life to lifting women from poverty.

'So, what happens now?' I asked. 'Are you out of a job?'

'No. They have kept me on a salary while they try to figure out how to change the modus operandi.'

'Who's "they"?'

'A bunch of Norwegians,' he says. Now I do hear a bit of passion – just shy of a sneer.

He shrugs and looks into his plate.

'As if they'd have any idea of how to operate it. They show up twice a year and they don't even speak the language.'

I resist asking more. Though I have so many questions, clearly he doesn't particularly like to talk about any of this; he must know that this bare room looks nothing like an efficient NGO. Maybe there will be another opportunity, later. Maybe we both need a little time.

He fills my glass with water. I wonder if it's filtered but I don't dare ask. I could do with a drink, actually. It would really help me to soften up the edges and get through this more smoothly.

When I retire to my room in the evening I discover that Farida has scattered pink frangipani petals on my bed. The scent is sweet and heady. I would like to take a photo of it, but the power goes off just as I start fumbling inside my bag for the camera. A couple of minutes later, Farida knocks lightly at the door and brings in a kerosene lamp that fills the room with a warmer glow. Now that we are alone, she covers her mouth, repressing a laugh, and reaches for my hair. She holds a strand between her fingers for a moment, testing its texture.

Later, once the sounds of closing doors, splashing water and coughing have ceased next door, I lay awake on the hard mattress, lending an ear to the other side of the wall. I am not ready to handle any intimate sounds that might seep through their bedroom walls.

Time here moves as slowly as inside a dentist's waiting room.

I am trying to figure out what Andrea's routine is, to get a sense of his existence, but his life keeps eluding me. There has been a procession of visitors throughout the whole morning, all of them men who sit out on the porch with him and talk very loudly in Swahili. I watch Andrea as he slaps his thigh and raises his voice, joining the chorus. He's a different person in this new incarnation – that cool aloofness, that lightness of touch he had when I knew him, seems gone. Swahili sounds like a language that needs a strong vocal emission, wide gesticulation and theatrical facial expressions. The men wear shirts over colorful *kikoys* wrapped around their waists, bantering and laughing on the stone bench that I've been told is called *baraza*. It could be local gossip, or perhaps they are just recounting a fishing expedition; I notice one of them is moving an open hand like a knife slicing his forearm, perhaps demonstrating the size of his daily catch. Andrea hasn't introduced me to any of them.

After lunch – another disappointing meal of plain white rice and fried fish with too many bones – I tell Andrea I'd like to go out and take some pictures of the village. I have begun to feel hostage to the house, as though – inexplicably so – there's an unwritten rule that I am to stay put and not wander out. It is decided that Farida is to accompany me in my wanderings. Apparently it doesn't look good for any woman – *mzungu* or local – to be out on the streets by herself. This has of course not been openly stated, but somehow I get the drift. Farida reappears clad in her black *buibui*, showing an unforeseen eagerness for the assignment she's been given, and off we go. The minute we are alone she urges me in sign language to enter a neighbour's house. I try to protest – I've had enough of being shut inside – but she won't relent. Evidently she's no longer so scared of me.

We enter another squared house with a small inner courtyard where an old lady wrapped in a bright pink cloth sits quietly next to a goat with her withered legs stretched out in front. She looks blind, and strangely beautiful. Farida ignores her and we enter a dark, stuffy room. I hear giggles coming from its depths. There are two young women about Farida's age who get up from the floor and come toward us. Farida shows me off to them with pride, like a girl with a new doll. I have a feeling that news of my arrival has been spreading and the neighbours are expecting to get a glimpse of me. There is a brief discussion, then the young women decide I have to follow them to the next room, darker than the first one. Here they pat the floor mat till I sit down. More women, both young and old, join us now, appearing from the recesses of what looks like a big house, and sit across from me, making sounds of appreciation. I am surrounded. The room smells of cheap lotions, cloth, sweat, boredom and sleep. Farida must have told them it'd be OK to go ahead and touch me, because now they tug at my hair, at my clothes, they inspect the fabric, grab my wrist, discuss my rings, my watch. The room is stifling; my clothes stick to my back as sweat rolls down my spine. I glance at my watch and I see it's only half past three. The end of the day still feels a long way ahead.

After two more visits in the neighbourhood, we are back on the road, although the way Farida grips my arm enhances the feeling of being her prisoner. We walk past the mildewed Soviet tower, toward what looks like the centre of town, but soon I realise there is no centre, no pretty square as such, no leafy gardens, no latticed verandas, no bustling heart of the village, but only more cement buildings decaying among heaps of trash. The market – the destination I have so eagerly prepared for – sits underneath yet another concrete structure, built by the same ghastly planners. At this time of day it's half empty except for packs of stray dogs wandering through the leftovers of market day.

I look around, searching for a view of the ocean. It comes to me that since I've landed I haven't seen a single shade of blue. I look in every direction, walk this way and that, but the sea is nowhere to be seen. How can this be possible? How can an island – especially such a small island – conceal the water surrounding it? My anxiety mounts. There must be an outlook, a promontory, a belvedere from which one can see water. I pose the question to Farida. Where is the sea? The sea! I ask in an almost desperate tone. Water? But she shakes her head, amused. I try with Italian. *Mare? Acqua? Eau?* No, she doesn't understand a word, and I didn't carry my *Teach Yourself Swahili* with me. Suddenly I must see water. My heart pounds. This must be what a real attack of claustrophobia feels like.

It is then, from out of the corner of my eye, that I get a glimpse of khaki. My brain registers the shade, the texture of the fabric, and instantly flashes a message. Your tribe. It is indeed a man in his thirties, in a light blue shirt and shorts. Right behind him are the loafers of Carlo Tescari. He and his friend Jeffrey Stone – tall, with thick blonde sideburns and round across the waist – are chatting as they come out of the fishmonger's with a parcel wrapped in newspaper.

My brain flashes again. I know exactly what's happening here. They will have delicious peppered shrimps in chili sauce for dinner. I raise my arm and yell.

'Hey!'

It has not been easy to get rid of Farida. She was very upset when I began to smilingly signal 'You can go home, it's fine, I know the way. Just go home now, I'm OK.' But the stubborn girl didn't want to move.

'Who is she?' Jeffrey Stone asked. We had just been introduced by Tescari, who had rejoiced when I had invited myself for a drink.

'You need a break from that madman, eh?' Tescari said, and I think he winked, too. 'What did I tell you?'

'Who is this girl now?' Jeffrey Stone asked again.

I didn't reply and Farida didn't budge.

'Can you speak to her in Swahili? Please tell her she can go home, that I'll be fine, I know my way back.'

Both Tescari and Stone spoke to her with the brisk tone people use with servants in this part of the world. Farida seemed hurt. She gave me a look under her long eyelashes, perhaps expecting me to explain her role to these men. She was my hostess, her face said, she was responsible for me. We must go home together. But I didn't obey her silent request. Instead I moved my hand again toward what I figured was the direction home.

Please. Please go.

Then a couple of words from the Swahili book resurfaced.

Nyumbani, tafadhali.

Reluctantly she turned and started walking away.

Jeffrey Stone lives in a slightly nicer concrete box than Andrea's, although no building on this odd, seemingly seaview-less island meets any of the requirements that might elevate it to something even remotely romantic. Stone has made an effort to make the place look cosy, though. He has a few colourful throws scattered across his sofa and armchairs, a Moroccan rug on the floor and a few coffee table books with old photographs of hunting expeditions or East African interiors. We sit outside on the veranda on plantation chairs and an older man with a severe expression in *kanzu* and *kofia* brings out a tray with iced gin and tonics and freshly roasted cashew nuts. Apparently Tescari has brought the booze all the way from mainland Tanzania and, judging from what's left in the bottle, they've had quite a lot of it already.

Tescari has an appointment tomorrow morning with the Ministry of Land and he's pretty optimistic that he'll get his permits without a problem.

'Despite,' he adds, turning to me, 'what your friend claims.'

I ignore his remark and say yes to a refill of my glass.

'He has married a local, right?' Jeffrey Stone inquires as he pours.

'Was that her?' Tescari asks.

I nod and feel both men's eyes on me. I know they expect me to make a remark or to crack half a joke as a sign of solidarity to the white man's cause when stranded on such unfriendly land, but I keep my straight face and ignore the question, asking Jeffrey what his job involves and whether he's planning to stay here much longer. He isn't, he's applied for a post in Uganda. Come the end of the year and he'll get the hell out of this hole.

This short parenthesis in the colonial world on the island has had the power to rejuvenate me, probably because of the alcohol intake, but I walk home strengthened, and full of ideas.

Andrea's on the porch, crossed-legged on the *baraza*. Pretending to be looking into some miraculous cloud formation in the sky. I know he's been waiting for me, but when I walk in he just says hi, as though he's not interested in where I've been. I move to sit next to him and he scoots over to make room. We sit quietly for a moment, though I am not quiet inside. I am energised and determined to pierce through the armour with which he has been shielding himself. We enjoy a moment of silence, then I begin.

'How come one never sees the ocean on this island?'

'On this side of the island it's more difficult to see it.'

'Then take me somewhere where I can. Otherwise I'll never believe this *is* an island.'

He stares into nothingness.

'Come on. Let's go. Just you and me this time.' I make my voice sound as conspiratorial and commanding as I can.

But he looks up at me, as if weary.

'Why?'

'Because I've come all this way to see you, and you, Andrea, haven't spent a minute with me. You've either handed me over to your wife, or talked to me like a stranger.'

He doesn't reply and looks away. I can feel him retreating, curling up. I raise my voice.

'Come back!'

He looks at me, startled, almost frightened. 'What do you mean, *come back?*'

'Just come back, for God's sake!' I shout. 'Come back into yourself! Come back! I feel you have turned into an alien.'

'Have you been drinking?'

'It doesn't matter and who cares? It's exactly what I think. This *person* you are pretending to be – is not you.'

'Oh really? And who am I then?'

'I've known you a long time. Longer than anybody else here. I know this is not you.'

He stares at me and doesn't say anything. I hold my breath. Does he hate me?

'No you don't,' he says coldly. 'You think you know me, but you don't.'

He glances toward the door of the house. 'And please lower your voice.'

Fifteen years of never eating fresh vegetables, but only rice, chapatis and fried fish in coconut oil have modified his shape, the texture of his skin, the molecules of his inner organs. Fifteen years of not having access to decent books, but just airport paperbacks snatched from the few foreign visitors, must have starved his mind, shrunk his intellect. Fifteen years of not speaking his mother language, forgetting its poetry, its songs, its sonorities and rhythms. And how about going to prayer five times a day, kneeling on a mat, his forehead touching the ground? In which way might that strict discipline transform an agnostic, a free spirit, a biker with long curls?

'*Why* are you still here?' my voice breaks. I had no idea I'd be so crushed.

He doesn't say anything.

I think about my boyfriend of five years, Gregorio, whom I'm not sure I'm still in love with but who has become my family, our sunny two-bedroom apartment in Monteverde Vecchio, my old dog, Olga. My daily morning run in the park, my small, cluttered office at the faculty, a couple of my brightest students. The list of my life's highlights is not that long and maybe not that interesting.

Who am I to judge? Maybe Andrea didn't come here seeking adventure. Maybe he has chosen this place to venture inward rather than expand, since everything here – the people, the buildings, even the geography – lacks beauty and brilliance. Maybe he was relieved when he found a place where he could shrink and settle into a smaller life, away from the eyes of others. From all our expectations.

'I am here because this is my home now,' he says, looking up again, to somewhere far away, above the mango trees across from the house.

'Don't you ever miss Rome?'

'Rome?' he asks, as baffled as if I'd said Mars. 'No. Never. I never think of Rome.'

'And us? Don't you ever think of us?'

He shakes his head slowly.

'No I haven't. In a long, long time.'

That's fair, I think. I hadn't been thinking much about him either. I hadn't truly missed him till now.

'Take me to see the ocean, Andrea. Just the two of us.'

He stares at me and something shifts in his eyes – is it tenderness? Or maybe just a spark of it.

───────────────

We drive for almost an hour in his battered Toyota with the NGO's logo painted on the side, heading north through a thick forest and then turning west, toward the setting sun. We walk on a sandy path through the bushes and suddenly it's as though a curtain has been lifted. Miles and miles of open view, of deep blue sea and sand lined with the vibrant green of the forest. The sand is as fine as talcum powder and snowy white, just as Tescari's brochure described it. I fill my lungs with the salty air, exhilarated by the open space. We sit, and watch the sun go down. It's low tide and the water has just started to retreat, its rivulets are sculpting wavy furrows in the sand, the crabs running obliquely on its translucent surface.

'This is beautiful,' I say.

The sun looks like an egg yolk ready to plop into the sea. I stand up and quickly strip off my shirt and unbutton my trousers.

He stands up, too, alarmed.

'What are you doing?'

'I'm going for a swim.'

'No. You can't go in like that.'

He quickly picks up my clothes and hands them back to me.

'Yes, I can. There's nobody around for miles and miles. And you've seen me naked before.'

'Stella!'

I drop my panties on the sand and I slide off into the velvety, luke-warm water. I dive in and swim until I'm almost out of breath. When I re-emerge I see him standing on the edge of the water with my clothes crumpled in his hand.

I swim out and out, where the sea gets bluer and darker, and after the last strokes I can muster, I wonder if I should worry about sharks.

Suddenly, I make out a shadow, as a dark, elongated shape darts past me. I shoot up screaming, and he emerges from the froth, like a shiny dolphin, stark naked.

We drive back in silence. It's a good kind of silence, as if the swim has exhausted us but also washed something away. The opaque film that has shrouded my days here has dissolved and now everything looks brighter.

By the time we reach the village it's night; there has been a power cut, and the house is wrapped in darkness, but for the faint glow of the kerosene lamp flickering through the windows. I can tell that Farida has been looking after our supper, there's a smell of curry wafting onto the porch. Before entering the house Andrea stops for a moment and rests a hand on top of my shoulder.

'You are the first person from my old life who has come to visit. It was a shock to see you. It was a shock to be speaking Italian again. I am sorry if I've seemed distant. It just felt like – well, like a lot to contend with.'

'Of course. I understand. Don't worry.'

'The day you arrived I was up all night, I just couldn't go to sleep. I was reminiscing, you know – all this stuff that I thought I had forgotten started coming back.'

'I'm sorry I barged into your life just like that, I didn't –'

'No. No, it's great. It's really good to see you, Stella. Yes.'

I reach for his hand, which is still resting on my shoulder, and I wrap my palm around it.

'Do you see me as a failure?' he asks. 'Like some kind of beached hippie?'

'No, I don't,' I say, and I squeeze his hand in mine, hard. 'I really don't.'

We enter the house and in the semidarkness I discern Farida sitting still on the floor, slightly slumped, her head hanging low. Only now I realise how worried she must be, seeing that Andrea and I have disappeared together. After all I am an impenetrable mystery to her – an older *mzungu* woman – an enigma she cannot even converse with or maybe even begin to grasp, like all of Andrea's life before her.

But as she hears us coming in, she leaps up and comes forward, and her face lights up. Maybe I'm wrong again here, I keep misreading the signs. From the way they look at each other, the way they gently exchange a few words, I see their bond is even stronger than what I'd glimpsed earlier. I look at Farida again. No, she isn't concerned after all. I'm not a threat to her. She knows her husband intimately.

And far better than I.

The next morning they drive me to the airport in the NGO's car. I'm flying back to Dar and from there on to Rome. Gregorio is coming to pick me up at the airport with Olga. Strange, how home has never felt so blurred.

For the occasion Andrea and Farida have put on their nice clothes – immaculate white *kanzu* and embroidered *buibui* because there will be people they know leaving or arriving on the small plane from the Big Island and there will doubtless be polite conversations and exchanges of news. Andrea moves around the tiny airport with ease, he weighs my bag on the scale, has a chat with the man in overalls who checks my ticket and passport, greets the people he knows. Farida has once again been holding my wrist tightly all along and now that Andrea has gone to get me a bottle of water she keeps repeating something to me in a hushed voice, something urgent, which he's not meant to hear. She repeats it two, three times and I turn my palms up. I don't understand. She reiterates the same words, more forcefully this time, but I widen my eyes.

'*Nini?* What?' I ask.

She laughs. And then Andrea comes back and tells me it's time I go, they are about to board the plane, so I am going to have to leave without knowing what Farida so urgently wanted me to know. Though I'm aware this is not the right thing to do here, I hug her and kiss her on the cheek. And yet I don't shake hands with Andrea because I've been told that's another taboo, one I don't wish to violate as my parting gesture.

'Wait! Just a second!' I call out, before they get back to the car. I have pulled out my phone. Farida immediately strikes an awkward pose, as I take the picture of the two of them. This is the only picture I've taken during the whole trip. I peer at the tiny screen. It's a good one.

I know they will have beautiful children.

'Same flight again, eh?' I hear a voice behind my back.

'Yeah, same flight,' I say to Tescari. Today he wears another freshly ironed blue shirt and orange trousers, hair still wet from a shower.

I see Jeffrey Stone in the lot, too, standing next to his brand-new SUV into which he'll soon climb and drive off.

'I bet you're happy to be heading back. At least I know I am,' Tescari says under his breath. 'This place would drive anyone nuts. Mosquitoes, crazy people, no booze, mangroves. It's hopeless.'

I know that Carlo Tescari will sit next to me and talk nonstop for the entire length of the flight. He'll feel even more entitled to do so now, given our newly born comradeship, which we'd sealed earlier with gin.

After all, haven't we come from the same place, and aren't we headed in the same direction?

MADE

David Hayden

The weight of unintention can make itself happen. I was in New York City. I had a friend that I was to visit. She was staying with her sister in Park Slope. I was meant to sleep on the couch but, in the early hours, Lia, my friend, appeared and implored me to join her in her bed. For the comfort. The sister hated me because of many things that I was not and, also, because I was a bad friend. I was a bad friend. I am still a bad friend. To her sister, who still I love.

We slept in the same bed and nothing happened. It was too much. I was asked to leave. It was agreed that I should leave.

Walking down the grey stoop, I meant to head for the subway but when I reached the sidewalk I saw a flash of yellow and put out my hand. I was before the frame, in the frame, behind the frame, the windscreen – and the city picture shook and altered and re-composed itself. There was no end of making, and every image was familiar and new, complete and unfinished, material and immaterial. The seat was soft and the air enfolding and oven-warm; there was a barely-smoked cigar at my feet and a smell of orange zest all around. The space was cramped but felt natural to me; the best way to travel. I thought vaguely about not arriving, about leaving decisions behind, outside. For the comfort.

The car stopped at a red light and I looked up, into the eyes of the driver who looked at me, learning what he needed to know. I was a picture to him too.

The avenue was broken into patches of light and movement held by the central grey-gold mass of the museum, which drew together people as they were and shaped us into a seeing crowd. The main exhibition gathered Mexican art; giant murals that, wherever they are now, are still made of smooth, flat-seeming areas of paint: blue-greys, clean, consistent but varied ochres, subjects, arguments, made broad and risen, brought to a single point of being. A wide depiction of dense foliage. Glossy green tongue-like leaves flourishing from thick, black, serpentine boughs that grow from bright yellow fibre-matted trunks and, behind this excessive life, eyes that cannot be seen but which are surely there, looking out, not seeing.

The flow of people slowed, coagulating in a narrow room where the most popular paintings hung; pictures of a woman giving birth to herself in bloody travail, of the artist, her fingers digging into her chest to hold back flesh and rolls of bright skin, her heart exposed and livid, her eyes still and fixed, above which was a tall shining forehead and a cloud of black hair.

A short woman in a lavender tweed suit jabbed me with her elbow, barged me with her shoulder and, finally, stamped on my foot to get a better view of the painting. I looked down, surprised; she was adjusting her wig and swearing fluently. She was as old as I am now but seemed as if she had a thousand more sour years left in her. She stared at the bloody woman, drinking her in. I could see, or imagine, that she lived the picture as a mirror, as a memory, as a mystery, and I wanted to know what she knew.

Another mass of bodies surged in through the entrance. No one was leaving. There was carping and shoving. One man spat in another man's face. He didn't wipe the scum off but let it slather down, all the while smiling, showing his teeth and leaning towards the spitter. A young man wearing an old man's hat was pressed, crying, into a corner, close to a picture of a blood transfusion with monkeys perched on the white steel bedhead, dark red cables entering the naked artist's body. One guard slouched, dead-eyed in a chair; another loitered nearby, looking on in disgust at no one in particular.

I needed to find a lonely painting.

Pushing counter to the heave of still-contending bodies, I moved from one bright room to another until I found one more sparsely peopled. A knot of neat young people staring pinch-mouthed at a vivid scene of collapsed sunflowers; tar-black seeds, twisted, elliptical petals, sulphur-yellow, under a sky of gathered smoke and other nameless filth. One of the men looked to me, to my legs, and did something with his tongue. He might have been beautiful in his own moment. I couldn't bear this for long and left, darting out and past the elevators and up, or possibly down, the staircase, the marble steps soft and mute underfoot, my fingers trailing on the cool brass railing; the light in the well being the light in the well.

On a new floor, which on reflection must have been a higher one, I found several empty rooms and wandered until a picture caught me. A drypoint etching on a large rectangular sheet of heavy-grade paper, rough-edged, dressed-over carefully – splashily – with acid greens, bloody, liverish reds and browns, shadowy, pus-like yellows and coal black. After the mass and colours it was the shapes, simple but unresolving, and the lines, that I found present; fat and crude, densely-scratched, faint, crazed and desultory, until the figures became more of what I knew about the picture. A man and a woman – a couple, according to the title – standing in profile, facing left; what there is, was, of light suggesting a winter, a city, with a crowd of rotten buildings nearby.

There is no inhibition in looking at made faces for as long as there is something to see. There are not the consequences of looking there would be with a person. There are other effects; what happens after the gaze is broken, the long bearing of the picture memory, should any arise; the discontinuity, the broken presentness. The picture memory can become a recurring event with its own rhythm and sense; its own story, even. Such as now, as I recall all I can of the faces and what the pictured felt; all that was figured in line and colour but perhaps did not show on the surface of their bodies, their faces; all that was was alive in their minds, heavy, sparking, unconsidered ... should there have been any such pictured people; should there have been anyone other than the artist and I.

The hats: hers plain, red and risen to a toadstool peak, his a white sugar-loaf. His bright cloak, her shabby coat; his curtain of drab hair, a steep, sloping chin, a long neck. One velvet eye, one eye shining dark in the corner of his face; her hair fluffed in feathers, blonde, out of the hat's brim. Her eyes, keen face-dents slanting with the slope of the land behind, her mouth sloping against this, closed but ready to open. His mouth, pursed plump lips, his two hands clumped in fists that pull the cloak to, flagging it out; her hands pocketed, perhaps, but not visible. This couple are travellers. So many of their journeys are pictured here; the place-to-place, the time-to-time; the journey into, out of, love, together or apart (together *and* apart); the journey – every moment the journey – the journey out of life.

Lia was in Austin. I got the call in Boston. Pills had been taken. Many pills. The right amount to cause the vomiting that would bring them all back up. Otherwise the right amount to shut down the liver, perhaps to provoke a sudden cardiac arrhythmia that would cause – between beats – blood to puddle and clot before being hurled out of the heart and into the brain, causing a massive stroke. The right amount to take the body rapidly along one of many paths to death.

Lia collapsed in the kitchenette, striking her head on the sharp edge of the counter as she fell to the floor where she rolled on her side, puked and passed out. Sara, who – after much trouble, untold trouble – was moving out, returned moments later, early from her boyfriend's place.

It was Sara who saved Lia, not me.

I remember standing in the hall holding the telephone, looking at the tawny rug, the over-large mirror, but I don't recall who called me with the news, or whether it was a man or a woman. I can hear the voice now; low, steady and unreproaching. I asked, 'Should I come? Should I come?' and 'What should I do?' 'Nothing,' said the voice. I waited a long time, listening to the hiss twisting on the line. 'Nothing,' said the voice; and they hung up. I didn't have to take instructions. I could have made another decision but I made the decision not to make a decision and I stayed. Made worst worse.

There was bustle in the gallery a room or so away. I shrank from the wall. I wasn't ready to be not alone. The voices faded back from where they had come. I looked to the painting and could no longer take sight of it. There had been a sudden failure of appearances from inside – but it was not the picture that had failed, it was me. My professor had said, 'hesitate with awareness before the limits of what is possible to know'; he had reached out and put his hand on my throat. He had sat not quite still; the hand was cold and rigid. He had time, he had his time and after this, he gasped long and said: 'with awareness before the limits.'

I looked around, glad not to be seen, searching for another picture, a steadying purpose, and noticed, for the first time, the shadowed spaces on the walls where what had been had been. I turned to the entrance and saw a trail of red-and-white tape on the floor between two hip-height metal stands. I walked out and past a room and another room and through a darkened arch. There was a high gurgling sound, which suddenly ended, and a hard white light that came on with a thump. The new room was huge, more a hall, and blank except for, at its centre, a confession booth. I at once felt bored and wondered how boredom could be thought of as a weight and a tide but, finally, wasn't interested enough to follow this through to an idea. I walked over to the box as I supposed I was supposed to do. The first door I tried did not open, the second did and I entered and sat down. My feet felt sore and hot and I shucked off my shoes. Vinegary fumes filled the tight booth.

I heard the artist's voice.

'*I.*'

The voice was too physically close, almost as if it were coming from within my head. I wondered how this was done.

'*I* ... ' there was a long, breathy pause, '... *suffer.*'

I felt bored again.

'*I ... suffer. I ... suffer.*'

I wondered when this would end. I decided to wait.

'*I ... suffer.*'

There was an anvil bang and darkness began. There was a dense pause and the artist spoke again; the voice thicker, wetter and – if this was possible – still closer.

'*I ... suffer.*'

I blinked, seeing white chrysanthemum blotches before me. This was vapid; silly even. Wasn't it? I felt like peeing. I felt like a little girl. I laughed and it wasn't me – it was me, laughing.

'I ... suffer.'

All feeling receded in me. I touched my face and sat still.

Lia had bought a loft in what was still the Meatpacking District. She showed me a sign placed on the sidewalk a block over that read *Fresh Killed Lamb,* done rather obviously in red paint that had slipped bloodily down the white board. The taxi driver told me that a man he knew of, but had never spoken to, had a few days earlier been pulled from his cab and stabbed to death for fifteen dollars and change. 'Killed by children,' the driver said, 'and they weren't even his own.'

Lia had a lover living with her – a lover whose story I cannot tell – and was studying writing. I was confused by how undefended she seemed; how warm, how kind to me, how solicitous, how direct and yet, somehow, appearing out of focus or to the side of herself. I saw a novel on her desk by a famous under-read novelist; one whose books I had also considered but had not read. I spoke, saying 'Oh ... ' in the book's direction, and she grew angry. The book, she said, was just about passing, about passing time; it was held together by nothing but light, descriptions of light, there was a lot of stupid fucking in it, her teacher should never have demanded that she read it. She fell silent mid-sentence and looked out the window that took up most of the wall, that displayed the old working side of the city, that was bitter cold at this season when you stood close to it, and I could see that something was broken but could not name it.

———————————————

I had grown comfortable in the box. The voice kept repeating the statement. The wide *I*, the sibilant *s*, the soft *f*s; the word clipped at the *r*; the long, floating, not entirely silent pauses. These became all the song I needed. The space grew closer, warmer. Eyes open or closed were all the same for what I saw. I was surely sleeping, dreamlessly away; without time or colour, without care.

'I ... suffer.'

I wanted nothing to keep happening. That would have been for the best.

'I ... suffer.'

An acrid, chemical smell – I wasn't thinking it, I was sensing it. A slick sliding noise and a blunt crack, and the raw white light of a single bulb shone through the screen aperture. The shutter had opened and I could see the waxy, sweaty yellow skin, the naked body of a man; brown and red blotches covered his chest, his eyes red, lashless, his lips white, cracked, his teeth black stumps. He was holding – he is holding – a silver microphone. He spoke again.

'*I ... suffer.*'

There were zinc white smudges on his forehead, on the bridge of his nose. Pupils filled his eyes with black. Prick and balls receded into a dark froth between his legs. A tiny sketch of burst vessels surfaced, red on each cheek. Arms were long and bony, their skin bagging and dry. There seemed to be less of the artist the more I noticed of him. His brown tongue sagged forward, lolled back.

'*I ... suffer.*'

I wondered about touching him but that would have meant reaching out. He was seeing me, and I saw myself, and I thought I should think less of myself, and I realised that I had become, once again, momentarily distracted from what I should be most attentive to, regardless of whether I was able or willing to reach out, to move beyond the knowing that is seeing to a more committed knowing; one that might bring about change, or not; an understanding of more than apparency. I closed my eyes.

Lia is standing on the boards of an L platform waiting for a train north. I am with her, just. In the background is the upper mass of a sixty-storey office building, 1940s, faced in dark brown stone that steps upwards towards the sky ending in a grey steel needle. On the corners of each indent above the middle floors are grey eagles that, even from this distance, can be identified as crude, unintentionally stylised; nothing that could be mistaken in any condition of light for a real bird. The windows are tiny and narrow almost as arrowslits on a castle tower. Lia's face stands out in the foreground, large and round; her hair is short and soft-looking, her cheeks are rosing in the cool spring breeze, her brown eyes are huge and wet and smiling, her mouth turned sweetly at the edges in the moment before a wisecrack, a plosion of pungent abuse or of some wordless utterance never to be repeated. There is nothing moving. There is no futurity. I have a photo of this. I am behind the camera.

There is a ringing which becomes a banging. The door opens and a night watchman stands in front of me in the dark, holding a flashlight, aimed to avoid dazzling me. I try to speak but my mouth is tacked shut.

'Lady, it's time to go home.'

I crouch forward, head tapping the box ceiling, and stagger into my shoes. The light beam hovers around my middle and I see that the shutter is down. I chew around my tongue, swallow drily and speak.

'Where is the artist?'

'I don't know, lady. I just work here.'

The guard walks off and I follow him out of the hall, down the corridor and I lose my way with where I might be, and from there rely wholly on him and what he knows. We turn into a tight passage and stop. There is a click and a throb from below, a door slides open, and we step into a service elevator standing, by a silent, mutual effort, as far from one another as the space allows.

We exit in the basement and pass through a corridor, through its sweet scent of floor wax; the shadows, the echoes of our passing. We move past a statue in night-coloured bronze of a man, nearly dead, spiralled-round by a large, swelling snake. We go through a steel door and up some steps, and – too soon it seems – I am out on the street.

'Night,' says the guard, and nothing more, and he closes the door, and I hear at once the noise of the city as a single music; not as the sounds of separate vehicles below or above, or of cries and laughs and conversations, or of buildings working, or of other machines that cool or light or make. I pull down my skirt and lift my foot – a cigarette paper is stuck to my heel – and as I try to shake it off, a man steps forward from a fragment of crowd and he crouches and angles his hands and from the space between them there comes a flash. And he laughs and stands, and I blink through inky clouds and I see the man, his wrinkled suit, his red and shiny face, the camera bulking on a strap around his neck and he cries out.

'Hey, baby! We made a picture!'

PALOMINO

Mark Doten

The Americans were coming up the road. They were walking a cart. The road was visible from the hotel. There was no running water, no electricity, but we had our rooms, and in the basements boxes of canned food stacked high on a dozen pallets, and in the courtyard a well with cold water. We had staked our claims to our rooms, and at night we closed our eyes and if we dreamt, the dreams were of each other – all of us, in all of our rooms, dreaming of each other in a cutaway version of our hotel, rooms visible, beds visible, sleeping, heads on hand, cups of cold water on end tables. Or so it seemed, some nights. Just as by day it sometimes felt as though we all moved as one, all reached for our doorknobs as one, then stepped back, and listened, and waited.

Our rooms faced the long straight road. On this day, we all sat at our windows, watching. They were a mark on the pale road that grew in size, until it was visible for what it was. The cart they were walking must not have been so heavy – there were six of them, but only two or three had a hand on the traces at any given moment, and the cart glided along almost without effort up the dusty road.

On the back of the cart was a horse. It was dead, you could see that from quite a distance. It was evening by the time they reached the hotel. The lead soldier, he was smiling as he greeted us.

What are you doing here? we asked. We had gathered in front of the hotel. The Americans had not been here in a long time, and in fact the treaty did not permit them in our town.

It was the horse, the soldiers said – couldn't we see that the horse had died?

The uniforms of the soldiers were covered in pale dust, but the creases were still sharp. The teeth of the horse protruded almost horizontally from the mouth, huge and gleaming.

We can't just leave the horse, the soldiers said. We have to do something about this horse.

Yes, of course, we said, but what can we do?

They were already manoeuvring the cart around to the courtyard, to the well.

We will need you to take the roof off this well, the soldiers said, almost apologetically.

We argued with them. Why should we take the roof off our well?

But the roof came down.

Then the crossbar and bucket, soon they were gone, too – and the old rope lay loosely at our feet.

We'll need a hand, the soldiers said. A hand with this horse.

The horse seemed to shiver, but the horse could not have shivered – the horse was dead. The soldiers grinned, almost apologetically.

It took all of us to lift her. She went in headfirst. She entered the water noiselessly, but all the way down there was the shrieking and cracking of huge teeth against stone.

CITY INSIDE

Porochista Khakpour

For the first time in his life, Henry was living in a famous city. Even his apartment building had a well-known history – the broker had told him some tale about a famous deli owner and his famous death in the building. His whole block was bustling. There were rough-looking bars meant to attract college kids. There were Japanese-looking hair salons full of the Japanese. There were convenience stores run by men of ambiguous origins, selling cold fish, canned pantyhose, prayer cards, everything. Dry cleaners with signs that boasted 'delivery.' A nameless store that sold only a dozen plain white t-shirts. The block was packed. In that first week, it was enough for Henry to just walk up and down it. He decided to save himself and take it slow with the city: content to sit in his new apartment, listen to the radio, read the Classifieds, make phone calls, check his balance, nap. He let entire portions of the day escape him. He let the day exist only as it did outside his one and only window.

He lived in a small studio on the third floor, which he accessed by elevator. The elevator was a good alternative to the strange traffic of the steps, which had presented itself to him on his first day, as he lugged the last of his boxes and found himself overtaken by a pack of howling children. They were in a bad rush. Henry was shoved against the railing. He was not convinced it was an accident. He suspected one child had even tried to trip him. He also felt mildly sure he had heard another mutter *old man*.

Henry had just turned 33.

It felt right to be paranoid. The city seemed to say to him, *I am a city of the strange, a city to interpret paranoically.* He was adjusting. Still, he felt it would not be wrong, in the adjustment month or two, to stay in more, to know his space a little better, and then branch out. There was no hurry to know the city in full, to know all his neighbours. He already got his share of the outside world just sitting there. He could even count on some socialising, as he could count on daily visits from maintenance.

Since he had moved in, the building's two maintenance men had been constantly at work in his apartment. The maintenance men were remarkably active, while their landlord-boss remained entirely anonymous. (Henry sent his rent cheque to a name whose source was shrouded in absolute mystery: 'Bettina.' He didn't know what – agency, person, or what – 'Bettina' was.) Their work never ended. They were constantly checking radiators, unscrewing and re-screwing knobs, tapping at ceilings, flushing toilets, running water, stepping on things, talking in hushed voices between themselves. One night, Henry awoke to the taller one standing on the ledge outside his window. He was painting. The maintenance man explained that they had painted the outer window frame just before Henry had moved in, but that they now had to repaint them, because 'Bettina' didn't like white; the building, after all, was *off*-white. What annoyed Henry even more was how they almost always left their tools in his apartment, knocking hours, sometimes days, later to retrieve them. The first few times this happened they had not even knocked; they had keys, and they let themselves in. Henry didn't have to be there, they reminded him, but Henry let them know he was always at home, he did his work from home, and that knocking was nice. They respected this.

The city said to him, as if with a playful rib-jab, *Deal with it, jerk*, and so he dealt with it. He reminded himself that the maintenance men were really a minor complaint. It was worth it – worth the thrill of the city that he felt more than enough, perhaps even more strongly, he thought, bottled in as he was, looking out.

The window was not for everyone. The broker had even shrugged at it, emphasising the high ceilings instead: *You know you're in the city when your ceiling is high!* In the other cities that Henry had lived in (towns, really), they had only had short buildings with short ceilings, wide roads full of lanes, parks packed with giant trees and picnicking families, and he was sick and tired of that stuff. In a city like this, a man required height, he thought, and a high ceiling symbolised this nicely. It also somehow made up for the many square feet his floor space lacked. *In the city you give up a few things – space is one – to be in the city, to really BE in the city, get my drift?*

So, beside the window, he set up his swivel chair – the one he had stolen from his old office on his final day, duct-taping it to the floor of the cargo van for the 180-mile-drive up the coast. He adjusted the height so his head got a good bottom quarter's perspective of the view.

The view was sky-less. All he faced was another jutting part of his building, the portion of it which, he imagined, contained one- and two-bedroom apartments. All he had was another person's window and its insides.

It belonged to a woman.

In his down-time – mornings when he waited for his mind's fog to clear, evenings when he fought a gassy restlessness behind his ribs – he watched her. Mornings and evenings were good times, because they were the only times the woman appeared. The woman worked.

She was alone, always. She was not the type of woman men watched, he figured. Sometimes it did occur to him to feel strange or even guilty – after all, in those other towns, good citizens regarded such watching as suspect, even *bad*. But he was in the city now, he reminded himself, and he was just looking out; it was allowed; he paid a high rent; it was not his fault there was a woman in his view.

Plus, her sight was not seductive. She was a thick, although not fat, woman. What little he saw of her flesh – wrists, neck, face – revealed a body solidly clotted and permanently flushed. She had an ample bundle of carpet-brown hair that she tied back with a rubber band. She did have nails, however, long and red and professional. He could not tell her age.

His interest was innocent. He admired her *substance*. The first time he saw her – his first night there – one word instantly popped into his mind: *decency*. She looked decent. Here was a woman who respected the right things in life and in return got respect. She did not seem to participate in 'going out on the town'. She stuck by a routine. She came home at roughly the same time each evening, in suit-sets of respectable shades (gray, navy, brown, black) and tasteful makeup; then she would disappear and return in sweats, a t-shirt, and a scrubbed face. She would pop a meal in the microwave, lie on her couch, and watch TV. Shows and more shows. Once in a while, when her face was lit with the battling flashes of the television, he could see her mouth something to herself. Sometimes she would smile. Once he saw her sneeze. Then when it came time to end the day, to get the recommended eight hours of sleep, she would one by one switch off the lights, and shade by shade, in dimming frames, simply disappear.

Then the day came when Henry suspected she might have caught his eye catching her. He was not sure but felt it was possible. She had abruptly turned away from the television and walked over to her window to get something left on the sill, he figured. As she reached out for it, Henry sensed her seem to become, for a quick second, conscious of him. He was not sure. After all, it was possible that her eyes might have accidentally fallen on the air-space that corresponded with his exact eye-level. Who knew? All that mattered was that she had looked away and gone on with her business.

But an hour later when his doorbell rang, Henry felt the stirring of a small yet staunch fear, like the unlodging of old gum in the gut. He quietly walked to his door and looked through his peephole, hoping for the main-tenance men. It was not them, but it was thankfully not *her* either.

It was a child.

Of course. The building was teeming with children. And sourceless children, children whose parents were invisible. He did not expect this of the city – he was sure the city would say, *I am a fucking-nice city, but not a good one for families (at best, couples with dogs.)* But not his building. His was full of them – children seemingly on their own, children with big words, children with money in their pockets, children going places, children with authority and agenda. Children who made their presence known.

The child was a girl, a wisp of a little girl who Henry had not yet seen.

She said, 'Sir, do you have heating, sir? We think the boiler's down and that we should call maintenance.'

He assured her that he had heat. He went as far to ask which apartment was hers. She said she lived downstairs. Henry smiled, relieved.

The girl suddenly said, 'Hey, sir, wait, I have something for you!' She darted off and came back with a black plastic suitcase, which she dramatically flipped open before his eyes. Inside: knives.

'*Steak* knives,' she said, the words glowing through her almost. 'We're selling them to family, friends. And neighbours! I'm sure you could use a new steak knife set, right? I mean, really think about your steak knives – when was the last time you got around to buying one? We got it all, eight-piece, nine-piece, all made in Germany, with high-carbon-stamped-stainless-steel, micro-serrated-four-and-a-half-inch blades, with three-rivet polypropylene handles, full tangs, on birch wood blocks or in pine gift boxes or plastic carrying cases, 61% off the list price, sir. We got real beauties ...!'

Henry looked at her gleaming, sharp, deadly things, and her freckles and glasses, and explained – tenderly – that they were very nice, but that no, thank you, he couldn't. Still, a part of him was sold; since the move, with his silverware still boxed, he'd been working at meats with plastic knives. Plus he had never owned steak knives, and he could believe they were nice.

'Whatever, sir!' the girl snorted, skipping off.

Minutes later, his doorbell rang again. This time it rang several times in a row, with an urgency that worried Henry. When he looked out the peephole, he saw a young gangly boy who looked somewhat like the girl – same freckles, same frame.

The boy held his middle finger up to the peephole.

Henry opened the door, for the sake of being natural, once the boy had galloped off. Although he realised it was a gesture not uncommon in the city, and maybe not even intended for hostile interpretation, he was glad to avoid confrontation. He didn't know what a child like that could do to him.

Exhausted, Henry slumped into his swivel chair. The evening had been congested with events. He turned to the window until the woman's lights went out and he decided it *was* time be done.

But it was bound to occur; that he knew. So when the moment came, only days later, that she noticed and made it known that she had noticed, when she didn't, even out of politeness, break the stare, Henry felt its inevitability like a bad knee ahead of a rainy day.

He did not lose control. He paced. He cursed the placement of his window – better yet, the architects of the building, for not thinking ahead and knowing better. He cursed his space – he wished he had other rooms, any room, that he could go to. He thought of the bathroom; he dashed into the bathroom. He was embarrassed to have 'dashed.' He sat on the lid, cursing his own alarm. He was disappointed in himself for letting a minor sensation of dirtiness loiter inside him, for something he hadn't done – or rather *had* done, and a lot, but for an altogether *other* purpose; namely, no purpose. None at all.

He flushed the empty toilet bowl and decided to go back out. He would just turn off the lights and go to bed, just like that. Then he realised there was the possibility he would look all the more conspicuous and guilty and dirty – what if she thought the darkness meant him wanting to be alone with and discreet about and enraptured by the whole mess? – and he did not want that.

When he finally walked out, he tried his best to avoid the window. But by the time he made it to his chair, out of the corner of his eye he could sense something. Something big. There was suddenly no flashing of a television, no other light. Her world was blocked off by something else in his view.

There she was, in sweats and a winter coat, standing on the ledge by his window, her red, red nails tapping away on the pane. Her knees were shoved up against the glass. He did not have to look her in the eye to know she was quite, considerably, pissed.

He did not know what to do. There he was, staring her up with his head only at her shin-height – and there she was, glaring him down, a mad tower of woman, taking up the full length of his window perfectly – just as he envisioned those Amsterdam red light window girls – standing and waiting, her face wearing the worst expression he had seen on it yet, tapping away with her nails (square-tipped, he noticed now), probably not banging only because it was glass – now *that* was decency – because by her expression, if she could, she would be *banging*. He felt the throb of a stale heat inside him. He quickly banished the Dutch whores from his head.

He had options. He knew this. He could, for instance, just not let her in. Just look at her, shake his head, turn off the lights, and go. Where? He had no other rooms. He could go *out*. Grab his keys, his coat, gloves, hat, and leave. But then he'd be in their courtyard, and certainly she could follow him out to the street. That would not be getting rid of her; that would just be transporting her to another spot.

Or he could, for instance, open the window a tiny slit and say, 'Yes?' And she could say her part and he could apologise, no matter what she said; anything, anything just to make her go away. But what if she didn't go away? What if she yanked the window up over on her side, crammed a thigh in, and then what?

Or, he could, for instance, just try to communicate with her through the window – certainly they could hear each other, somewhat at least, through glass. But what if they couldn't really? What if the outside world – the cabs, the kids, the city – just didn't allow it? Certainly that could anger her more? What if she grew frustrated and went back, to her window, to her living room, to her door, out her door, down his hall, to his door, knocking, banging – then what?

He sat there, spinning idly from side to side. He went to the corner that served as a kitchen – where the minifridge heaved atop the micro-wave, next to a table topped with rice maker and blender and juicer and hot plate and hot pot and toaster oven – and he found his mug. He dumped in three spoonfuls of instant coffee, turned on the 'H' tap, filled it halfway, and drank.

He couldn't avoid the window altogether. She was not going anywhere. Sometimes the tapping would stop and that would only worry him more – her just being there. Then he would look over, just for a quick scan of the hard white of her face, or the hazy blur of her hair's wild brown. And then it would start again. Tap, after tap, after tap.

After a while, it occurred to him that outside it was probably cold, and that the cold could kill a person. He decided he had to do it. It had been a while. He could not let the cold get her. He was not that kind of character.

'What the fuck were you looking at?'

She had repeated the sentence over and over. Her dirty diction hurt. *Fuck*: the right word – maybe; a city word – yes. But from her: bad, wrong, out of place, mislead, unforgiving, overeager ...

She said other things too.

She said, 'You know, that wasn't the first time. I see you, you don't know that, but I've seen you do it, asshole, and I want to know what the fuck ...'

He thought of the gangly boy and his middle finger. The city said *Be tough and you'll BE tough.*

She said, 'How would you like it, bastard, if someone was doing that to you? You like being watched? I mean, what the fuck were you looking at? You like being a spy? You think it's some kind of joke ...'

He felt embarrassed that his house was so bare and ill-lit and that still, weeks into his arrival, there were boxes everywhere. Her voice sounded different than he had imagined, but somehow familiar and still nice, in spite of the words. He considered putting them away, pushing them to the side, something.

She said, 'I mean, I am not leaving until we get this fucking nightmare sorted.'

He nodded to himself.

He would have to find a nice way to get rid of her.

She said, 'Busted, bastard!'

Busted: he had a history. He remembered the feeling as a child. Getting busted for busting, for example. He remembered kindergarten, and in particular, their lunch hour. He remembered the rules. Like the one about saving the dessert for last. The teacher had even reiterated it that day: *meal first, then dessert.* The dessert that day had been cantaloupe. His peers, no matter how dull the dessert, always wanted to go for it first. Henry never did it; he understood the rules and respected them. The disobedience of his peers annoyed him. And on that particular day, he had really had it –

―――――――――――――――――――――

She said, 'Bastard! You hear me? Son-of-a-bitch!'

―――――――――――――――――――――

So when the kid next to him reached for her cantaloupe slice, he shot his hand up. He had something to say about that. Teacher came over and he told on his neighbour, just like that. His neighbour began to cry. Teacher looked at his neighbour, the crying girl, then at Henry, over and over, thinking long and hard about it. Teacher put an arm around the crying girl, and turned to Henry, and tagged him with a word he knew well from the playground –
      She said, 'Mute! Retard! You want to just sit there? Creep!'

―――――――――――――――――――――

She said, *Snitcher!* 'Snitcher' from a teacher – the adult world's adoption of a children's insult, used to label those who had done an allegedly bad thing that was really an intended good thing that might look like a bad thing for a good reason, or, a bad reason. The buster had gotten busted. The world had turned itself upside down on him. The misunderstanding, miscommunication, misinterpretation; it still sickened him.

―――――――――――――――――――――

She said, 'Sicko! Motherfucker!'

―――――――――――――――――――――

She said, 'Fuckingmotherfucker!'
      He remembered what her voice reminded him of: a voice he had loved in childhood, the voice of the man in the chocolate syrup commercials who went on about the thick, rich, deep, dark, milky, velvety stuff. That man had the ideal voice for chocolate. That was it. Hers was the voice of the thick-rich-deep-dark-chocolate man.

He popped a bagel into the toaster. He ate it slowly and even managed to look her in the eye a few times as he ate.

She ran out of names to call him. She sat on the floor, like a retired puppet. He had no other furniture to offer her but boxes, and of course his chair – but he could not get himself to offer the chair. She was still bundled in her coat. When he was convinced that she was done shouting, he toasted her a bagel and placed it on a plate.

She grabbed the bagel in her hands, squishing it down to dough, in the manner they handled complimentary stress-relieving balls at his old office, and said 'I'm gonna kill you.'

'Look who's looking at you, asshole.'

She had undoubtedly grown up in the city. She did what they did not do in the city unless out of hostility – she stared. She stared at him with a mean resolution. He stared back. For a very long time, lengthy paragraphs of silence, they just stared. Until she got up, shuffled aimlessly, kicked a couple boxes, and made a noise.

It was apparently a sob.

She said, 'Do you know what we go through? We go through hell, asshole.'

We. It terrified him. It could also mean she had causes.

He wondered what she could do. She had said it plainly: *kill*. That was her goal. That was that. That plus the fact she could have other causes. Plus the fact she could have causes and be crazy. He thought about it harder and concluded it wasn't too much to think she was crazy. The city said, *Crazy yourself.*

But he was worried; about her causes. If she was right, if she was crazy, where to draw that line; her misunderstandings, his. Because at an early age, he had learned. He recalled a certain sundries store of his youth, where the young son of the owner, roughly his age, had worked. They were almost friends. The young son had asked Henry if he could draw. Henry said he had done it before, he *could*, but maybe not well. The young son asked him what he drew. Henry shrugged and named various school projects, maps of the world, dinosaurs, dead presidents. The young son concluded that he could draw people. Henry shrugged. The young son phrased it differently: *would* he draw people? Henry said he would if he had to. The young son went further: what about *naked* people? Henry thought about this, and admitted he'd rather not. The young son told him there were free cigarettes or ice cream or whatever he wanted from the store in it for him. Henry thought further. Before he knew it the young son took out a piece of paper and a pencil and ordered him to draw. He wanted a naked woman. Henry choked back the lump in his throat. He took a while to lightly sketch a smallish naked woman. The young son told him it wasn't so great but it would do OK. Henry got a free Astropop that day. Another time, he got a radio. He got other things as well. One day, the young son demanded a naked man. Henry told him he would rather draw naked women. The young son told him to do it, he had to, and besides, it would be easier. Henry did not know what to do, so he did his best. The young son looked at it and suddenly got angry, accusing Henry of drawing men and women the same. He suddenly wasn't so sure of Henry's naked women. Hadn't he seen a woman? Hadn't he seen himself? What was he trying to do – hustle, steal, *shoplift?* The young son told him to get out or he'd call the cops. He crumpled the paper and Henry ran out, thinking of course he knew, of course men and women were different, of course. It had just been a mistake, a mis-rendering, a bad translation ...

She said, 'Do you hear me?' over and over again.

Then, 'I am tired,' she said, done.

It wasn't the window – the window hadn't done a thing but gotten conceived in a bad spot. It was the chair's fault. He wondered why he had ever put his chair there. He remembered: because his desk was there. Maybe it was the desk's fault. He had spent a good deal of time thinking about it. In a studio, you had options, too many options. Desk near radiator? Dresser near desk? Bed near radiator? Bed near window? Radiator near dresser? Desk near window? Desk near window. He thought it would be the best thing. He had read it somewhere, that it would be good for him, as well as for the general wellbeing of the room, to have his desk beside the window.

He wondered why he had never put up curtains. He remembered: nobody had curtains in the city. Blinds at most, and usually open blinds. In those other towns, people were always worried about privacy and protection and inner lives, things like that. Here the city said, *What the fuck are you looking at? Oh, you're looking at me? Go the fuck ahead,* the city said, *go the fuck ahead.*

———————————

It was different watching her in person, up close, and 'live.' It was like running into a famous film star taking out the trash (something he had not yet seen, but anticipated he soon would once he began to go out in such a famous city).

She was herself with him soon enough. He recognised that.

She would scrape her nose with the tip of a nail, raking up dead cells.

She would scratch her shoulders, crossing her arms over her chest to reach the opposite shoulder.

She would whimper, rant, yell, choke up, go quiet.

She would pace and then sit down again, always at the one corner under the window, sometimes with her thick legs wrapped around each other, often in a peculiar knot, which made them look slimmer and limber.

Once, she did something he liked. She got up and put one foot up onto the sill to tie her white nurse-style sneaker. It reminded him of that certain girl who lived in his old teenage mind, the girl in the short skirt on the spring day, hiking a leg up against the bark of a tree to tie her shoe. He did not know who exactly that girl was, only that it was a girl he was sure had romped through the minds of most men at some point in their lives.

He thought it looked nice, but he did not understand it. Tying her laces when she wasn't going anywhere.

———————————

Constantly, like a child's wind-up toy car, he bumped into the wall that was the idea: *what-to-do.* He sat down next to her, wondering what she would do. He imagined abuse. To his shock, she said nothing. She reached over to the distorted mass of bagel, ripped off a piece with her teeth, and chewed. She kept chewing. He thought she might need water. He went to get her water, but by the time he returned, her head was tipped back and her eyes were closed. She looked asleep. He sat down next to her again and tried to fall asleep as well.

When he opened his eyes, her eyes were open too. He had one thought: they had done it. Almost, in a sense, with a few of its intimate connotations intact, they had slept together.

The idea bore a bad acid. He felt sick. The city had a saying, he thought, and he remembered: he told the idea to take a walk; *Take a fucking walk, jackass.*

'Sex, is that it? You want me? Is that what we're getting at?' she said.

'I have kids, you know,' she said.

'I'm not afraid to admit that I'm scared,' she said.

'They don't live with me,' she said.

'But you know that, you know I live alone,' she said.

'God, what time is it,' she said.

'You think I do this every day?' she said. 'I do not do this every day.'

'How are you going to pay me back, asshole?' she said.

She took the plate beside her, and with both hands slammed it against the floor. She could break things, this woman. He worried that the broken pieces might be the only weapon he would have to defend himself, when the time came.

When the doorbell rang, they both looked at it, then each other, accusingly. He wondered if there was any chance she had called the police and he imagined she wondered the same thing.

He looked through the peephole. It was the young girl from downstairs, in pink flannel pyjamas, squinting through her glasses with sleepy eyes, smothering the shaggy blue rabbit tucked snugly in her armpit.

He looked back at the woman: biting her lip, staring at the ground, in plain view. It wouldn't look right. He would have to be careful. He opened the door just a bit. He fought the urge just to run out, and instead stepped out on the doormat.

He asked if he might help her.

'Can you turn the TV down, sir?' she said. 'Some people have to be up early, you know.'

He apologised. She had started to walk off when he had an idea. He yelled for her to wait, adding that he would like to know more about those goods she had been selling the other day ...

'Yeah, sir, I got the knives. I'll show you tomorrow again, if you want 'em.'

He told her he needed to see them now, if possible.

Certainly it was possible. She rolled her eyes. 'Which one? I have my two best sets left. Bundy, Bush. Your choice, sir.'

He was going for cheap, sharp, big, impressive, *safe*.

'Bundy. That'll be $129.99, 61% off the list price. Cash or cheque, sir?'

The price was still very high, didn't she think?

'Whatever, sir!'

He fished out his chequebook and pen and filled it out. She tucked the cheque under her arm. He asked her when he would get the knife set.

'Oh, soon,' she said, 'I promise. It's worth the wait, sir, it's a *steal*!'

He told her to run right back with it. She sprinted off with a quick careless wave that he hoped meant *goodbye* and not *whatever*. Had he not written her a cheque that was guaranteed to bounce, he could fear that she had just robbed him, mugged him in the most professional way possible.

He closed the door and prayed the woman hadn't heard a thing. The transaction seemed ripe for misreading.

Instead, he found her lost in her own world. With her back to him, with hands gently resting on his glass, the woman was gazing out his window, at the light beyond her own window.

'I am tired,' she said, later.

It was later. He hadn't stayed up all night in ages. All he knew was that they were somewhere around the point where late meets early and things get really confused.

He was ashamed not to own a clock yet. He used the radio announcer on the AM news to tell the time, but thought it would be inappropriate to turn on the radio.

He tried to look past her and out the window. He saw nothing but the dim light of her living room. With windows like theirs, there was no telling what shade of blue the sky outside had in store that moment.

Suddenly there was song. The silence was singed with a tinny chorus. It was a tune he knew and a tune he liked. It was a tune from his childhood.

It was 'Take Me Out to the Ball Game'!

It was her cell phone.

The woman, who worked, of course, had a cell phone. She fished it out of her coat, with little surprise.

She said, 'Morning.'

She said, 'Oh, geez, yeah, thanks, sorry I didn't tell you earlier, but I can't ride with you today. Can you tell him I might be late? Tell him, in fact, I might need the day off. Can you do that?'

She said, 'Just stuff, you know. Oh, no everything is fine, really.'

She said, 'Love you!' and hung up.

She put the phone away. Her face suddenly collapsed into her palms. Even muffled, he could make out the words 'What the hell am I doing.'

He had instincts; he did not have answers.

When he heard the knock on the door, he thought one thing: the Bundy. He rushed to the door and opened it, without looking through the peephole. He was eager for the girl and her gift.

Instead there stood the two maintenance men. Their greetings, as usual, came in the form of nods, which Henry returned.

'Bettina has sent us to check your locks,' the shorter one said.

'May be a problem with your locks,' the taller one said.

Henry told them he had no such problem, no such complaint. He told them to come back some other time.

'Bettina has sent the order,' the shorter one said. 'It will only take a second.'

'Good safety to have your locks checked,' the taller one said.

He told them he was not arguing with that, but it was late, or early, in any case, a bad hour, he had things, work, affairs – until he remembered: *their tools*. He knew how this went. The men would come, 'work', leave their tools ...

The Bundy would have won, but tools could do too. He seemed to remember hearing that women backed down at the sight of tools.

He *did* believe in safety. He told them to go ahead.

'It will be very quick,' said the shorter.

They fiddled with the doorknob, shaking it, jiggling it, oiling it, each taking turns standing outside and then in, opening and closing the door, over and over.

'The door is fine,' the shorter finally announced. And he began to place their tools inside his bag.

Henry announced that there was no way they could leave – yet. There was more work to be done, he was sure.

'Please call Bettina if there is a problem,' the shorter said.

'Back once Bettina sends the order,' the taller said.

He tried to plead with them, that there were other doors with locks, the bathroom door, certainly that was what the damned Bettina meant –

'Bettina said the front door,' the first man said. 'We will gladly check the other doors once we have an order for them.'

He stood in their way, trying to reason. They were adamant. Eventually they pushed; pushed their way right through Henry, as if he were just some insignificant ghost.

As they speed-walked down the hallway, Henry called to them, asking if they could just lend him something, a screwdriver, a power drill, anything, so he could just fix things himself –

'Please call Bettina and place the order,' the first man said.

'Other doors to check now,' the second man said.

He closed the door, and leaned his forehead against the wood, thinking, until he heard her 'Shithead' – suddenly too loud, loud enough to be too close.

'Oh, I heard that. I'm on to you. I know what you're up to, bastard!'

He must have forgotten what the city always said: *Always, always, keep your bags packed.*

'I want to sleep,' she said, 'in your bed. Now.'

He wondered if in the pockets of her coat – the pockets that had housed her cell phone, after all – the woman could be harbouring a weapon.

He wondered how to hold a plastic knife with dignity.

She said, 'Oh, c'mon, at this point, isn't this what we're expected to do?'

He had not yet heard her black, black laugh. It was bad.

She got up and grabbed his hand. Her hand was colder than he expected. What he expected was the moment when the nails dug deep into his palm.

He did not remember her name, but he could never forget *her*, that certain young girl in his schoolyard. The girl had only been at their school for a day. It was enough. At recess she singled him out, said, *You, come over here, you.* She grabbed his hand with her nails, nails he noticed were torn jagged and dirt-packed. She led him behind a trailer in the schoolyard, an empty trailer the kids called 'the Matson,' because painted on it was the enigmatic word 'MATSON.' The kids never had much use for the Matson. It was too obvious a spot for hide-and-seek, too appendage-less for proper play. She, however, had a purpose for it. Without warning, still holding his hand, she kicked him hard in the crotch. She said, *There.* He bent over in pain, trying to hide his tears. She ran off, and the next day she was gone. Nonetheless, he told the teacher – not the full story, not *where* she had struck him, but that she had struck him, and hard.

Teacher had smiled, and patting his head, explained, *Oh, that's just what girls do when they like you!* She had made it sound like sunshine. It was something that he, and apparently all adolescents at some point were told of – how a kick in the crotch could (sometimes) mean a kiss, how it would come like a hurt that was not meant to hurt, how situations were often just situations but also sometimes their inverse.

She said, 'What else do men and women do?'

She said, 'Isn't it what they want us to do?'

They. He froze. How did he know what those *theys* really did, what the other *theys* really wanted? How did anyone really know?

He opened his eyes. She was at the window. She was standing on the inside ledge, leaning carefully on his glass, hands clutching the frame. She was looking straight at him.

She said three words: 'Take it easy.' That was all.

She walked out the window, one sizable thigh after another, out of his world and back into hers. She left his window open. He watched her shut and lock her own.

He locked his own door; once, then again, just in case.

And he stopped watching.

NEW ZEALAND FLAX

Éilís Ní Dhuibhne

The early purple orchids are plentiful this year. So plentiful that Frida wonders if they really are as special and rare as she believes. In her field they're as common as the other flowers of June, the clover, the buttercups. The yellow one. Bird's Foot Trefoil, sometimes called scrambled egg. Still, she swerves around any patch of grass graced by the chubby little orchids – turgid, phallic, episcopally purple – but mercilessly slices through buttercups and clover – the latter is the bees' favourite thing, and smells nicer than the orchids, when the sun shines. Little islands of long grass with an orchid or two dot the 'lawn' – that's not the right name for it. The patch of field that she cuts, so it's like a pond of short grass in a forest of long rough stuff.

'Why don't you get someone to do it?' Her son is exasperated on the phone. Perhaps a tad guilty? He hasn't been down here in over a year, to cut grass or do anything else. It's time to paint the walls, and the windows, and he likes doing that. He says. 'You shouldn't be going all the way down there just to *cut the grass.*'

'I'll get somebody,' she says. 'Before I leave.'

She has figured out, recently, that the best way of dealing with advice from him, or anyone, is to pretend to take it. Some people realise this when they're four years old, but better late than never. The thing is. Having to cut the grass provides her with a reason for coming down. That's why she doesn't get a boy or a man to do it. That, and the cost, although it would most likely cost less than the price of the petrol for the drive down and back. And then, a man or a boy on one of the lawnmowers that look like toy tractors would not avoid the early purple orchids, or the two little hydrangea bushes, or the clumps of New Zealand flax that she planted last year and that have survived the winter storms, the spring storms, and the early summer storms. *Barely* survived. The spikes of flax look like soldiers who came home from the Battle of the Somme, battered, their skin burnt, and minus a couple of limbs. A man or a boy speeding around the field on a big lawnmower would certainly cut them down. A man or a boy wouldn't even see them.

Well. There is only one other person on earth who would see those clumps of pathetic flax.

Did she think, *on earth*?

She wipes the wheels and puts the lawn mower back in the garage. Just come and take a look, would you. When the sun goes down. The lawn-mower feels wounded. It has been rattled – the grass was more than a foot high, no ordinary lawn mower should have to deal with such stuff, it was a job for a big lump of farm machinery. The blade may have loosened. After two hours pushing against the gradient, doing the work of a combine harvester, the last thing she wants to do is examine the insides of the lawn-mower. But she forces herself to take a look.

Yes. There is a screw loose on one of the wheels. Now, where does he keep the toolbox?

The grass is so long because she has been away for the month of May. You can't let the grass grow for the month of May and expect anything other than a hayfield. She'd been in Finland; she's not sure why. Since this time last year she has travelled to all the countries Elk had ever lived in, or loved. Four or five, the north of the world. There have been different reasons for going to the various countries: a book launch, a 60th birthday party, a conference. A funeral. The ostensible reasons were many. But there was always another reason under the surface and that never varied. Constant as the northern star, it was. Dreams have an overt narrative, which is usually repeating random bits and pieces of your recent conscious experience, and a latent one, a broken record churning out the same old message for all of your life. Apparently her waking life is now operating on the same principle as her dream life. This doesn't particularly surprise her.

Why travel? To get away from Elk, on the one hand, and to look for him, on the other. Why else go to his places, far flung northern islands and archipelagos, rather than perfectly nice warm countries that might cheer her up? The only reason for the choice, which seemed not like a choice, was that he might be far away in the north, hidden in the deep evergreen forest, or sitting on the edge of a lake, fishing for pike? Or climbing the side of a volcano?

But maybe he's here, in the south of Ireland, in the cottage in Kerry, in his own study, which he always dignified with the name of 'library', or sitting on the side of the ancient volcano at the back of the house, looking out at the Great Blasket?

The red toolbox is in the corner at the back, hidden behind an old dustbin. She takes out a screwdriver and tightens the loose nut. When she is replacing the tool in the box, something catches her eye.

A bottle of wine.

Empty?

No. It's a Chablis. 2007.

They must have bought it one year – 2008? – on the way down, from the farm shop in Nenagh where they often stopped for a coffee, and to buy treats. Cheese from France, country butter from Tipperary. Mango chutney with caramelised onions that somebody in Cloughjordan makes. Mostly they drank the wine on the first night. But he must have tucked this one away in the garage for a special occasion and forgotten about it.

Or maybe she did that herself.

Once a year he wanted to drive to Brandon Creek; often on a Sunday afternoon when there was that Sunday afternoon feeling, that mix of nostalgia (for what? For nothing you can put your finger on) and boredom. The sound of football commentaries, wildly excited, from car windows and cottage windows, which filled Frida with a strange ennui, a longing to escape to somewhere, she knew not where, even when she was eight years old. One of the great things about Elk was that he couldn't care less about football, and didn't even know that that was an unusual gift, in a husband.

But even so.

Let's go to Brandon Creek.

Cuas an Bhodaigh. St Brendan is supposed to have sailed from there, in a naomhóg, and landed in America. But there is another tale associated with it, the story which gives the inlet its name in Irish, and that's what drew Elk to it. The story of the Big Bodach. The Big Bodach was a rich Kerryman who built a huge castle here on the coast; he had just one son. The Bodach wanted his own name to live forever, and he married the son off as soon as he could to a rich young woman. Then, when everything was in place, he died himself. But fourteen years passed and the couple had no children. Every day in summer the woman went for a swim at Cuas an Bhodaigh. One day, when was drying herself after her dip, a sea man came sweeping in from the ocean and took her in his arms. She fell asleep and when she woke up he was gone. Nine months later she gave birth to a son. He was a wonderful child, clever and handsome, but he had a problem: he could never sleep. Because he was half human and half merman, as only she knew. The Devil's Son as Priest, it's called in the international index of tales. Although he's not a devil; just not human. Not someone you should be consorting with.

Frida reads the story today, for the umpteenth time, in a collection of tales by Peig Sayers. She wants to have the story in her head when she's looking at the place. It has often occurred to her in connection with the tale that nobody in their right mind would go for a swim in Brandon Creek. A long narrow inlet, a fjordful of black water, fathoms deep, a ravine, a chasm, loomed over by Mount Brandon at the back and grim cliffs on each side. The creek crashes angrily down, and the water slurps ominously into crevices in the rock. There's no beach of any kind.

It's like an entrance to another world – and not a very nice one, if the gateway is anything to go by. You can understand that Brendan, obviously fond of high drama, would sail from here to the unknown, and that a big bodach from beneath the wave, a merman, Neptune, would emerge here. Here, rather than some golden sandy cove or long stretch where children play in the frilly shallows and where any normal woman would go for her daily swim.

Frida parks the car high above the creek, in a sort of layby, and walks down a winding boreen to the water. A young couple are on the way up, the girl with long black hair, the boy a redhead. They are dancing up the road, laughing, sort of waltzing and humming like bees in the sunshine. Or two butterflies.

They don't see her at all, have eyes only for one another.

At the start of the pier Kerry County Council has a warning: Do Not Enter This Pier if the Sea is high. DANGEROUS. The sea is not high, on this fine summer's evening. Down to the end of the pier she goes. There's a car parked on it. People drive the whole way down sometimes; it always amazes her. They'd rather risk drowning than walk a few hundred yards. A man in a navy blue jumper. Hello. A bit cheeky. Lovely day. She doesn't look at his face, but walks to the end and looks down into the water. It's not black when you're beside it. Transparent. You can see right to the bottom. Small fish darting about, in a great rush to go to somewhere. Bubbly kelp, and a huge clump of seaweed with long waving fronds, rather like the New Zealand flax. They say that everything found on land has its match in the ocean. Even that.

Behind her, she can sense the man in the blue jumper.

His eyes on her back.

She becomes conscious of how lonely it is here, at Cuas an Bhodaigh. Alone at the end of a pier, with deep black water all around. This happens, a lot. She's in a place she likes, a place that is familiar and was always safe, and she suddenly feels, I shouldn't be here. Why am I here?

She turns and walks back along the pier and up the winding hill to her car.

The man is at the back of his car as she approaches, doing something in the boot. She tries to look carefree as she strides past.

'Here!' he hails her again. She jumps out of her skin. There's a pause, as he eyes her with amusement. 'Have you any use for crab claws?'

He extends a plastic bag full of them.

'I've more than I need.'

'Thanks,' she takes the bag, since that seems to be the easier option. Forces a smile. Elk loves crab claws, and so does she.

'A treat for your tea.'

'Thanks!' she repeats. 'We like them. Thanks.'

She walks slowly up the hill. The young couple have disappeared. Before she climbs into her car she looks down at the inlet. The man in the blue jumper is reversing, down the slip, towards the water. She can hear it lapping and slapping against the stone, friendly, before it deepens and becomes a dark other world.

Driving back, southwards through Muiríoch and Baile na nGall and Ballyferriter, through little hayfields and purple slopes, the story is still on her mind. It dawns on her that it's about a kind of incest. Is the merman the woman's father-in-law, impregnating her from beyond the grave to ensure his line? Once she spots it, it seems obvious, although Peig doesn't spell it out. She'll have to ask Elk. It's the kind of matter to which he would have given some thought: what really happened in a story about a man who lives under the sea and a woman who never existed.

————————————

They'll have a nice dinner to celebrate the cutting of the grass and the survival of the New Zealand flax. She has the crab claws and the wine. New potatoes and salad and spinach. Lemon and parsley.

She peels the potatoes, puts them on. Slices spring onions and tomatoes; chops parsley. Spreads the white table cloth, and sets it with the best cutlery she can find. Flowers. Buttercups, clover, and two of the orchids, which may be a protected species but since she has saved the lives of about fifty of them today her guilt is minimal. In the small glass jar they look lovely, against the snow of the cloth. When it gets dark – which won't be till about half past ten – she will light the white candle.

She has Beethoven's 'Pastoral' beside the CD player for when dinner is served. One of his favourites. One of everyone's favourites. Now she's listening to Kathleen Ferrier's hits although she shouldn't, because it opens with 'Blow the Wind Southerly', a song of longing for a sailor who won't come home, because he is drowned. Blow the wind southerly, southerly, southerly, bring my love safely back home to me. And somewhere on the CD – it is towards the end – is Orfeo's lament for Euridice. What is life if thou art dead? The saddest song in the world. Tradition doesn't hold back on emotion and neither does opera, though few get as close to the bone as Gluck.

She travels to get away, to look for something, to forget and to remember. But coming home all she wants is to tell him about her travels. Coming home, she realises that the main point of going anywhere is to report back.

Which is why she has invited him to dinner tonight. There are so many aspects of the recent trip to Finland that only he would have the slightest interest in. She wants to ask him about the loan words, how the Finns seemed to drop the 's' from some words they borrowed from Swedish. *Kuola* from *skole*, for instance. *Tie* instead of *Stig*. And other words which are so strange. He would know why the Finns call a book *kirja*. You'd expect the word for book to come from Latin, or Greek, or Swedish or even Russian. Where did they get 'kirja' from?

Who cares about this sort of stuff?

Elk and Frida.

Into the thick goblets from the local pottery she pours the old wine. Sits down, and raises her goblet.

'*Kippis!*' she says, to the empty chair opposite her.

The Finnish for *Sláinte!*

She sips the wine.

'It is very good,' she nods.

'I can never sort out what the Finns did during the Second World War,' she says. 'Can you explain? So I get it straight?'

The sun is still high, in the South-west, over the island they call the Dead Man. Frida prefers the other name, the Northern Island.

Euridice! *Eurid eeeeeeche.*

What is life without your love.

At last the sun starts to sink behind the Northern Isle. Elk loved it when they showed that scene on RTÉ, back in the days when they played the national anthem at close of programming.

The blue of the night.

And when the sun slides down behind the Dead Man he comes out of the library and sits in his own place at the table.

'Will you have some wine?'

He looks at the bottle as if he has never seen one before. Puzzled, shakes his head.

He is like himself. Not pale and thin as he was in the last year, or panic-stricken as on the last days in the hospital, with his horribly swollen stomach and tubes shoved down his throat. He's wearing his navy blue jumper, which is odd, because that's the jumper she keeps under her pillow at home in the city.

'Now you're here I don't know what to say to you.'

She leans over to take his hand. His long fingers, thin and agile from a lifetime of typing, like a pianist's. But he pulls it away, not unkindly.

'Well.' She says the first thing that comes to her head. And yet she knows the time is valuable, like the time you've got for a job interview. You've only got half an hour so don't waste it saying unimpressive things. 'I miss you.'

'Yes, my darling,' his voice is his voice. Soft, round, robust, male, like a mellow burgundy. Like a purple orchid. It was one of his great attractions. 'Well, I am glad to hear that, even if it is selfish.'

'I miss you a lot.'

No need to repeat yourself.

'Yes, yes. It's terrible.' He sighs. 'But spilt milk.'

'I went to Finland.'

'Good for you! Did you learn some Finnish?'

'*Anteeksi! Huomenta! Päivää!* Excuse me. Good morning. Hello!'

'Good woman!'

'That's all I learnt.'

'Did you have a sauna?'

'Nearly every day. You'd have loved that. We should have got one, for your back.'

He is blurred, like a photograph that is not in focus. Sometimes the photos are like that, on the computer, and then after a little while they swim into clarity.

'I was listening to that song, Euridice.'

'Maybe you could find something more cheerful?'

'I've got Abba's *Greatest Hits* in the car.'

'*Ush!*'

'I cut the grass yesterday. I came down specially to do it. It was over a foot long.'

'My dear little darling.' Nobody ever calls her that any more. Well, of course not. 'But you shouldn't come down here just to cut the grass. Why don't you get someone to do it?'

'I will,' she promises.

There is plenty to tell him. About the funeral. About the tributes, the obituaries, the solemn ones and the funny ones. That he has a new grandchild and their other son is going to get married at the end of the summer. And especially that she has found out how much she loves him, that she always loved him and should have told him that more often. She should have told him that every minute. She needs to tell him these things, and to ask several more questions. Where is his article about 'The Dead Lover's Return'? The introduction to the book he was collaborating on with the guy in Galway? Is the Bodach in the story of Brandon Creek the father-in-law of the woman?

What used he do on Sundays, before they were married?

That's before she even gets to the big issues.

'I got a man to level the field.'

He walks to the window. The field is not actually very level. The man came with a digger or a bulldozer or something and dug it up, then put on some grass seed in last August. It cost about a thousand euro but nobody has noticed that it is any different from before. Apart from Frida herself.

'It's very nice, my darling!'

He doesn't comment on the three New Zealand flax plants. She points them out to him, down by the septic tank. They look like nothing. Like a few rushes that the lawn mower missed.

'They're a bit scrawny but they'll get bigger and make a shelter belt and then I can grow other things.'

'That will be just lovely, won't it?'

He can be ironic and kind at the same time.

There is one thing she really has to tell him. She can't say it so she puts on the CD and the voice comes pouring into the dim room.

'What is life if thou art dead?'

He leans over, and his face is close to her, his woollen jumper.

'Dear darling. I miss you too.' He looks around the room, at the fireplace and the bookshelves. The picture of Peig. 'I miss everything. And there is so much work I didn't get done.' For the first time his face is sad. 'But you don't want to come with me.'

'I do.'

It strikes her that this is the solution. It's simple.

'No, dear darling. You went to Finland. You cut the grass. And you've planted those ... scraggy things!'

'New Zealand flax.'

He laughs.

'Yes, New Zealand flax! You've got to look after the New Zealand flax, and make sure it grows big and beautiful.'

Frida doesn't know why it has that name; probably some sort of cloth can be made from it. But it looks nothing like ordinary flax, that misty blue corn which you never see any more and from which rare and lovely linen is made. New Zealand flax is not blue, and the flowers it gets look like brown withered prunes. It seldom flowers in this climate, and the leaves look like green spears, rusty from the west wind, with pointed tips that cut you if you touch them. There's only one reason for planting it.

'It survived the winter!'

'Yes, my darling, it survived the winter.'

He gets up.

'Don't go.'

Please don't go.

'Yes, I must go. Before the sun rises. You know the rules!'

He walks towards the door.

'The sun won't rise for ages.'

'It has already risen in Finland.'

She runs after him.

'Will you come back?'

He turns.

'One of us had to go first. That's the way it is.'

They warn you. Till death do us part. You hear it but you don't take it in. The small print. You throw it away, into the bin, like the wrapping paper on a beautiful present.

He puts a hand towards her shoulder, but not on it. If only he could hold her in his arms for one second!

'Make the most of the time you have left. It will be over soon enough. There's plenty of work to do.' He winks. ' You can do mine, if you don't want to do your own.'

'Yes,' she says. 'I will.'

He always gives good advice.

———————————————

Imagination is supposed to be a great thing. A gift. It can conjure up, it can invent. But its creations are as nothing, really, compared to the real thing.

The man on the pier didn't reverse into the water. He attached a rope, which was dangling from the back of his car, to a small boat in which he must have been out before she came, fishing for the crabs. And he pulled it up after him, to dry land.

TRANSITION

Maria Takolander

N othing could have prepared her for this. The blackness is rich and thick, like velvet. The sun is a white star and the earth an immense orb revolving silently around it. The moon hovers nearby. It is a rock, but also the ghost of a rock. Everything is still but at the same time in motion.

Dawn, when it falls upon the planet, appears as an arc of blue so vivid that it is shocking. Then the sunlight chases the darkness over the sphere, revealing the white arteries of rivers, luminous oceans, bleeding deserts, the geometric scars of farmlands and cities; all protected by a radiant layer of atmosphere.

She had seen images of it, but the reality is altogether different. It is as if she had been watching a lion on a screen and then the creature itself was suddenly panting in her living room, its fur framed by muscle and bone, its breath heavy with the odour of flesh, its yellow eyes inhuman.

Things have never seemed so real, but at the same time unreal. Floating near the transparent ceiling of the cupola, she feels like she is dreaming. She has broken free. She has escaped the sordid weight of herself. She is a pure spectator, akin to a heavenly spirit. She approaches the camera fixed at the apex of the cupola and observes her likeness in the depthless surface of the lens. It is this disembodied image of herself that she wants beamed back to the earth.

She presses her hands against the cold glass. She sees where topsoil has stained the ocean alongside the deforested island of Madagascar. The depleted body of the Aral Sea is exposed to her, as is the smog over Beijing. A vast cyclone covers the north-western coast of Australia, the outer areas of cloud pocked by soundless bursts of light. Then the world falls into darkness again, its cities like the embers of smouldering fires.

It is then she remembers why she is here. She will be the first to leave all earthly problems behind. She will make a clean start. It is time to quit orbit. It is time for her transition to the new world.

She feels a muddying confusion, almost like panic, as if she has forgotten something of utmost importance – but the opportunity for hesitation is long gone. There is no choice anymore. She leaves the cupola and floats back to her operation seat in the illuminated alcove of the control room. She straps herself down.

To escape the pull of the earth, there is an acceleration, both mysterious and atrocious. The lights are extinguished, and she is pressed deep into herself in the inscrutable darkness, becoming heavier than she thinks she can endure. She is almost sure that she falls unconscious. Certainly she drifts into a kind of sleep, although there are no memories or dreams. The emergence back into wakefulness is marked by a feeling of disease or disgust, abiding in her flesh and bones. It is not what she had expected.

The lights flicker on. She squints at the shining ceiling. She sees the glassy eye of the camera lens embedded there and makes out her reflection. She is bound to the padded chair in her pale jumpsuit, some grotesque unfortunate from a bygone age. She is a blight in the immaculate space. This is not what she had envisioned.

She allows herself time to recoup. She remains in the reclined seat, her head cushioned in a stout brace. With the pressure against her ears, she can hear a fleshy percussive noise, her heart sounding like something unborn. She lifts her head and observes the undulating zipper down the front of her suit, rising and falling with each breath. Something has gone wrong.

She unbuckles herself and gets to her feet on the gleaming floor. Her weight is cumbersome in the new semblance of gravity. She listens to the reverberation of the ventilation fans and takes in the metallic taste of the air, like the vile residue in her mouth when she coughs sometimes. Her nausea is strong. She feels as if she is standing still, but in fact she is being spun and hurled through endless space and time. She had understood the plan, the mechanics of it all, how she would be sent on her way, but now she feels only as if she is in a carnival ride gone wrong.

She looks around her. The space is so white that at first it is hard to distinguish anything. Then she makes out the circular walls of the control room. There are a number of doors. One of them returns her to the cupola. There she sees instantly that the view has changed. It is all gone. Looking at the hemisphere of glass above her she sees only blackness, unbroken by any stars.

The dome looks close, much closer than before, its blackness like morbid ceiling paint. The radiation shield has closed over the craft. Beyond is eternity, silent as an iceberg. She will never see the earth again.

Her nausea settles into a dead weight in the pit of her stomach. She leans against the wall of the cupola, triggering the release for the door. The door slides shut, and she is sealed in. The blackness is so dense that it is like blindness. She cannot even see herself. She lowers herself cross-legged to the floor, heavier and sicker than she has ever felt before.

How brief her life on earth had been, she thinks. It is as though it had never happened.

She should be looking ahead – it is what she has been trained to do, a habit in which she has come to trust – but sitting in the dark she finds herself almost paralysed. She ought to be following a new routine, enacting life, this afterlife, as it is to be from now on, but she has no wish to move. She is not even sure that she can. It feels as if the hardness and coldness of the floor is merging with her legs. Her chest and throat are becoming rigid too.

Looking up, she notes the green glow at the centre of the ceiling. It is the power signal on the rim of the camera lens. The light is too weak to provide illumination, but it lends the blackness around her its texture. She is a statue buried in a catacomb.

She should open the door to the control room and let its light enter the cupola, this sole room exposed to the elements, but she has no desire to do this. She has been cast into an abyss. This is no fantasy of starlight and glittering dust. Let people see what awaits them after life on earth. Let them cleave to each other. Let them cleave to their home in fear.

The anger is irrational and strong, a resurgence of life, but it leaves as quickly as it comes. In the blackness her body becomes frigid again. She thinks of her own home, remembering not her apartment in Moscow but the farming town in Finland where she grew up. It was less a town than a collection of timber houses built in fields hard-won from the taiga forest and, in times gone by, from their Russian neighbours.

She closes her eyes – it is easy in the darkness – and sees the skeletal trunks of the birch, pretending to the winter that they do not exist. The pine and spruce are burdened by snow. She hears the sliding of her skis, smells the freezing air, feels the weight of ice on her eyelashes. The sky is only half-lit. She spies a lone elk in a white clearing, its antlers stark as an outcrop of rock. The wings of a black grouse break the silence.

She used to ski for kilometres through the forest to get to school.

In spring the snow ruptures and thumps from the trees, melting into slurries of earth, releasing the stench of things dead and buried. Summer crawls out as if it had been waiting. The mosquitoes come in swarms, rising from the soupy ground. She feels the sticky grass on her calves, smells the pine needles and soil, hears the sucking sounds of a creek somewhere. The sun is eternal. In her bedroom fox-skins hang from the wall. Even there she cannot escape the reek from the barn of her father's pigs, sulphurous and cadaverous.

That stink had followed her everywhere.

She opens her eyes to the void. The ventilation system hums like a refrigerator. She had hated everything about her home, she recalls. At least she could admit it. Everyone who lived there hated the place, though they kept silent as if it was a national virtue.

In the warmer months farmers dragged what they could from the earth to feed themselves and their beasts; in winter they cut down trees with calamitous machines. Drinking was another kind of labour. People took to it early and stuck with it until the end. Every Sunday they gathered to receive the promise of another life from an old man whose hands, as he raised a chalice of wine towards the pine ceiling, trembled as much as those of his parishioners. The age of pagan worship had well and truly passed. Still, child after child was born onto that patch of earth. People were no better than animals.

She crosses her arms over her abdomen. There is a faint scar on her torso, shaped like an inverted crucifix, a reminder of her own sordid mistake, when life briefly had its way with her. It does not require her attention.

She stares until she feels as though the black air is silting into her eye sockets, into the cavity in her skull. Life, she thinks, never cared about anyone. It was the biggest animal of all.

Immersed in the darkness, she knows that she has escaped. But it does not feel as it should.

Something has gone wrong, but she does not understand what it is. Her body is cold, like stone, though she feels sick to her core. She wants nothing more than to lie down and retreat from it all. It happens, she knows. Back home, men were found under bridges every winter. Her father was one of them. Drunk on cheap alcohol, cowering from the night like some kind of ape-man, he drowned in his vomit.

He had been too weak to survive. The Finns had a word for his kind: *nassu*. She remembers how he showed up at her confirmation, lurching into the pine church in his funeral suit. His blonde hair was sticking up in tufts. The stink of him was faint but nevertheless present: pig-shit, sweat, alcohol. She and her mother had not seen him for days. Steadying himself at the end of her pew, he had begun stroking her hair, the colour of his own, his fingers clumsy on her skull. '*Niin kuin vauvan,*' he had mumbled to the old pastor at the altar. *Like a baby's*. She had been fifteen.

She liked to think that she had never believed the earth was anything other than a rock circling the sun, but the truth was, dressed in her white gown that day, she had hoped to be one of God's children. She had turned to look at her mother in a pew behind, the lights from the ceiling burnishing her hair, which in those years was brown as soil. '*Anna hänen olla,*' her mother had said to her and then to those around them. *Let him be*. The pastor had continued with the service, and she had pretended that her father's hand was not upon her, that his stench was not contaminating everything. When she got home, she had fled to the sauna and washed. She never went to a service again.

She is not the daughter of such men. She rises in the black pit of the cupola and fumbles along the wall for the release to the door. The white control room appears in front of her, a floodlit bank of snow. She raises her arm to defend herself. When her eyes adjust to the gleaming light, she observes her chair, with its abandoned padding and bindings. It looks like a thing thrown clear from a crash site.

She assesses her body. She is colder than she has ever been, though there is no shivering. The nausea is enduring. There is a weight in her chest, as though a fist is pressing against her sternum, and there is a pressure in her throat. It is as if something powerful is trying to erupt from her flesh.

She glimpses the reflective lens at the apex of the white room. She must take care of herself. She crosses the lustrous floor and presses the release to her sleeping cubicle. She falls to her knees at the side of the bunk inside and unlatches a drawer beneath it. The medical supplies are kept there. She removes a transparent tube of pills.

She has never had a sedative before. They have always struck her as dangerous. She watched her father, night after night, drink himself into oblivion. He would sit in the kitchen alone, tipping the liquid from one bottle after another into his mouth, until he was bleary-eyed and could no longer see.

She saw him, though, when she crept past in the hallway to go to the bathroom: slumped and snoring on the wooden chair. She saw her mother too, tending to the pigs in the morning when her father was too wretched to get out of bed, or on those occasions when he simply disappeared. Her mother, a midwife, had her own work to do, but the pigs made such a racket when ignored. Their grunts and shrieks rose from their hidden sties like the noises of the damned.

Her mother might have accepted life as it came – she helped the pigs give birth as much as she helped women do the same – but, unlike her mother, she refused to even enter the barn. It was the eyes of the animals that bothered her more than anything: the way they looked at her from beneath their pale lashes, their snouts hovering just above their own shit on the earth. Not that it mattered. They were bred to be killed.

She thrusts the chalky pills into her mouth and forces herself to swallow. Then she dims the white lights in the cubicle and curls up on her side on the thin mattress. The room is still too bright for her liking. It reminds her of the witching hours of summer, those hours after midnight when the sun cannot be seen but its light silhouettes the creatures of the forest that ought to be in darkness, that ought to have their time in hiding. She stares at the pallid wall and focuses on the cold surface of the pillowcase against her cheek, waiting for her body to become numb.

The bed grows soft. The tension in her chest and throat releases, and her respiration finds a rhythm in the steady reverberations of the ventilation system. She is breathing easily, as if breathing is the easiest thing to do. She is barely responsible.

There is horror at her failure, at the miscarriage of her transition, but it is a distant feeling, as if she might have dreamed the whole ordeal. She is aware of the space outside the vessel and her distance from the earth, vaster than anything she can imagine, but her horror of that has subsided too.

There is no pain. She can remember everything without fear: even that she once fell pregnant and lost a child. She had been in a science laboratory at the university in Moscow, when a burning pressure had grown in her abdomen. She had walked to the hospital in her white coat, along streets wet with spring melt. The pain had become excruciating. It was a long walk; that is what she remembers most. Yet it also feels as if it took no time at all.

She was lucky not to be killed by the child. After the operation, with the scar fresh and sore, the nurse had led her downstairs to the morgue, pulling out a single drawer in a wall lined with steel cabinets. The stored foetus looked prosthetic, a prop for a film. Days later, in the hospital chapel, a priest, in a grotesquely extravagant gown, conducted a group funeral. There were no fewer than six small coffins arranged at the base of the golden crucifix. The corpses had already been cremated in the hospital incinerator, and the white coffins at the front of the room were empty, ready to be used again. Still, the would-be parents, hunched on the pews, had cried as if those babies were there.

The father of her baby had sobbed with them, a sound like her father made when he was drunk sometimes, loose-lipped and wretched. Some time later in her apartment, drunk himself, he sat opposite her at the dining table, flicking the stubs of one lit cigarette after another in her direction. It was a novel kind of violence. When the cigarettes came close, she simply batted them away. Soon he got up and left. She was glad not to see him again. It had all been a mistake, her body leading her astray, as it had done from time to time in those days.

The wall in her cubicle begins to look thick and blurry. Her body on the mattress is barely present to her anymore. She remembers how she and her friends, as teenagers, thought that sex might save them. That feeling of power made the world momentarily seem larger than it was. The romance, though, was short-lived. Her friends began to have children, who would grow up and have their own children, and so on – all on the same patch of earth. Life was using them. It wanted to live, just for the reckless sake of it, at the cost of anything, of anyone.

So many babies were born; the earth was a factory for them. When she was still a child, her mother, unable to leave her at the farm alone, had sometimes taken her along to births. Through doorways she had glimpsed woman after woman, working through their pain in the closeted warmth of saunas, each one of them riven by the gluttony of life as it begat itself over and over again. Their infants were born in gushes of flesh, protesting as the air filled their lungs, as they felt the weight of themselves for the first time.

Then there were those who emerged silent as fish.

She imagines her child, spilling into her abdomen four months into term, asphyxiating in the hostile atmosphere of her body. She had a double uterus, she told her mother some weeks later on the phone. She was sitting on the closed lid of the toilet of her apartment near the university in Moscow. She had not told her mother that she was pregnant; she had not wanted to admit that she had ended up in such a common bind. Her mother was alone in the farmhouse. Her father had died years previously, and the animals were gone. There was silence, and then her mother replied: '*Niin kuin yksi isäsi porsaista.*'

Like one of your father's pigs.

The wall across the floor from her bed becomes one with the hazy whiteness of the room. Her body is a distant memory. She closes her eyes, hoping for a dreamless sleep, like the one she had under anaesthetic, when she had been set adrift from her pain, released into the ether until there was nothing of her left.

It is only towards the end that her body returns and, with it, a dream. She is pushing at the sides of a box, which are strangely soft. It is a struggle to wake. The white walls of her sleeping compartment appear and disappear like the white walls of the coffin in her dream. When she finally surfaces, she is lying on her back in the confinement of the cubicle. The room is dim, the ceilings and walls the uniform colour of plaster. The door to the luminous space of the control room is discretely closed. Her compartment has a clear finitude, unlike the space in her dream. It is, she realises, because of the obscene weight of the void outside.

She catches the eye of the lens embedded in the low ceiling. She knows that she should get out of bed. She is supposed to follow diurnal rituals, regardless of the fact that there are no longer days and nights, no longer time, except for that time buried in her terrestrial body, in the bodies of every creature borne of the earth.

She wipes the dried spit from the corners of her mouth. Her body feels calm and slow, like when she awoke in hospital after the surgery all those years ago, but there is something else lurking inside. She does not understand why it has not been removed. It is best to keep still.

Perhaps she has woken from the sedative too soon. She remembers once seeing a bear emerge early from its winter sleep. It was in the forest behind her childhood home, the world there still blotted by snow. It was standing behind a frozen pine, lost like a sleepwalker.

She listens to the electric sound of the ventilation system and takes in the battery taste of the recycled air. She thinks of the vast emptiness just outside the membrane of the walls, of her remoteness from the earth. Her chest grows heavy, and tension mounts in her throat once more. She crosses her arms over her abdomen. It is her body, she realises. It is trying to betray her.

She remembers the dogs, on her last night on earth; how they tried to lure her into doubt. She had been quarantined at a complex at the launch site in the snow-strewn Kazakh steppe. Lying in an old steel-spring bed in a windowless room, she had listened to the staccato bursts of fireworks, erupting in the icy sky. The world had been celebrating her impending escape, but the dogs had begun lamenting. They had started straightaway, with the first explosions, though their howls had continued long afterwards, as if, once the fluorescent arcs had drawn their attention to the night sky, they could not forgive what hung over them.

She recalls the granite statue of the dog she had seen in the lobby of the complex when she arrived. A stray captured in the streets of Moscow, it had been the first living creature blasted away from the earth. It had died alone in its capsule, surrounded by a titanic blackness, before the vehicle crash-landed back on earth.

She observes her reflection in the fathomless surface of the lens above. Laid out on her white bunk, in her grey bodysuit, she looks like a corpse in a mortuary. She is not dead. There is something stuck in her throat, pressing to get out.

She opens her mouth.

The squealing is so high-pitched that her ears ache at the alien sound. Then the snorting and grunting come, beginning in spasms in her abdomen, before squeezing through the cavities of her nose and mouth.

The camera transports her body back to the earth.

About the Authors

GINA APOSTOL

Gina Apostol's last novel, *Gun Dealers' Daughter* (W.W. Norton & Company, 2012), won the 2013 PEN/Open Book Award and was shortlisted for the 2014 William Saroyan International Prize. Her first two novels, *Bibliolepsy* (University of the Philippines Press) and *The Revolution According to Raymundo Mata* (Anvil Publishing, Inc.), both won the Juan Laya Prize for the Novel (Philippine National Book Award). She is working on *William McKinley's World*, a novel set in Balangiga and Tacloban in 1901, during the Philippine-American War. She was Writer in Residence at Phillips Exeter Academy and a fellow at Civitella Ranieri in Umbria, Italy, among other fellowships. Her essays and stories have appeared in *The New York Times*, the *Los Angeles Review of Books*, *Foreign Policy*, *The Gettysburg Review*, *The Massachusetts Review*, and others. She lives in New York City and western Massachusetts and grew up in Tacloban, the Philippines. She teaches at the Fieldston School in New York City.

KEVIN BARRY

Kevin Barry is the author of *Beatlebone* (Canongate, 2015), *City of Bohane* (Jonathan Cape, 2011), and the story collections *Dark Lies the Island* (Jonathan Cape, 2012) and *There Are Little Kingdoms* (Stinging Fly Press, 2007). His awards include the IMPAC Dublin City Literary Award, the Sunday Times EFG Short Story Prize and the European Union Prize for Literature. His stories have appeared in *The New Yorker*, *Granta*, the *Stinging Fly*, and many other journals. He also writes screenplays, stage plays and radio plays. He lives in County Sligo.

SARA BAUME

Sara Baume studied Fine Art at Dun Laoghaire College of Art and Design before completing a Master's in Creative Writing at Trinity College, Dublin. Her short fiction has been published in journals and newspapers. In 2014 she won the Davy Byrnes Award and was named Hennessy New Irish Writer of the Year at the 44th annual awards in Dublin. Her debut novel *Spill Simmer Falter Wither* (Tramp Press, 2015) has been long-listed for the 2015 Warwick Prize for Writing, and will be published by William Heinemann in the UK and Houghton Mifflin Harcourt in the USA in 2016. It is also due to be translated into Spanish, Dutch, French and German. She lives in Cork with her two dogs.

MARK DOTEN

Mark Doten's first novel, *The Infernal*, was published in 2015 by Graywolf Press. He wrote the libretto for *The Source*, an opera about Chelsea Manning and Wikileaks that premiered at the Brooklyn Academy of Music in 2014 and appeared on the *New York Times* list of best classical vocal performances of the year. He is senior editor at Soho Press, and co-host with author Adam Wilson of the literary podcast *The Consolation Prize*. He has an MFA in Creative Writing from Columbia University and is a recipient of fellowships from Columbia and The MacDowell Colony. He can be found at markdoten.com.

NIVEN GOVINDEN

Niven Govinden is the author of four novels, *We Are the New Romantics* (Bloomsbury, 2004), *Graffiti My Soul* (Canongate, 2007), *Black Bread White Beer* (HarperCollins, 2013) most recently *All the Days and Nights* (The Friday Project, 2014), which was longlisted for the 2015 Folio Prize. He has been twice-shortlisted for the Green Carnation Prize, and was a winner of the Fiction Uncovered Prize in 2013.

DAVID HAYDEN

David Hayden's short stories have appeared in *The Dublin Review, The Warwick Review, gorse, The Moth*, the *Stinging Fly, Numéro Cinq, Lighthouse* and *Spolia*, and poetry in *PN Review*. He was shortlisted for the 25th RTÉ Francis MacManus Short Story prize.

POROCHISTA KHAKPOUR

Porochista Khakpour is a novelist, essayist, journalist, and professor. She is the author of the forthcoming memoir *SICK* (HarperPerennial, 2017), and the novels *The Last Illusion* (Bloomsbury, 2014) – a 2014 'Best Book of the Year' according to NPR, *Kirkus, Buzzfeed, Popmatters, Electric Literature*, and more – and *Sons and Other Flammable Objects* (Grove, 2007) – the 2007 California Book Award winner in 'First Fiction,' one of the *Chicago Tribune*'s 'Fall's Best,' and a *New York Times* 'Editor's Choice.' She has had fellowships from the NEA, Yaddo, Ucross, the Sewanee Writers' Conference, Northwestern University, the University of Leipzig, and many others. Her writing has appeared in or is forthcoming in *Harper's, The New York Times*, the *Los Angeles Times*, the *Wall Street Journal, Al Jazeera America, Slate, Salon, Spin*, the *Daily Beast, Elle*, and many other publications around the world. She is currently Contributing Editor at *The Offing*, a channel of the *Los Angeles Review of Books*, and Writer in Residence at Bard College. Born in Tehran and raised in Los Angeles, she lives in New York City.

SAM LIPSYTE

Sam Lipsyte is the author of the story collections *Venus Drive* and *The Fun Parts* and three novels: *The Ask,* a *New York Times* Notable Book, *The Subject Steve* and *Home Land*, which was a *New York Times* Notable Book and received the first annual Believer Book Award. He is also the recipient of a Guggenheim fellowship. He lives in New York City and teaches at Columbia University.

BELINDA McKEON

Belinda McKeon is the author of *Solace* (Picador, 2011), which won the Geoffrey Faber Prize, the Sunday Independent Best Newcomer Award at the Irish Book Awards and was also voted Irish Book of the Year 2011, and *Tender* (Picador, 2015). McKeon's essays and non-fiction have been published in *The New York Times*, the *Guardian,* the *Paris Review* and the *Irish Times*, as well as in a number of anthologies. As a playwright, she has had work produced in Dublin and New York. She lives in Brooklyn and is an Assistant Professor of Creative Writing at Rutgers University.

FRANCESCA MARCIANO

Francesca Marciano is the author of three novels, *Rules of the Wild*, a *New York Times* Notable Book, *Casa Rossa*, *The End of Manners*, and *The Other Language*, a collection of short stories which was shortlisted for the Story Prize in 2014. She was Writer in Residence at the Wurlitzer Foundation in Taos and at the M Literary Residency in Sangam House in India. She has written several film scripts, mostly for the Italian cinema. She uses both Italian and English in her writing, although English is the language she uses when writing fiction. She has lived in the US and Kenya and now lives in Rome.

ÉILÍS NÍ DHUIBHNE

Éilís Ní Dhuibhne was born in Dublin in 1954. She has written novels, collections of short stories, several books for children, plays and non-fiction works. She writes in both Irish and English. Her short story collections include *Blood and Water, Eating Women is Not Recommended, Midwife to the Fairies, The Inland Ice, The Pale Gold of Alaska* and *The Shelter of Neighbours*. Among her literary awards are The Bisto Book of the Year Award, the Readers' Association of Ireland Award, the Stewart Parker Award for Drama, the Butler Award for Prose from the Irish American Cultural Institute and several Oireachtas awards for novels and plays in Irish. She received the Irish Pen Award for an Outstanding Contribution to Irish Literature in 2015. The novel *The Dancers Dancing* (Blackstaff Press, 2000) was shortlisted for the Orange Prize for Fiction. Her stories are widely anthologised and translated. Her next novel for young people, *Aisling*, will be published in autumn 2015. Éilís worked for many years as an assistant keeper in the National Library of Ireland. She is now Writer Fellow in UCD (University College, Dublin) where she teaches on the MA in Creative Writing. She is a member of Aosdána.

YOKO OGAWA

Yoko Ogawa has published more than twenty works of fiction and nonfiction, including *The Diving Pool, Hotel Iris, Revenge* and *The Housekeeper and the Professor*, which was adapted into a film, *The Professor's Beloved Equation*. Her fiction has appeared in *The New Yorker, A Public Space*, and *Zoetrope*. She has won every major Japanese literary award.

KRISTÍN ÓMARSDÓTTIR

Kristín Ómarsdóttir is the author of four novels, three short story collections, seven books of poetry, and seven staged plays. Her work has been published in Swedish and French. Ómarsdóttir has been nominated for the Nordic Council's Literature Prize and the Nordic Council's Drama Prize. She has also received the DV Cultural Award for Literature, and the 'Griman,' the Icelandic prize for best playwright of the year. She lives in Reykjavik and is currently at work on her new novel.

E.C. OSONDU

E.C. Osondu was born in Nigeria, where he worked for many years as an advertising copywriter. He won the Caine Prize for African Writing in 2009. He is the author of the book of short stories *Voice of America* (HarperPerennial, 2011) and the novel *This House Is Not for Sale* (Harper, 2015). His short stories have appeared in *The Atlantic, Guernica, AGNI*, and many other magazines. With William Pierce, he coedited *The AGNI Portfolio of African Fiction*. His *AGNI* story 'A Letter from Home' was named one of the Top Ten Online Stories of 2006 by *storySouth*, and his *AGNI* story 'Jimmy Carter's Eyes' was a finalist for the Caine Prize. He was interviewed in the *World Books* podcast for Public Radio International's *The World*. He holds an MFA in Creative Writing from Syracuse University, where he was a Syracuse University Fellow. He is Associate Professor of English at Providence College in Rhode Island. His writing has been translated into German, Italian, French, German, and Belarussian.

ELSKE RAHILL

Elske Rahill grew up in Dublin and was educated at Trinity College. Her short stories have appeared in various literary journals and anthologies. Her first novel, *Between Dog and Wolf* (2013) is published by the Lilliput Press and a collection of her short stories is scheduled for publication this year. She lives in Burgundy with her partner and their three sons. She would like to thank Dr Joseph Roche for his generous assistance with her research for 'Terraforming'.

ROSS RAISIN

Ross Raisin's second novel, *Waterline*, was published in July 2011 (Viking, Penguin). His first novel, *God's Own Country* (Viking, Penguin), came out in the UK in 2008. The book won the Sunday Times Young Writer of the Year Award in 2009, the Guildford First Novel Prize, a Betty Trask Award, and was shortlisted for six others, including the Guardian First Book Award and the IMPAC Dublin Literary Award. In 2013 he was named as one of Granta's Best of Young British Novelists. He has written short stories for *Prospect, Granta, Esquire, Dazed & Confused,* the *Sunday Times*, and BBC Radio Three and Four, and done journalistic feature work, mainly for the *Guardian*.

SUZANNE SCANLON

Suzanne Scanlon is the author of two novels, *Promising Young Women* (Dorothy, A Publishing Project, 2012) and *Her 37th Year, An Index* (Noemi Press, 2015). She lives in Chicago, where she writes about theater for *Time Out* and the *Chicago Reader*. She teaches Creative Writing at Columbia College Chicago, Roosevelt University and in the University of Iowa's Summer Writing Festival.

MARIA TAKOLANDER

Maria Takolander is the author of a book of short stories, *The Double* (Text 2013); three collections of poetry, *The End of the World* (Giramondo, 2014), *Ghostly Subjects* (Salt, 2009) and *Narcissism* (Whitmore Press, 2005); and a work of literary criticism, *Catching Butterflies: Bringing Magical Realism to Ground* (Peter Lang, 2007). She is currently writing a novel, *Transit*, for Text Publishing. She is an Associate Professor in Creative Writing and Literary Studies at Deakin University in Victoria, Australia.